Somewhere Between Dreaming & You

by : Kailey Brown

Published by Eleven Legacy Press

ISBN: 979-8-9949097-4-4

Prologue

It began with a boy I invented and ended with one who lingered like a memory.

Sometimes I wonder if I dreamed him into existence. Back then, it didn't feel like much, just another story I told myself to fall asleep. There was this boy who lived somewhere between dusk and dawn, showing up in my dreams, going on carnival rides, quiet walks, and game nights at coffee shops that never existed.

Every time I woke up, I'd write him a letter. Each one started with "Dear L," as if I were keeping a secret even from myself.

The box is still under my bed, the dark blue one with carved moons and gold stars. It's strange, the things you can't bring yourself to throw away. What kind of eighteen-year-old keeps imaginary love letters like treasure? Maybe the same kind who still secretly half believes in them.

When I think back, everything about that time feels warmed and loud: the clatter of pots from the kitchen downstairs, the sound of Italian pop music through the walls, the faint smell of garlic and basil that never quite left our house. My world was small, but it felt full, steady, and wrapped in laughter.

Maybe that's why I wrote to L. Even surrounded by love, I wanted something all mine, away from the noise and expectations.

My parents met at thirteen. Part of me thought I'd missed my chance—maybe true love skipped generations, or you had to *imagine it first* to recognize it.

My Nonna used to say real love isn't loud; it's quiet. "When someone really loves you, tesoro, they remember the little things," she told me once, stirring the soup she always made when I was sick. "The ones who make your heart race are fun, sì. But marry the one who stirs the pot when it's about to burn."

That's the kind of love I was raised on, the kind that smelled like Sunday sauce and second chances. The kind that made me believe in magic, even when I swore I didn't. Sometimes I wonder when the dreaming stopped and the living began, or if it even has.

Somewhere between the girl who wrote to L and the woman I'm trying to become, life kept moving. It's brought me here, to Copperridge, to the smell of garlic and basil, to the place where everything still feels the same.

One

The lunch rush hits before noon, and Nonna's restaurant already smells like the signature scent of the Morettis, garlic and basil. The steam from the pan blocks my view of my Papà, who is shouting his usual orders in half English and half Italian. Fresh bread sits cooling in front of the oven, so of course, I grab a piece on my way to the dishwasher, these napkins won't roll themselves. The fog of the kitchen makes it hard to breathe, full of steam and the trace of flour that never seems to leave.

I love it back here. It's sensory overload, but it feels like me, it feels like home. It's just another Friday at my parents' restaurant, named after the most inspiring woman I've ever met, my Nonna. It's the kind of day where the routine you've practiced since you were seven makes you unstoppable. You know exactly when to sneak that piece of bread, exactly when to sip the espresso, when to laugh, and when to disappear. Steady and predictable. Except there's a small piece of me that feels like the safe routine can sometimes be suffocating.

"Remilia Moretti!" Papà shouts my name from behind another cloud of steam. "Table 4 needs more Parmigiano, and don't forget your smile." He adds.

"I'm smiling on the inside," I said, which earned me an eye roll and an inaudible Italian phrase.

I wipe my hands on my flour-covered apron, grab the cheese grater, and roll my shoulders like I'm auditioning for *Top Chef: Copperridge Edition.* Copperridge, Tennessee, isn't famous for much, unless you count gossip, beautiful sunsets, or my family's marinara sauce. Anyone driving into town can smell the garlic before they see the 'Welcome to Copperidge' sign. That's us, the Morettis.

My parents opened Nonna's twenty years ago, and somehow it's still the heart of this one-stoplight town. We've had first dates, last dates, proposals, break-ups, and everything in between. Some people go to church on Sundays; Copperridge eats my Nonna's famous 'Sunday sauce'.

I balance the cheese grater in one hand and step through the kitchen doors. The bell over the dining-room entrance rings, and the familiar mix of laughter, clinking glasses, and the faint thump of an old Italian song wraps around me. For a second, I forget I'm just the girl giving you extra parmesan. For a second, I feel like I belong to something bigger than the routine, and I guess I am. This kingdom belongs to me, I am the legacy. This should be everything I want, wrapped up in a pretty bow. Emphasis on *should.*

Mrs. Patterson sits at table four, and I love her, I really do, it's just that sometimes she acts like she's a part of this legacy too. She may as well be, she's been coming here since before I could spell linguine. "Tell your mamma this sauce tastes different today." Pointing her accusatory fork at the pasta in front of her.

"It's the same recipe, Mrs. Patterson." Adding the parmesan to her plate, my voice laced with annoyance. "Maybe your taste buds decided they wanted the brick oven pizza today." I quip.

"You sound just like her, you know, your mamma," she points the same fork over to the bar where my Mammà entertains a couple I've never seen before.

Giving her my best *that's not a compliment* smile, I hurry away.

When I pass by the register, Mammà is leaning across the counter enthusiastically telling a story, her story. Her accent always thickens when she tells the story of how she and Papà met. It was a random Rome vacation, a spilled drink, a promise that turned into a restaurant, and a family. She catches my eye mid-sentence and winks. Her smile is effortless, like she never stopped being the girl he fell in love with.

The night slows the same way the sauce thickens, with time. When the door is locked, and the dining room is finally empty, I make my way to the kitchen, where I can practically see the wafts of garlic flow from the saucepan. Papà wipes down the counters as Mammà stirs what's left in the pan, tasting it every few seconds like her life depends on it.

"I didn't want her to be right, Nico, but she was." He held a spoonful of sauce up to his mouth. "It needs more basil."

"You always say that, Elena," Papà huffs out.

"And you never listen, Amore Mio." She plants a kiss on his cheek.

"Mrs Patterson said it was the best she's ever had when I went to her table." Papà gently hits her leg with the towel.

"She said *different,* not best." Mammà plants a hand on her hip. "That woman knows when you've changed the recipe."

"I didn't change it, I improved it." Papà shrugs.

I lean against the counter, arms crossed, watching them, my head volleying back and forth, threatening to give me a headache. Twenty years married, and they still flirt through arguments. She gestures wildly with the spoon; he smacks her arm with a towel. It's loud, ridiculous, and somehow still romantic.

"This is why Mrs. Patterson said the sauce tasted different," I mutter. "You're both secretly trying to out-cook each other."

Papà points the towel in my direction. "Dream girl knows everything, eh?"

"Don't call me that," I say too fast. He raises an eyebrow, amused.

Ugh, not this *dream girl* crap again.

"I call you that because you're always a thousand miles away," he says, tapping his head and going back to wiping the counter. "One day you'll drift right out of here and forget all about us."

Mammà smiles softly. "She's not going anywhere. She just has big dreams like her papà."

I pretend to be busy myself with stacking chairs, but their words stick. Maybe I am a thousand miles away. Maybe that's safer than being right here, watching two people who make love look effortless. They move around each other like music, bumping hips, laughing, tasting each other's sauce just to prove a point. It's the kind of love that fills a room and leaves no space for doubt.

That's when it hits me, why they call me dream girl. It's not because I'm lost, it's because I *want* something this real and terrifying. Something that big could swallow a person whole. What if I loved someone like that and never came back the same? Lose myself in the process, only to be left behind like my Nonna was without my Nonno.

"Remi, lights," Papà says, breaking the spell.

I flip off the light switches in the restaurant, one by one, until only the sign outside glows, warm against the Tennessee dark. The fresh air against my skin tempts me into going for a walk or even a long drive, but the comfort my bed brings is the biggest temptress of the night, and I'm going to fall straight into her trap.

At home, the quiet feels louder than the restaurant ever did. There is comfort in the noise; silence always sounds like questions that I don't want to answer. Tossing my keys into the bowl by the door, I head straight upstairs, needing to wash this day and this mood off. Crawling into bed with too many thoughts and damp hair, I can still hear my parents' laughter echoing out of some corner of the house.

I sit up, reach under the bed, and feel for the box I swore I'd stop touching. The wooden box is cool against my fingers, the blue faded from years of hiding. I pull it out and set it on my lap. So many memories stuffed inside this box my Nonna gave me when I was a young girl. I shouldn't open it, I should stuff it back under the bed. Actually, I should throw out the contents. I'm not that girl anymore.

I was never very good at listening to my inner self. I run my fingers over the carved stars and moons and flip open the box before I can change my mind. The letters stare back from the same place I left them years ago, folded, fragile, and more than a little ridiculous. My handwriting looks younger, braver. They are all folded differently, and the one folded into a heart catches my eye first.

Dear L,

I think you'd like it here tonight. The fireflies are out, and the sky looks close enough to touch. I sat on the porch steps and pretended you

I run my thumb over the closing line. It's strange how even at thirteen I knew exactly what I was looking for. That's the thing people never understood. L was never some silly fantasy. He was every good thing I believed could exist: the gentleness, the warmth, the safety. I fold the letter back, running my fingers over the edge until it softens under my touch.

A thousand memories live in this box, the majority of them good. Moonlight walks, porch swing talks, cicadas singing their song outside of my window.

Buried beneath those good memories is the night that rewired something in me. I don't even mean to think about it, but it always finds me when I hold these letters. This memory overpowers all the good ones. There's fairy lights, nail polish remover, microwave popcorn, and the evil laughter of girls I once called friends.

Sleepovers are supposed to be filled with movies, gossip, painting our nails, braiding each other's hair, and you know, pretending we weren't thirteen and terrified of boys our age. Someone put on music, someone asked who we liked, and someone else, Jenny freaking Carver, found the blue box.

"What's this?" she'd said, already opening it before I could speak.

I tried my best to move quickly, jumping over my bed, trying to get to the other side. But by the time I reached her, she was already reading my letters out loud.

"Dear L," she singsongs. "I think you'd like it here tonight..." her tone laced with mockery.

I remember that night like it happened last night. The laughter filled the room before she even finished the sentence. Not giggles, full belly laughs, and they were all at my expense. One girl gasped, another shouted, "She's writing to an imaginary boyfriend!" The words landed like heavy stones. In my memory, I stand there pretending to laugh too, pretending it didn't hurt as badly as it did. I can still smell the betrayal; it smells like Jenny Carver's pomegranate shampoo, and I still feel my cheeks burn with embarrassment.

Later, when they all finally fell asleep, I gathered the letters from the carpet one by one. Some were crumpled, one torn. The fairy lights still glowed, soft and pink, as if the room were trying to apologize. I packed them all up, everything back into the box, and told myself stories like this didn't belong in the real world. That I didn't either.

The morning after that sleepover, the whole school already knew. Someone must have told everyone. That someone was Jenny Carver. By the first period, whispers were floating across every corner of every classroom: *"Love letters to nobody."* By lunch, someone had taped a heart-shaped note to my locker with a giant L drawn in the middle.

I remember ripping it down fast, pretending I didn't care, pretending it was all some inside joke I was too cool to explain. Thank God Maddie and Joss weren't there that night, they would've burned the school down before they let anyone laugh. But it didn't matter, by the end of the day, the story had its own life.

Mammà called it *girls being cruel.* Papà said *people laugh when they don't understand magic.* Neither of them knew how to make the heat in my chest go away.

That week, I threw away every letter except the ones that didn't mention love. Then I dug them back out of the trash the next morning, wiped the coffee grounds off the envelopes, and hid the box under my bed.

I stopped writing after that. Stopped hoping anyone would ever see the world the way I did.

I blink back the pain. The memory dissolves as fast as it came. I tuck the letter back into the stack and close the lid.

Maybe that's why I stopped writing. Not because I stopped believing, but because believing started to hurt. Believing in a love so effortless became out of reach. I slide the box under the bed, turn off the lamp, and lie back in the dark. The ceiling fan spins lazy circles above me.

Two

((

The front door creaks embarrassingly loud as I open it up, like it's announcing something the entire town needs to hear. It's just Joss, my best friend. She's holding a gallon of my favorite ice cream, pistachio! She pushes through the door as her long black hair flows over her shoulder, walking in like she's lived here all her life; she may as well have.

"I heard Bocelli playing and decided I'd better grab the ice cream and come over for that delicious sauce I know your parents are cooking up in the kitchen." She wiggles her shoulders as she heads for the kitchen.

Joss, short for Jocelynn, has lived next door to me for as long as I can remember, and yes, my parents are blasting music so loud my neighbors can hear. Heck, I saw movers moving someone down the street. My parents' music is so loud, I bet they are regretting their decision to move into that house right about now.

"Well, hello to you, too," I say to the air as I slam the door, Joss nowhere in sight.

Making my way into the kitchen, Joss has already begun pulling plates out of the cabinet and is setting the table. My parents, however, are still dancing. Have they even noticed Joss has invited herself over for dinner? It's like my Papà can read my mind. I finish the thought at the same time he pins me with a '*what is she doing here?*' look.

"Joselynn, it's nice to see you knocked this time," Papà calls over his shoulder, which causes Joss to choke on the air she's inhaling.

"I even used the front door this time, Nico," she places a kiss on his cheek, greeting him.

She makes her way over to mammà, wraps her arms around her slender waist, and places a gentle kiss on her cheek. "He's on one again, isn't he mammà E?"

My mammà gives her a knowing smile paired with her signature wink that says, *You know he is.*

Papà and Joss have always had a back-and-forth, banter-filled relationship. She spent a lot of time with us when we were about five or six years old. I'm talking about staying over for weeks at a time and taking baths together. Nonna would always shake her head at Joss, smiling down at her, saying, "Her heart is louder than her mouth, even when the world can't see it." She has always been here, always been loved.

We finish eating my favorite meal, vodka rigatoni, when Joss and I make our way to the patio outside. She's going on and on about how some girl named Millie was talking crap about her in the restroom at the mall. Apparently, Millie had no idea that Joss was in one of the stalls. I'm doing my best to stay engaged in this conversation, but I cannot let go of the flutter in my chest ever since the doorbell rang. Of course, it was Joss; it just felt like something new, something exciting was going to knock on my door for once, someone.

I reach for the half-eaten carton of ice cream she brought, digging my spoon into it.

"Gross, are you going to get a bowl?" she twists her face up in disgust.

I point my spoon at her, "You brought over a half-eaten carton of ice cream, and I'm the gross one?" I roll my eyes and continue digging in.

"Whatever..." She continues to fill me in on all the gossip of the town, plus all the gossip of the school.

"You do know I go to the same school...right?" It's my turn to look disgusted.

She rolls her eyes, but continues on with her story as if I didn't see it unfold in real time. There aren't many times that Joss lets silence fill the air, this is one of those times. She is looking at me quizzically, studying me.

"What's up with you, Rem?" She looks down at her hands."You look like your mind is elsewhere. Are you okay?"

"Yeah, I'm perfectly fine," I shove another spoonful of ice cream in my mouth. "Stop staring at me like that." I swallow. "It's weird."

She doesn't press me on it; she grabs a spoon and dives right into the carton of pistachio ice cream. *Now, who is gross?* I think to myself.

"You know this stuff is terrible, right?" gulping down a spoonful. "The only good thing about this ice cream is it's your favorite color." Her eyebrows scrunch up, and she cocks her head to the side. "Come to think of it, that's why you like it, isn't it?"

I want to tell her yes, but when I look up at her, she gives me a knowing look. I shrug my shoulders and dig my spoon back in. She's my best freaking friend, she should be able to connect those dots by now.

"What is that look for Remi... Seriously, I'm worried about you." Her voice is low.

I shove another spoonful of ice cream into my mouth, buying myself a few more seconds to decide if I'm going to tell my best friend the truth or cover this up and keep my feelings hidden. I settle on the truth; she may be dumping gossip on me, but she would never dump mine elsewhere.

"Do you think I'll ever fall in love?" I set my spoon and the carton down on the patio table. "Or do you think I've peaked emotionally?" I pull at the hem of my shirt, distracting myself from the question floating in the air.

Her eyes balloon, "Are you serious?" She scoots her patio chair closer to mine.

After a long pause, I give her a Kanye-sized shoulder shrug. " I don't know Joss," throwing one hand in the air, still not making eye contact. "I just feel like no one out there gets me. I think I've peaked." I finally looked up, meeting her eyes. "What if I will only ever be loved by my parents and you?"

"Didn't you write like a thousand letters to your future soul mate?" She deadpans, sitting back in her chair.

A thousand memories flood back in, good and bad. I hate that people know that part of me. Joss wasn't there that night, she and Maddie were off traipsing around on Maddie's family's estate in Aspen. I begged my Papà to let me go with them that year, just like I do every year. The answer is always the same, it's always no.

"Are you ever going to let me read them?" her voice low, unsure. "I only ever heard the stories from the whispers in the hallways when we got back that year." Pity fills her eyes as she looks over to me.

"Josselyn," my tone is sharp. "What makes you think I'd share that part of me with anyone?" my voice dropping to a whisper. "Ever."

"Whoa," her eyes ballooning again, "We're using full government names?" she spits out. "Well, Remilia Guessepinna Moretti. I never asked because you didn't tell. I would have never let them make fun of you that night, nor would I" putting her finger in the middle of her chest, and then pointing to me "make fun of you myself."

I flinch at the use of my full name. Why my parents decided to name me after my Nonno, I'll never know. I've never even met the man. Yeah, that's right, I'm named after a man, Guisepee Moretti. Anyway, back to the problem at hand.

"It's not the weirdest thing I've seen you do," her voice low as she tries to lighten the mood. "I mean, sure, you write Dear No One letters like you're Tori Kelly. But..." She trails off, rubbing the inside of her wrist. "I did try to carve initials into my skin with the end of a paperclip that I heated up with a lighter... for a boy I can't even stand now." Her eyes meet mine. "So yeah, tragic."

I push out a pitied laugh, but it sticks in my throat.

"Maybe we're all a little tragic." She pushes the carton of ice cream in my direction. "It's nothing to be ashamed of." she reassures me, pushing my hair out of my face.

I close my eyes, let my head fall to the back of the chair, and breathe.

Joss stands and drops a kiss to my head before she says, "I'll see you tomorrow at school, Rem. Tell Nico and Elena I said thanks for dinner, would ya?" looking down at me with soft eyes. "I love you, Remi."

I scrunch my nose up at her as she makes her way to the side gate. That's the good thing about having your best friend live next door. Lying my head back down onto the back of the chair, I can't help but close my eyes and think of the boy who occupied so much of my time at thirteen. What would it be like to sit with him one more time, letting his silence give me all the answers I need?

Pushing that feeling deep down, I head upstairs, grabbing my headphones and my shoes. I've got to get out of here, get some fresh air, and forget about the thirteen-year-old version of myself who wrote letters to an imaginary boy, or this eighteen-year-old version of me who feels like love is unattainable.

"I'm going on a walk, be back soon-ish," I yell over my shoulder, not waiting for a reply. I shut the door, eager to be anywhere but in my head.

This small Tennessee town is so beautiful at dusk. The smell of pine in the air, the wind pushing my hair in every direction but the good one. I push air in and out as I blast "Drive by Sza" over and over again. The burn in my calves from these hills tells me I will be sore tomorrow. I make the mental note to grab my keys and go for a drive next time.

So what, I wrote letters to an imaginary boy. My Nonna had just died when I started seeing him in my dreams every night.

My heart was broken. I think it was my way of searching for the kind of love she always gave me, warm, safe, unconditional.

I turn the corner, lost in my thoughts, lost in my memories of her. So lost, that I don't even see the figure ahead of me until it's too late. I run straight into something solid. Correction, someone. A barricade in the shape of a boy, but *why is his body so hard?*

Oh.

Black boots, fitted jeans that hug his hips, a simple black t-shirt, and a jaw sharp enough to slice right through mozzarella, cleaner than any knife we have at Nonna's, that's for sure.

He's standing between the road and the edge of a driveway, struggling to pull a box from the back of a beat-up truck. I can feel the annoyance make its way to my mouth, but it dies on my tongue, right as the wind blows my hair in front of my face again. The air feels charged with something electric.

Wait.

I freeze where I stand, one hand clutching my non-existent pearls, the other gripping invisible air like it might hold me up. He must hear the gasp that slips through my lips, a small betrayal, because he drops the box and turns.

"Are you okay?"

His voice, *Where have I heard that voice?* I've heard that voice, somewhere. I just can't place where. He lifts his head, searching my face, his eyes drop down the length of my body, and then his eyes find mine.

Everything stops. I know those eyes. Honey colored eyes, the kind I've only ever seen in one place. My dreams. The boy I imagined isn't a dream at all.

He's standing right in front of me.

And those eyes...

They're his.

Three

"Hello," he waves a hand in front of my face. "I asked if you were okay?"

I blink hard. My brain refuses to catch up to what's happening. There's no way this is real, but he's still looking at me. I can't form a word—he probably thinks I'm mute. *Quick, Remi, say something.*

"Um, yeah," I say, though my voice doesn't quite sound like my own.

He studies my eyes. Eye contact with a stranger is getting awkward. His brows knit, like he's trying to remember something. Maybe he's been to the restaurant? I don't know, but I'll find out—maybe.

"You sure. You uh," he reaches up to scratch the back of his head, and I try not to stare at the stretch of muscle poking out from his shirt. "You screamed."

"Oh, yeah. Sorry, I saw a.. Uh… a spider." Smooth Remi, real smooth.

He tilts his head, clearly not buying it but too polite to press. The corner of his mouth twitches, almost a smile.

"Well," he says, voice a little softer now, "spider's gone, I think." holding his hands out and looking around on the ground.

I nod, pretending to laugh, but my heart's still hammering against my ribs like it's trying to get out. The air feels heavy, making it hard to breathe. Everything about this moment is off-kilter, like the world tilted half a degree and no one but me noticed.

He shifts his weight from one side to another. "So uh." stuffing his hands in his pockets. "Are you from around here?" he pushes out nervously.

"Yeah. um Im Remi." I trip over my words, my hand flying in front of my face. *Speaking with your hands, Remi, when did you start this?* " I live at the house on the corner covered in vines, its white but you would never be able to tell by all the vines and trees, it reminds my parents of home, not this home though, my parents think it reminds them of Nonna's village back in Italy, where ivy climbs up every wall like it's racing for the roof."

I stop to catch my breath. His eyes are getting bigger by the second, like he is watching a train wreck happen right before his eyes.

"My family owns Nonna's, down on Main." I blurt out, throwing my hand up in the direction of the restaurant. The one with the red sign in town." I can see I'm scaring him. "You've probably driven past it."

"Yeah," his eyebrows raise. "I've seen it," he nods.

"Sorry, I'm rambling. I tend to do that when um.. I'm alive." *I'm alive, what the..*

That gets the smallest laugh out of him, quiet but real, and it does something weird to my chest.

"Guess I'll have to stop by." his voice is low, steady.

"You should," I say, trying to sound normal but hearing the breathlessness in my voice. "Best garlic knots in town. Probably the only ones, but still."

He smiles, just a little, one side of his mouth lifting like he's not sure if he's allowed to yet.

"Noted," he says.

Neither of us moves. Cicadas cantan. The sun presses on my neck. The air between us is thicker than Joss's failed attempt at Italian bread.

Then he clears his throat. "Well, uh, see you around… Remi."

"Yeah," I manage, fingers still twitching in some kind of nervous encore. "See you around."

My feet start moving on their own, even though I never want to leave this spot.

"Hey uh, Remi?" his voice was low.

I whip my body back around. Maybe he wants me to stay in this spot forever, too.

"You probably shouldn't tell strangers where you live." That half smile shows itself again, except a little deeper this time.

"You might be right." I huff out in a half laugh. "I have to go, stranger," I hook my thumb over my shoulder, pointing backwards towards my house. "I'll see you around." I turn back and take a wobbly step back towards my house. "Or," I find myself announcing as I turn back towards him.

He cocks his head to the side, dropping the box once again and putting his hands back into his pocket.

"Or you won't, do you even like Italian food, or garlic knots..." I scratch my head. "We don't even make garlic knots, actually." I twist my face up in disgust. My Italian heritage just threatened to cancel me, I can feel it.

Awkward silence stretches between us, both of us taking turns looking at each other and then anywhere but each other.

"I have to go.. I'll see you around, stranger." I turn back towards my house, not waiting for a response.

Never have I word vomited like that to a boy I just met. I've also never wondered how a boy would *look in a tux at the end of an aisle with me in a white dress.* But here we are.

I open the front door, and the creak that sends sound waves throughout all of Copperridge snaps me out of whatever *im getting married soon* trance I was just in. I shut it quickly, leaning against it, letting the coolness of the wood calm my heated skin.

Could this really be the boy from my dreams? Surely not... right? Still, the thought won't leave. The voice. The eyes. The way the air felt when he said my name.

"Mamma mia," I mutter, dragging a hand down my face. What else can an Italian girl say when the boy from her dreams has a name, biceps, and hair worthy of a shampoo ad?

"Did you say something, Tesoro?" My papà's voice breaks up my thoughts. He pokes his head out from the kitchen, staring at me like I am crazy for talking to myself.

"No Papà." Standing at attention like I'm going off to war. " I'm going to take a shower and go to bed." Finding my footing, I take a step towards the stairs.

"I'm meeting Joss at The Copper Café tomorrow for brunch, and then I'll be at the restaurant to help you with the lunch and dinner crowds. Goodnight papà," I tell him, trying to escape his gaze.

I dart up the stairs as fast as I can and barricade myself in the restroom. I can't let him see my face. Papà has this way of knowing exactly what's happening just by looking at me, and I'm not sure I'm ready for that just yet.

It's not until I'm lathering up my hair for the second time that I finally come down from whatever roller coaster of emotions I was just on. Which in itself is a problem, because nothing about a three-minute conversation with a boy I don't even know should leave me acting like I just lived an entire lifetime in five seconds. This is a whole new level of pathetic. Who gets this worked up over a boy they just ran into? Me apparently. Great. I scrub harder, like I can wash the weird déjà vu off my skin. It wasn't some cosmic moment. It was just a cute boy with nice arms and annoyingly familiar eyes. End of story. My heart can take several seats, preferably in the back row. The universe doesn't just hand you the boy from your dreams with a "congrats, you're unhinged" sticker attached.

Oh my gosh, what is Joss going to say when I tell her about the boy who just moved onto our street? I quickly finish up my shower so I can send her a quick text. I don't think I'm ready to see her reaction in person yet. This is the kind of news that needs to be broken behind the safety of a screen, with at least three layers of sarcasm so she doesn't hear the actual panic hiding under my voice.

I still wonder. And in a way that feels dangerous. Here's the thing: if I let myself think about him for more than two seconds, I start imagining things. Things I absolutely do not have time for. Like a fling. Or a crush. Or anything with a boy who looks at me like he's known me longer than five minutes.

I have plans. Or… okay, not actual plans. More like the outline of plans. The rough sketch of a life everyone keeps telling me I should already have figured out. I don't know what I want to *be.* I don't have a five-year plan, or even a five-minute plan, most days. All I know is that everyone around me seems to be sprinting toward their futures while I'm still tying my shoes, hoping no one notices. And now, on top of all that pressure, the universe decides to throw a boy with perfect hair into my path like I needed a side quest?

College brochures keep showing up in the mailbox like little paper threats. Teachers keep asking what major I'm leaning toward, like I'm supposed to know. My dad keeps trying to talk about internships like I'm not still trying to survive high school chemistry. I don't even know what I want to be, let alone who I want to be. All I know is that I'm supposed to be "focused on my future" and "taking things seriously," which leaves very little room for mysterious boys with good hair and confusing eyes.

I squeeze the water out of my hair for the final time. Turning the water off, the steam from the shower starts to dissipate as my mind travels to Nonna. She would un-dig her own grave if she heard me say the words *garlic knots* and *Nonna's* in the same sentence. That woman treated those little dough spirals like a personal insult. "Real Italian bread does not look like a twisted pretzel," she used to say, dramatically condemning anyone who enjoyed them.

"I miss you, Nonna," I whisper into the fog.

I wrap myself in a towel and grab my phone, fully intending to scroll mindlessly and forget everything that just happened on my front porch. Instead, my fingers unlock my phone faster than my brain can catch up, which is how I find myself drafting the most dramatic message possible.

Me:

Hey, *I think my Nonna is haunting me or something. I took a walk after you left to clear my head and ran right into the new neighbor down the street. He looks EXACTLY like the boy from my dreams, so I'm thinking instead of brunch... do you want to go wedding dress shopping?*

Joss is quite possibly the only person alive who encourages my chaos. She is also allergic to delayed reactions.

Her reply appears in under 10 seconds. But it's not a text. Oh no. It's a GIF. A very dramatic GIF. Megan Thee Stallion is gasping for air like she's seen a ghost. Followed by Cinderella spinning into her dress like she's preparing for her royal engagement photoshoot. I'm not sure if she's telling me to slow down, speed up, or start practicing my future signature for our invitations.

Joss:

BESTIE, WHAT DO YOU MEAN HE LOOKS LIKE DREAM BOY???

SEND DETAILS. LOCATION. BLOOD TYPE. HEIGHT. HAIR SITUATION.

DO I NEED TO GRAB MY BINOCCULARS???

I choke on a laugh, then swipe my hand diagonally down the foggy mirror. My reflection appears in the streaky clearing, a mess of wet hair, pink cheeks, and wide eyes that look like they just saw their entire life flash before them. Or maybe their past. I don't know anymore.

I blink, but she doesn't. I stare at the girl looking back at me. She looks… startled. Like she just saw the first page of a story she didn't realize she was in.

"Who are you?" I think, not expecting an answer.

The weight of the silence feels like I got one anyway.

Four

☾

I woke up from what feels like the best sleep of my life with the sounds of Bad Idea by Olivia Rodrigo, a ringtone that fits Joss perfectly. Great song, terrible alarm. Hitting the ignore button, I snuggle back into the comfort of my warm bed. My mind instantly replayed meeting him last night, quickly becoming my favorite moment of the week, beating everything else by a mile.

Wait.

Hold on…

No, no, no, no.

I don't even know his name.

My eyes snap open. I sit up so fast the room tilts, and suddenly I'm wide awake for the worst possible reason. I search the memory front to back, side to side, upside down, mentally hitting replay on every second of our less than five-minute conversation.

I never did.

I met the boy who looked exactly like the one my brain had been inventing for nearly a year, and somehow skipped the part where normal humans exchange names. My pulse starts doing jumping jacks. *What were you thinking, Remi?* I collapse back on my bed, cover my face with a pillow, and let out a muffled, pathetic groan.

Of course, that's the exact moment Olivia Rodrigo decides to enter the room again. I stare at the screen, more annoyed than the first time she called. She better not be canceling on me. Then I swipe to answer.

"Jocelynn, if this is you canceling on me, cancel our friendship too." I declare.

"Girl," Joss always pauses for dramatic effect. "Get up, brunch just turned into breakfast, I need all the tea before Maddie meets us. You know, as soon as she hears about a new boy in town, her hormones will be doing backflips. I'll be there in seven minutes, and you better not have sleep in your eyes." She takes an exaggerated breath. "GET UP!" She yells and hangs up in my face.

I swear, she's so demanding, it's way too early for this. I throw my grey comforter back over my head and sulk over the fact that I don't know his name for five more minutes. I finally get my eyes to close again, and I'm hit with the same Olivia Rodrigo song. She is insatiable, I swear.

"Im up, Joselynn. Leave me alone." I grunt into the phone.

I can hear her laughing, which makes me hit the red button on her immediately. She knows I'm not a morning person until I've had my caffeine. I'm Italian for crying out loud. I peel my comforter from my tired body, and I climb my way out of this warm, comfortable bed. I pull on my favorite pair of jeans and a slouchy black sweater, perfect for the pre-fall chill settling over Copperridge. Or, more accurately, perfect for surviving The Copper Cup Café, which Georgia Whitlock insists on keeping at subzero temperatures year-round. I tell myself she does it to chase us teenagers out, but really, it's probably a clever strategy to sell more coffee.

I stumble out of my closet and grab my bag, filled with probably more books than anyone should carry at once, my restaurant uniform, and about three different flavors of the Essence Super Peptide Glossy Lip. All of it ends up in a pile on my bed, plopping my body down next to it probably wasn't my best idea. Mammà would probably murder me if she saw me propping my very well-loved black Converse on my bed, but I need to tie my shoes, and I'm in a hurry. As soon as Joss hits that door, there's no slowing her down. She has what Mammà calls the 'second child syndrome', she always says, 'Joss marches to the beat of her own really fast dub step drum, which no one else can hear. She is the chaos to my calm.

Making my way downstairs, the scent of coffee warms my heart before it ever warms my body. It also means Mammà is already awake. Morning coffee has always been our special time together; it's kind of like an Italian rite of passage.

"Hi Mammà," I say, leaning in for a hug.

I swear she always gives the right amount of pressure when she hugs you. Not too tight to where she squeezes you until you turn blue, but enough to where you feel like you're falling into the coziest bed you could ever dream of being in.

"Mmhmm, good morning, Teroso, I locked the top lock so Joss couldn't get in," laughing into the side of my head. "But if you don't hurry, she will go around back." She says, rubbing circles on my back.

I lay my head on her shoulder and tell her that I will be at the restaurant for the lunch rush. Kissing her lightly on her cheek, I head for the door. Joss said seven minutes about five minutes ago, which means she will be here any second.

"Hold on, Teroso, you'll need this." Mamma throws me a small bottle.

Stuffing the bottle into the bag hanging from my shoulder, I look up to see Joss' shadow coming towards the back door. The big floor-to-ceiling windows let her know we can see her, just as she can see us. I laugh and look up to see Mammà, shaking her head.

"La mammà sa tutto." She whispers, bringing her mug to her lips.

My smile grows as I turn towards the back door. I shoot her a grin over my shoulder. Mammà really does know everything, doesn't she?

"Uffa, che fretta! I was coming," I say, opening the door.

"Remi, I know enough Italian to know you just asked me *what the rush is.*" Her nose scrunched up in a scowl.

Joss' arms folded across her favorite blue sweater, and I can't keep my smile from reaching my ears. Instead of words, I choose to roll my eyes at her. She could probably carry on a conversation in Italian with all the time she has spent over here.

I push past her, "Come on, Joss, let's get going."

This town is pretty small, so the three block drive takes no time at all. Joss doesn't even question me when I climb into my car. There's absolutely no way I'm getting into her car, I don't believe we would make it there alive. She's been trying and failing at the drivers test for almost two years. She finally got her license three months ago and has already been in two fender benders. That doesn't include the time she ran over my childhood bike. I still don't think I've forgiven her yet.

On the car ride to the cafe, I word vomit again. This time, filling her in on all the details of my run-in with the stranger, whom she claims I'm 'madly in love' with already. My head is already pounding from all the eye rolls I've given her today, and it's nine in the morning.

"Morning Sugar!" We're greeted by Georgia Whitlock as we enter the Copper Cup Cafe.

Georgia has owned this cafe for as long as I can remember. She's slightly older, I can tell by the sprinkles of grey hair throughout her head. She doesn't miss a beat, though. I love this place, especially when it rains. There's something about a warm cup of my favorite Café Latte on a rainy day. The cups here all have unique shapes and colors. Georgia gets them from a potter a few towns over. I personally think the 'potter' is her boyfriend, but when I ask her about him, she shuts me all the way down. I don't think she notices the way her cheeks pink when she walks away, though.

I think it's my favorite part about this place. Each cup of coffee is unique to the person drinking it, so it fits. It could also just be Georgia's theme because it matches perfectly with the mismatched furniture. I come here to read a lot. Georgia hardly ever charges me for refills now, it's like she knows the way to my heart or something.

Joss and I place our order and make our way to our spot, a cute little wooden table right in front of the window. She sets her bag down and heads for the restroom about the same time Georgia is setting our drinks in front of us. The coffee shop smells nothing like Nonna's kitchen, but it's close enough to trick me for a second. I wrap both hands around my mug and watch the foam tremble with each passing bus outside the window. The milk is hot, the air thick with roasted beans, and suddenly I'm not here anymore.

I'm eight years old, my legs too short for the kitchen chair, and my feet swinging in the air. Nonna is at the stove, her back to me, humming softly. My Mammà leans against the counter, her hair pulled into a messy knot on top of her head, smiling over the rim of her cup.

"Your first Vero latte macchiato, bambina," she says, as if I've just been invited into a secret society. Nonna sets the cup in front of me as a cloud of steam rises, carrying the scent of coffee. She taps her spoon against the cocoa tin and dusts the foam's surface. "It's for the eyes and the heart." She says in Italian, sliding the cup closer. I lift it with both hands, and I can't help but feel comforted by the warmth against my palms. The first sip leaves a little mustache of foam across the top of my lip, and Nonna laughs, dabbing at me with a napkin.

Joss plops down at the table and breaks my trance. I pull out the small jar Mammà gave me this morning and dust my café latte with cocoa powder, just like my Nonna did. I'm halfway into my first sip when Joss nods towards the door.

Maddie breezes in, the third to our best friend trio, her blonde hair catching the light as her bright green eyes scan the cafe until she spots us. She's been part of our trio since middle school, she's quieter than Joss, but somehow pulls the spotlight in her direction without even trying. She's the kind of effortless beauty that half the world pays top dollar trying to imitate. She drops her tote onto the chair next to me, already eyeing Joss like she's waiting to be filled in on whatever gossip I've been holding back.

I take a slow sip and close my eyes as the foam melts on my tongue. It's good, but it's not Nonna's.

Hours later, I step out of The Copper Cup Cafè and let the fresh air pack away the memories of Nonna. I mostly sat and watched as Joss gave Maddie all the details of my run-in with the strange boy. Trying my best to keep the smiles to a minimum. Maddie has an unintentional way of demanding all of the attention for herself, and I selfishly want his attention all to myself.

The Cafè is two doors down from my parents' restaurant. It's a small town, and Nonna's is on the corner of Main Street, so my fresh air doesn't last long. I can already smell the basil and marinara. I like to pretend Nonna's isn't a big deal, but the truth? It's *the* restaurant to be at for at least a hundred miles. People plan for months and drive hours just to get a table. Friday nights, Saturdays, and Sundays, the place is stuffed tighter than the ravioli with reservations.

Nonna helped Papà design the menu back when it first opened. Most of the dishes came straight from her own childhood. Recipes her Mammà made in a tiny Tuscan kitchen with a window that overlooked the olive trees. Every time I pass through the doors, it's like stepping into her memories… just with customers asking for extra breadsticks.

Walking into Nonna's, I can already feel the tension. I just know my papà is throwing out orders somewhere in this building. I head for my papà's office so I can put my bag down and change into my uniform. The smell of garlic is so strong, it always takes me back to a memory or two of Nonna.

The kitchen smelled like heaven, garlic, butter, and fresh rosemary all coming from the oven. I was so proud of myself, pulling the baking sheet out without burning my hands, or legs, yes, I've done that, on the oven rack or door. When I set the tray on the counter, Nonna's eyes balloon and I know I've messed up.

"Oh, bambina," she pressed her hand to her heart, but the corners of her mouth were already twitching. "This garlic bread, she went on holiday without us." She grabs a wooden spoon and smacks the bread, "Straight to the beach, spent too long in the summer sun."

My face sinks, and my lips turn to the side, "It's ruined, im sorry, Nonna."

Nonna shakes her head, "No, no, just, she forgot her umbrella." She tears a piece off from the middle, where the bread is still soft and golden, and she hands it to me. "See, bambino, still good where it matters."

I took a bite, and the buttery center melted on my tongue. I close my eyes, and my shoulders come up towards my ears. "We will make another," she says, already pulling the ingredients from the cabinet. "And this time, we watch her together, Sì? You keep your eyes on her, and I'll keep my eyes on you."

That's how my papà finds me in his office, locked into this memory of my Nonna. "Teroso, where is your mind?" He asks as he hugs me and kisses the top of my head.

"Hi papà, the smell of your wonderful food sent me back into a memory of making bread with Nonna," I say, twisting my lips up, just as I did as a little girl.

"I miss her," I say into his apron. He sighs and rubs my back.

"Me too teroso, but she would tirare le orecchie," he says as he's pulling my ears. " to us if she knew those tables hadn't been greeted properly, I need you out there." He says as he squeezes my shoulders and walks out of his office.

"I guess that's my cue," I say to absolutely no one.

I spend the rest of the night taking customers to their tables and keeping them stocked with fresh bread. Don't worry, I'm not the one cooking it. The last table was left twenty minutes ago, but the smell of garlic and basil will never go away. The chairs are flipped onto tables, and the only thing you can hear is my Papà humming as he counts the register. I swipe my rag over the last table. The restaurant always feels bigger when it's empty, like the walls have taken a step back to catch their breath. My feet ache, and I smell like marinara, im ready to go home.

Throwing my towel into the laundry on the way by, I wave bye to papà as I slip out the door, the fresh air hitting me, making my hair blow like I'm on stage with Queen B herself. Copperridge is nearly still at this hour, streetlights and shadows, shop windows and neon signs. I inhale, trading oregano for the faint smell of wet pavement. I love this time of night, it's quiet, like the whole town is holding its breath. My steps echo against the sidewalk until I reach my car, climbing inside my cobalt blue Toyota Corolla. I take in the silence for a few more breaths before I roll my windows down and head home, a nice warm bath at the front of my mind.

I take my time driving, taking in all that Copperridge has to offer. I pass the florist's window, dark except for the glow of a single string of fairy lights, then the hardware store with its dusty display of paint samples and lawn chairs. Just as I round the corner toward home, the quiet breaks. I hear the low strum of a guitar. I pick up my pace to see where the sound is coming from. That's when I see him, leaning against the tire of that pickup truck.

I should keep going, I really should, but I don't. My body betrays me by making me pull over.

Five

☾

Yesterday I couldn't get away quick enough, today I find myself getting out of the car and walking towards him. He doesn't see me. He's so wrapped up in strumming the guitar slowly with his eyes closed, I almost hate to interrupt. I said almost. My body is still moving towards him; I'm trying to slow my breathing. On instinct, I pull out my phone and bend down to snap a picture of him leaning against the tire, making sure to get the glow of the fleeting sunset behind him.

"hey!"

Oh crap, that came from me. I shove my phone into my back pocket and close the gap between us. The strumming stops. He opens his eyes and lifts his head to look at me, and when he does, I'm stunned. He's so handsome.

His eyes look like barrels of sticky honey, and I'm certain it's me who is caught in the stickiness. I can't tell what he is thinking, but I can feel it. His eyes rake over my body, but when they flick back to mine, I can still see the hint of sadness. It makes me want to reach out and give him a hug, an Elena Moretti hug to be exact.

"You again," he pauses, his eyes searching mine. "Remi the rambler," the corner of his mouth lifts into the most devilish smirk I think I've ever seen.

Okay, this boy is a charmer, and I'm already charmed. I'm in trouble.

"Yeah," I push out nervously. "Sorry about that," I say, looking down towards my shoes.

My mouth twists to the side as I try to focus on the tiny speckles of flour on the shoes. Instantly regretting pulling that car over. I don't want to be charmed or stuck in honey anymore.

"No, I uh, don't be sorry." He fumbles over his words.

I don't know if Papà put something new in the marinara sauce tonight, but it feels an awful lot like boldness.

"May I?" I point to the ground and ask him if I can sit.

He looks at me, licks his bottom lip, and nods. He watches me intently, as if he is searing this moment into his brain forever.

"I uh," smiling at how dumb I'm about to sound. "Spent so much time throwing up my words that I actually forgot to ask your name." I finally spat out, throwing my hand in his direction.

I'm not ready for the smirk he gives me. It feels like time has stopped for a split second. The way my heart hammers in my chest has got to be unnatural. This ground feels cold, but my skin is burning. Without thinking, I tuck my bottom lip between my teeth and tuck my hair behind my ear, even though at this very moment I'm sure it should be covering my blushing cheeks.

"Zane."

I blink.

"Zane?"

He shrugs, eyes flicking over me like he's reading a page and deciding whether to turn it.

"That's mysterious," I say, tilting my head. "Or suspicious. Can't decide which yet." My voice comes out way breathier than I intended, which kind of makes me proud.

His smirk deepens, as I've just given him extra points in whatever unspoken game he's playing. "You're quick."

I look down at my hands in my lap, deciding on where to take this conversation. I shrug, "And you're dramatic, who says their name like it's a plot twist?"

"Maybe I like plot twists." He scoots closer to me, not enough to close the space completely, but enough that I catch the faintest scent of rain on him. "But you'll figure me out. Eventually."

My chest tightens for no reason other than the cool night air. "Bold of you to assume that I planned on trying."

He laughs under his breath, as I caught him off guard, shaking his head as he comes to whatever conclusion he just came to. The smallest smile fights its way onto my lips before I can stop it.

He laughs once, quietly. "Sure you weren't."

For a moment, neither of us moves. The street feels too still, like even the leaves are holding their breath with us.

"Well, Zane.." Emphasis on Zane, like it's something I'm not sure I believe. " I should get going. It's nice to finally know your name, I guess."

As I stand to leave, he stands with me and leans his guitar against the blue truck. He props one foot on the tire, and he leans his back against the body of the truck, crossing his arms and meeting my eyes. I've never in my life been jealous of a truck, but here we are. My eyes travel down his body, noticing every muscle his clothes are clinging to. When my eyes travel back up to his, his mouth twitches ever so slightly. Like catching me staring at him is the icing on his cake. He's looking at me like he wants to ask me something.

"What?" I ask hesitantly.

"What's your favorite place in this town, besides the one you're always running off to?" He says with that smirk I'm already etching into memory. "You know, the house with the vines." He says with a chuckle, like he's proud of himself for making fun of me in a moment of sheer panic when I word vomited on him last night.

"Who is trying to figure who out now?" I say with a proud smile.

His face doesn't change; he just stares blankly at me with the same smirk he has been wearing throughout this exchange.

"I love the Copper Cup Cafè" I finally say. " Or Ridgewood books, it's a pretty cool place. They have a loft that some of my friends hang out in after school sometimes." I twist my mouth to the side, debating telling him what my actual favorite place is, but I decide not to.

"Will I get to see you again, or are you the type to run when people start asking questions?" He stares at me hard, like he's trying to take a peek into my soul when he asks that.

I think to myself, end it here with a witty response, or keep him on his toes and see how far I can get him to go. I shouldn't feel this drawn to him, but I do. I really don't want this to end just yet, so I say the one thing that will take the longest.

"I live three houses down. Walk me home, ask your questions, and if I find them interesting enough, I'll come back to you tomorrow."

His eyebrows raise, and I can practically see the dare in his eyes. He doesn't know it yet, but he's playing with fire. His head cocks to the side a bit like he's trying to decide his own fate. His eyebrows raise again, and that smirk that I've already memorized appears on his chiseled face.

"Careful, Remi, I'm very good at interesting."

He takes his first step towards me, but I don't move. His scent is something I feel like I've smelled before, and his presence is something I find oddly familiar. His name is different, but this is him. I can feel it in my little Italian bones. I turn on my heels, making sure to look anywhere but at my car. He falls into step beside me, and for once, he's not rushing to fill the silence. I hate that it makes me curious. Maybe he is good at interesting.

"Why do I get the feeling you're harder to impress than you let on to be?" He says, stuffing his hands into his pockets.

His shoulders shoot for his ears. He's uncomfortable. I raise my eyebrows and think to myself, good. Something about him settles me, even when I don't want it to.

"Is that really one of your questions? That's not necessarily a question, more of a statement." I say with a shrug of my own, I slow my steps, it's only three houses down, and anyway you flip it, this moment is going to end way too soon.

"If I guessed your biggest secret, would you admit it?" He retorts.

I stop in my tracks as my eyes balloon "heck no!" I move my feet. "Next question, please." As I let out the breath I was nervously holding, I gave it a side eye. He's staring at me, and you know that little thing I just said about him settling me, yeah, it was all a lie. No part of me is settled right now.

"What's the one thing I could say right now that would make you stop walking?" His feet stop moving, and so does my heart.

I glance at him, the corner of his mouth tilted up like he already knows the answer. He doesn't.

I keep walking for another two steps before letting my lips curl into the smallest of smirks. So this is how those hallmark moments feel.

"Funny thing, Zane... I don't stop walking for just anyone. You'd have to make it worth it." I keep moving, he can't win that easily.

His laugh is low and warm, and I hate that it makes me want to linger. I shove my hands back under the sweater I'm carrying and keep moving, pretending not to notice his gaze lingering on me. We reach the edge of my driveway, and I stop just long enough to nod toward the house.

"This is it," I say defeatedly as we both look up at the house.

"Wow, you weren't kidding about the vines." He says, with a grin that stops my heartbeat in its tracks.

I match his grin but raise him a nose scrunch. I definitely don't want this to end, and if my gut is right, he doesn't either. He takes a step closer to me. I'm not sure if it's to nudge my feet forward towards the door, or to get out of the street. Either way, I like the closeness.

He takes his hands out of his pockets and reaches for the piece of hair covering my eye, and he slowly drags his fingers across my face until he reaches the back of my ear. I can't help the way my breath hitches as I gasp for air like im a piece of "come un pesce fuor d'acqua"

"You speak Italian?" He says, dropping his hand from my hair, and I can't lie, I miss his touch on my skin already, but wait.

"What do you mean, that's not a question," I say blankly.

"You said come uhh pesce fuor d' something which is Italian, I'm pretty sure." He looks at me strangely with one eyebrow reaching for his hairline.

Remilia Giuseppina Morreti, you did-freaking-not. "I…Yes, I'm Italian, I mean I speak Italian." Great, now I'm fumbling over my words like the Cowboys fumble the football on Thanksgiving. "I didn't mean to say that aloud. I'm so sorry." I stare at him, dumbfounded. "Fish out of water." I finally give it up.

"So what is that, *fish out of water*, what thought were you concealing, Remi?" His smirk grows as he asks this question, and it's not one I plan on answering.

"Is that your final question, Zane, because I'm going to be honest, that's not interesting at all," I say, a little breathier than I intended.

"Oh, it's definitely interesting. But no, that's not my final question. What's the best-kept secret in Copperridge?" He says, bringing his thumb up to his lip and swiping nervously like he just made a mistake.

"Easy." I shrug my shoulders. "The post office, that's where Mrs. Callahan works. She knows every secret in this town, but if you want your mail on time, you never ask her about them." I say with a wink. I take a step forward, and he gently reaches for my arm.

"Not yet," he said gently.

His thumb rubs back and forth on my arm, and I can't make myself look away from the spot on my arm he's touching. I inhale gently and lift my eyes to his, he's staring right into my soul again. I stare back, searching those honey pools, trying to find whatever he is looking for first.

"Ask me, Zane, I know you have one more question." I stare at him boldly now, heat humming between us.

His lips twitch like he's trying not to grin, but then he tilts his head, studying me in a way that feels like he's turning pages only he's allowed to read.

"Alright," he says quietly, almost like he's afraid of the answer. "What's the one thing you've never told anyone in Copperridge?"

My breath catches. That's not small talk. That's not safe. And judging by the way his eyes lock on mine, he knows it.

"Careful," I say, forcing a smirk even though my pulse is pounding. "You might get more than you bargained for."

He leans in just enough for me to catch the faint scent of rain and something I can't name yet. "That's exactly what I'm hoping for."

I take a step back, needing the air to simmer between us, the wooden step is the only thing keeping me upright. "Guess you'll have to wait until tomorrow then."

"I'll hold you to that, Remi." He retorts, and I'm loving the way my name rolls off his lips.

"I'm counting on it, Zane," I say as I drop my chin, bite my lip, and walk away.

By the time I crawl into bed, I'm still warm from the walk home. My hair smells faintly of rosemary and rain, and my brain is still tangled up with his grin. I pull the covers up, staring at the ceiling, replaying every word. Come un pesce fuor d'acqua. That's what I felt like. But maybe for once, I didn't mind being out of my depth.

Oh crap. My car.

Six

☾

I love the slow mornings, the ones where you're woken up by the sunlight and the smell of coffee. The kind of mornings where you can lie in bed for a while and replay all of the highs from your walk home. The same walk home, where I decide to leave my car just to spend two extra minutes with a mystery boy named Zane. Mornings when you get to take extra time in the bathroom mirror, noticing the subtle way your cheeks pink when a memory of him pops into your head.

Shaking that thought out of my head, I make my way downstairs, where I know the most perfect cup of caffè latte is waiting for me. Mamma always makes the best cup, second to Nonna, don't tell her I said that.

Mamma is already at the kitchen table, leaning back in her chair with both hands wrapped around her mug, like always. There's a certain glint in her eyes that makes me suspicious.

"Morning teroso." Her voice is light, but it's got that sly undertone she gets when she is circling her prey.

"Morning Mammà!" I say, sliding the chair across from her and pulling my mug towards me.

"So... " she sets her coffee down slowly, deliberately almost. "Who was the boy who walked you home last night?"

I pause mid sip, "Boy? What boy Mammà?"

She tilts her head with one eyebrow raised, and her lips turned upwards slightly on one side, like she's heard this one before. "The boy with the smile."

"Mammà, always watching." I say as my eyes balloon over the warm mug in front of me. Mammà hits me with a pointed stare. "His name is Zane." He took a sip to conceal the smile and, hopefully, the warm cheeks. "The smile is nice though."

"Did you see movers last week?" I say, trying to deflect from what I just admitted to her. "He moved in there. I ran into him on one of my walks. I find him interesting... I think." Hoping that my rambling will seal the deflection.

"Yes, I saw the movers," she says, rinsing her mug in the sink. "And I know the boy. His name is Zane. He came to introduce himself to your Papà and me yesterday. Went on and on about the vines covering the house, how beautiful they are. Said they reminded him of a picture he saw from Italy."

My eyes bulge right out of my head. There's no concealing the pink in my cheeks now. Did he say that to mock me? Or is he casing my parents to see how easy it'd be to win them over? I bet Papà talked his ear off after hearing that.

"Careful, *ragazza mia*," she calls me 'her girl' over her shoulder with a smile. "Sometimes the charming ones are the most dangerous." And with that, she's gone. I'm left sitting in this kitchen smiling like my Nonna did when I managed to finally cut my first noodle straight.

~

I have bags upon bags of things to drop off at The restaurant. Remilia, run and get this, make sure to get that. Before I left the house, he gave me a handwritten list of all the ingredients from the farmers' market and sent me a text with other things he needed.

I'm walking up to one of the three stands I'm allowed to get these supplies from, mentally going down the checklist of how to check for the ripest tomatoes, the fresh basil, and, let's not forget, the buckets of garlic bulbs. There's no way I'm walking into Nonna's without checking my list twice, just call me Santa Claus, the Italian version. I remember coming to the farmers market with Nonna and Papà, so I know what to look for and exactly which stands to avoid.

I can still smell those Saturdays at the farmers market, the air thick with basil, oregano, and sun-warmed tomatoes. Nonna's hand looped through mine, Papà on her other side with a basket already too full. They'd argue over which stand had the freshest ingredients, their voices rising and falling like music, equal parts love and stubbornness.

Nonna always swore by the woman who grew her tomatoes in plain old soil, "just like her mammà used to." Papà, of course, had to bring up volcanic soil and sweetness and the perfection of Gianni's stand two rows down. They made it sound like a debate that might decide the fate of our entire family's future.

I was used as the tiebreaker. They'd both turn to me, Nonna pressing a tomato under my nose, Papà pinning me into place with a glare, waiting for me to crown the winner. I didn't understand it then, but I do now. They weren't really fighting about ingredients. They were teaching me that food mattered, yes, but passion mattered more. That love could be loud, even stubborn, and still soft underneath. Or they could have just been teaching me how to pick the best tomatoes.

Sometimes when I'm at Nonna's restaurant now, sliding basil leaves into sauce or setting a basket of bread on a table, I catch myself smiling the same way she did when I chose her tomatoes over Papà's. For one heartbeat, it feels like she's still here, laughing beside us.

I miss you, Nonna.

I come back to reality and pull the tomato out of my nose; yup, it smells sun-warmed to me. I ask for an entire crate. They're not shocked. Someone from my family is here weekly to get the freshest ingredients while supporting local. Papà only gets some things from traditional grocery stores, which is where my next stop is. I put all of the tomatoes, garlic, and fresh herbs into my obnoxiously loud wagon. I should really stop at the hardware store today and get a new wheel. I tried to fix this one before I left, but my parents are chefs and an interior designer, there's not much in the tool department of our house.

I park this unstable wagon at the back of the restaurant and begin my trek up these three oversized concrete steps. Whoever mountain man made these steps had only a one-size-fits-all mentality, and let me tell you, this size step only fits one: him. Nobody has this long of legs. I'm doing a full workout just to get up the first one.

Marco, one of the managers, sees me struggling and swoops in just in time to grab the crate of tomatoes out of my arms. My heel catches the edge of the top step, and I stumble forward with all the grace of a newborn deer. Somehow, I manage to clutch the doorframe before my knees kiss the concrete.

He looks up at me and chuckles when he says, " Careful, Remilia, your Papà would drown me in pesto if he finds out I let you get hurt."

"Thanks," I sarcastically spat out, as my eyes went wide in annoyance. I run my palms down my jeans, straighten my shoulders, and pretend I didn't just embarrass myself in front of most of the kitchen staff.

"Nothing to see here," I say as I raise my hands in embarrassment.

"Remilia, thank you, teroso, what would I do without you?" My dad asks as he kisses my head and pulls me in for a big hug. "Are you hungry?"

I don't even have to answer that one because my stomach uses this opportunity to tell me I've only had Mamma's Caffè Latte today.

"Yes, I would love some food," I say, rubbing a hand over my empty stomach. "Teresa and Larry send you their love, and say they will have more garlic for you next week, Papà," I tell him.

He begins to make my favorite meal, Vodka Rigatoni. While it may be my favorite, I just know my Nonna is rolling her eyes from the other side, thinking of these modernized American options my Papà added to the menu a few years back.

I finish my meal and kiss Papà goodbye. It's almost time for the dinner rush to start, and I want to get out of here before I get tricked into staying and helping out tonight. I've got a date with my pistachio ice cream and the rest of my current read, but first, I'm going to grab a wheel from the hardware store across the street.

It's a perfect night tonight, the breeze hits my cheeks and pushes my hair back behind my shoulders, while the leaves dance to their own song on the sidewalk. Fall in Copperridge is so breathtaking that it reminds me I need to make my way up to the ridge. It turns the brightest shade of burnt orange for just a few short moments at sunset.

I'm too busy staring at the leaves and thinking about the ridge to notice the familiar voice I'm about to stumble upon.

Zane

I hear him before I see him. The way my body reacts to the timbre of his voice is nothing short of magical. It blankets me before I can even find him with my eyes. The way his perfectly sharp jaw moves as he talks feels like he's chiseling himself into my memory, line by line. His raven black waves move with the breeze, and his award-winning smile is almost enough to make my heart short-circuit. I shake myself out of the twilight zone just as he finishes helping Mrs. Ethridge put her sand in the back of her SUV.

He closes the lid, and that's when he sees me, his lip twitches and raises on one side, that smirk. I nervously bite the inside of my lip and push my medium-length hair behind my ears. I scrunch my nose under his gaze and find something, anything to pin my attention to on the ground because he's heading this way.

"Finally!" Escapes his lips as he brushes his waves back off his forehead, they fall like waves in the ocean right back into the place he just brushed them from.

For a minute, I'm stuck, my lungs aren't pumping oxygen, and my mouth isn't forming words. I give him this quizzical look, and he mirrors my face. We're in a steamy stare off, and good ole Mrs. Etheridge breaks it by telling him how much she appreciated his help today doing some landscaping for her.

"So, the strange new kid in town does yard work for elderly ladies, huh?" My entire face is scrunched, and I'm trying my best to conceal my smile. He rolls his eyes and sways his head to the side.

"If you're nice, I'll fix this rickety wagon you've carted all over town today." As soon as it leaves his mouth, he regrets it. He knows he's been caught spying on me, or at the very least, listening to the gossip of what I do on Sundays.

"Keeping tabs on me, so will you be professing your undying love today?" My smirk is easy, there's a twinkle in my eye, like I've just won the town talent show. He avoids eye contact and bends at the knee to check out my broken wagon.

"I actually have a wheel this size in a box at home. I can fix this for you in like 3 minutes if you'll let me." Keeping his eyes low and his voice even lower. It's like he's doing everything he can not to look up at me. Probably sure I'll say no, but I think I want to be around him, just as much as he wants to be around me.

"You help young ladies, too, not just old ones. Why so many nice things, Zane, paying penance for a past life I'm unaware of?" It sounds like sarcasm dripping from my lips, but I actually do want to know. I stare at him with one eyebrow practically touching my hairline.

"Maybe it's not penance. Maybe it's balance. Some people take more than they give…I just don't want to end up like them." He's still looking down at the wagon, but the underlined sadness in his tone he just revealed has me questioning who hurt him, and how many shakes of salt it would take to ruin their favorite pasta.

"So," he stands and gives me a pointed glare. "Are you going to let me fix this for you?"

I exhale the air and the anger I'm still holding for whoever hurt him. I bite the inside of my lip and say, "Thank you, that would be nice."

"I'll load it up in the bed of my truck. Let me help you get in first."

He turns on his heels, and I'm left standing there dumbfounded, because one, I don't need help getting in a truck, and two, who said I was getting in your truck? I stand there for a few beats as I contemplate what to do. Who am I kidding? Getting into the truck of the hottest boy in a hundred miles, yeah, I'm doing that. I nod my head, square my shoulders, and follow behind him.

I pull out my phone and send a quick text to Papà asking him to drive my car home for me.

Zane slips his hand over the handle, opening the door for me, and holds out his other hand for me to grab. I hesitate slightly before I slip my hand into his and step up on the step. I pause halfway up to look at him, his face void of any emotion as he watches me climb into his truck. When he shuts the door, the smirk I love to see is plastered on his face for all of Copperridge to see. He loads the wagon in, gets himself in, and the smirk is still there. He pulls the shifter down as his eyes travel my way, and he says, "You ready?"

By the way, my heart skips a beat, I'd say I'm not ready, I'm not ready at all.

<h1 style="text-align:center">Seven</h1>

☾

Zane

This house is too quiet. Too clean. Too unfamiliar. Boxes line the walls, serving as a reminder that everything here is new to me. My mind drifts to Greyson, my brother, his wife, and their baby that's on the way. Resting my head against the headrest, I silently remind myself that this move will be good for me. They needed this, they needed me to go. I owe him that. He has taken care of me for the majority of my life, he deserves to bring his baby home to a home that's just his.

Remi's scent immediately hits my nose, overtakes my mind, and gets trapped in my memory. It carves itself into a dark corner of my soul. Basil and coffee. A unique combination, the two have never smelled so good, probably ever. If I were smarter, I'd purposely get lost in this four-stoplight town. Drive around in circles. Get lost in something other than her. I can't. Something about her is so magnetic, it's like a part of me is already hers, and it's the part of myself I've been searching for my entire life. She feels like the sun looks. Warm and constant.

Parked in the driveway of my aunt Cami's house, my new home. Maybe this one will feel like a home. Although with the way Remi is staring at my lips, I'm already feeling the warmth. I saw her at the hardware store looking like a damsel in distress with that wagon she's been carting around all day. I never cared to be anyone's knight in shining armor. Until now.

She looks up at me with those stormy grey eyes, and she knows she's been caught. Her nose scrunches, she tucks her hair behind her ear, and looks away. *Please don't look away.* She pulls her lip in with her teeth, something I've noticed she does when she's nervous. If she keeps doing that, I'll never fix this wagon wheel. I can't take my eyes off of her. Yeah, she's a magnet for sure.

"Funny," I say, resisting the urge to reach out and touch her silky brown hair. "I didn't think fixing a wagon wheel would be the highlight of my day."

Her laugh slips out, I feel it more than I hear it. A vibration from deep in my chest. My eyes flick to hers, catching the sparkle in her eyes, and I can't stop myself.

"Careful, Polaris. Keep pulling me in like that, and I'll forget what I'm doing."

She blinks, nose scrunching again, but this time her eyebrows pinch. "Polaris?"

I grin, turning back to the wheel so she doesn't see how deep my smile is. I blink, preparing myself and her for the truth.

"Yeah, North Star." I run my hands down the length of my face. "You don't even try, but you've got gravity."

I leave it at that. Like a bomb just went off, I exit the truck and grab the wagon from the bed. She hasn't moved, and that makes me smile even bigger. Looks like Remi the Rambler is stunned for once.

I can sense her finally getting out of the truck, but I keep digging through this box of nothing. The urge to turn around and watch her walk towards me wins. It feels better than it should. A pull, gravity.

"Funny thing, Zane," her voice low, but not as low as her eyes.

Staring at those converse, she's walked a thousand miles in.

"Gravity might pull things together... but it also makes them crash. You sure you wanna test that theory with me?" Her eyebrow is high, it's a challenge, a dare.

I take two quick steps toward her. She might be unsure of what she's saying, but I'm not. I hook my finger under her chin and pull it up so she's staring me right in my eyes. The words I want to say die on my lips, I'm stuck. Her eyes were so stormy. I'm lost in them.

Unable to resist the pull any longer, my left hand begins to travel up her arm, her skin hot to the touch, but the shiver that runs up her spine tells another story. I take my time drinking in her features. I wonder if she knows how beautiful she really is.

Her freckles tell a story over the tip of her nose. Her eyes were full of thick, long lashes. Her lips, my newfound favorite shade of pale pink. I let my thumb trace the curve of her jaw, slow, deliberate, like I'm memorizing her shape.

"You think I'm afraid of crashing, Polaris?" My voice is low, lower than I intended, but steady nonetheless. "I'd rather crash a thousand times with you than keep orbiting out there in the dark."

Her eyes widen just slightly, and for a second, I forget how to breathe. My chest feels too tight, too full. I lean in, close enough that I can feel her breath catch against my lips, but I stop there. Just short.

"Gravity's already won," I murmur, letting the words hang between us before I finally take a slow step back. Already missing the way she feels under my gaze.

This is all too much, it's happening way too fast. It hits me all at once, the pull toward her, the way she looks at me like she's known me forever. Girls like her don't look twice at boys like me. Not once they see the cracks. I'm the new kid. Temporary. A distraction until the next shiny thing shows up. If I fall, I fall alone. With her, I think I'd fall hard enough to drown.

She takes a seat on the tailgate of my truck while I fix my focus back to the wheel I'm supposed to be repairing. I like having her here, even if she isn't saying anything. That's what confuses my mind. Tricking me into thinking she actually wants to be here. The pink in her cheeks matches the shade of lip gloss she keeps nervously applying. The look in her eyes tells me she has something to say, but she's holding back. I want her to feel safe. I think I want her to make me feel safe.

"Say it." Falls from my lips as I set the tools down and look into the face of the girl who keeps pulling me deeper.

"You feel so familiar to me," she looks down at her hands, and then back up to me. "Like I've met you before. Which I know is strange." Pressing her lips to the side, tucking her hair behind her ears, and looking down at her hands again. She's nervous.

"Remi," I pause long enough for her to put her focus back on me. "It's not strange, I feel it too." I stuff my hands as deep into my pockets as I can. "It's like I've been walking toward this moment my entire life and didn't even know it until you looked at me," I confess.

The air between us feels alive, we can both sense it. It's tangible. She looks away like she doesn't believe me. Truth is, I've never felt like I belonged anywhere until she looked at me for the first time. It was terrifying. It was like my heart knew it was home. She feels like sunlight.

"I'll bring the wagon back to you tomorrow. I need to find the right tool. Can I walk you home?" I say with a heavy chest. I could use a walk right about now. A moment to clear my thoughts, i barely know this girl.

I watch her hesitate, like she's weighing the danger of saying yes. That flicker in her eyes tells me she wants to, but she's not ready to hand me the answer without a fight. She presses her lips together, and I swear my chest tightens just waiting.

"Zane..." she finally whispers, my name carrying more weight than it should.

My lip twitches on its way up. I already know what her answer is, even before she gives me the smallest nod. Relief and something dangerously close to hope collide inside me. An unsettling combination.

"Good," I murmur, grabbing the broken wagon handle and tucking the tools under my arm. I move them towards the pile of boxes I need to find time to put away. "You first," I announce, my hand motioning towards the street.

We fall into step, the night closing in around us. Every brush of her shoulder against mine is a reminder: gravity isn't something you choose. It just is. And right now, it's pulling me straight to her.

Remi

That silent walk home was the best walk I've ever taken, and im Italian, we walk everywhere. The way he kept moving closer was as if being near me felt natural to him. Zane walked me all the way to the door, his hands glued to the inside of his pockets, like he didn't trust himself. When I turned to say goodnight, he finally looked up, and when he did, there was this tiny crooked smile on his face. Like it was unintentional but genuine.

"Goodnight, Remi." his voice was so low, like he was telling a secret.

Pinning my lips between my teeth, I nod and slip inside before my knees forget what we're doing here. The door creaks behind me as I close it. The smell of garlic and tomatoes hit my nostrils before the door was completely closed, the Moretti house's signature scent. The humming lets me know my Papà is in the kitchen. That's exactly what I need to come back down from the high that is Zane.

"Ciao, ragazza mia," he says without looking up, wrist flicking as he stirs the pot. Garlic and tomatoes bubble, filling the air. "You're smiling. That means either pistachio gelato or a boy."

I roll my eyes and drop my bag onto the floor. "Papà..."

"Mm," he hums, finally looking at me. His dark brows shoot upwards. "So it *is* a boy. Which one?"

"There's not a *which one*. There's just..." I stop, biting down on my lip.

That was a big mistake on my part. His grin widens like he's won a game. It's so easy to talk to him, things just tumble right out of my mouth.

"Let me guess," he plays, touching his chin with his finger. "Tall, dark hair, a dangerous smile?" He's having too much fun with this.

"Have you been talking to Mamma?" I give him a quizzical stare.

"She didn't have to tell me." He taps the spoon against the pot, leaning his hip on the counter now, giving me his full attention. "I can see it written all over your face. You're glowing like Nonna's Christmas tree. Plus, I knew he didn't care about the vines on the house when he came over to compliment them."

I groan, covering my cheeks with both hands. "You're impossible, Papà."

"Impossible, but right," he says, chuckling. Then his voice softens, quieter now. "He's the new one, yes? Zane?"

I peek through my fingers and nod before pulling them away. "You already know his name?"

"Of course. He came by my house," he pauses, "and the restaurant. Said he was picking up an order for Mrs. Ethridge. I like him, he's" another drawn out pause, like he is thinking of the right words to say. "kind." Papà stirs again, but there's something in the cadence of his words that he's leading up to a warning.

"But?" I ask, bracing myself for it.

Papà sighs, setting the spoon down with care. He wipes his hands on a towel, then meets my eyes.

"But…" he sets the towel down. "Ragazza mia, charm is like olive oil. Smooth, golden, useful" he shrugs, "but it can also make you slip if you're not careful."

I wrinkle my nose. "That's the weirdest warning I've ever heard."

He laughs, reaching over to tap my forehead lightly. "Then maybe you'll remember it." His expression lingers somewhere between amusement and worry. "Just take your time with him, sì? A man who smiles that much is usually hiding something. Sometimes good, sometimes not."

"Sì Papà, sometimes good, I hear you," I say with a smirk. Papà just laughs and walks back to the tomatoes, grinning as he stirs.

We fall into a rhythm in the kitchen, it's always so easy here. It's therapy for our family. Nonna always said, "When the hands are busy, the heart has room to mend." In this case, there's no need to mend a broken heart, but it's our way of centering ourselves. Many arguments die in the kitchen. This is where we laugh, have flour fights, and fix our problems.

Mammà comes home, and we sit around the table, where they tease me a little more. They have this secret language that only the two of them know. I've seen the remnants of it my entire life, but tonight at dinner, they keep looking towards each other, like this time the secret conversation is about me.

I make my way to the shower and then head for my bed. Mondays come quickly when your weekend is filled with anticipation and being held under the weighty gaze of a boy with honey colored eyes. My skin is still warm from the steam, my hair is still damp when I slide under the covers, and I let myself smile into the pillow at the thought of him.

My smile lingers, even when a faint pressure nudges at my temple. It's nothing dramatic, just enough to remind me the day was long and maybe I let my thoughts run too wild. I close my eyes, letting the weight of exhaustion blur everything into soft edges. The last thing I feel before sleep takes me is the pulse of a migraine. Small and steady, almost like a drum before it fades into dreams.

Eight

☾

Remi

The bell rings to end the third period, and the school is already buzzing with news of the new boy, my new boy, Zane. How pathetic am I? Already calling him mine when I'm not even sure I want to be liked by him or by anyone, really. That's exactly the kind of attention I've avoided for so long. That kind of attention messes up my plan, the one that I don't have locked down. I've really got to get my crap together and my head on straight.

I haven't seen him yet, but I know he is here. The air changes when he is near, as if it were filled with gas, waiting for a spark.

Filling Joss in on everything that happened this weekend with Zane was interesting. Her mouth was on the floor as I spilled all the details. At one point, she yanked my arm down to pull me closer to her. "Polaris?! As in North Star? Remi, are you kidding me? That boy just nicknamed you the literal guiding light of the universe, and you're standing here like it's casual Monday?" Her eyebrows raised, she blinked hard and shook her head in a circle for about 2 minutes straight.

"You ready, Rem?" Maddie calls out.

Nodding, I loop my arms with theirs, like we have every day since as long as I can remember. Only this time, as soon as we enter the doors, my gut stops me in my tracks and pulls my attention towards the right side of the room. I follow the feeling before I can talk myself out of it, and that's when I see him. Zane.

He's leaning against the wall, one foot braced behind him, talking to a group of guys I've never bothered to notice before. Who am I kidding? I've never really noticed *anyone*. My head's always been in a book, my safest hiding place.

That's when I hear Maddie say, "Wow, he really is better than they described."

My neck stiffens, and I whip my head towards her so fast with a look that would send a kitten into hiding.

"Who are they?" Not exactly trying to hide the bite in my tone.

"Let's introduce ourselves." She waves me off and skips in his direction.

I'm too stunned to speak. Too angry, too, for my feet to move. Pinching my lips between my teeth, I tilt my head to the side in pure aggravation, unsure what to make of the swirl of emotion hitting me or how I'm meant to act with it vibrating through me.

"C'mon, Rem, let's go watch her introduce herself to *your* man," Joss says with a nod and a wink, pulling me by the arm towards them.

I see the moment Zane notices someone is there. He looks up at her, slowly. Maddie is tossing her hair from side to side like Galinda in Wicked. Jealousy, that's the emotion wracking throughout my entire being. I've never been jealous before, never had the need to be jealous. Something about Zane has me wanting all of his attention. My head is definitely not on straight.

Zane's eyes are empty, his lips are flat, and there is no emotion on his face whatsoever, which makes my mouth turn up in a small smile. He must sense me here, because as soon as I get close, his chin turns towards me before his eyes get the hint and follow. It's like his body knows. His eyes go from empty to on fire in a matter of seconds, and I can't help but widen my eyes and look down. I tuck my hair behind my ear and let Joss lead me, still linked at the arm.

"You're missing the show, Remi," Joss nudges me. "Maddie just realized it's you and not her."

I look up about the time he pushes off the wall and takes a step towards me, his hand coming up to brush his waves back. I'll never tell him what that move does to my heart. His eyebrow reaches for his hairline, and he gives me that signature smirk, his eyes soft. We stop just inches before running into each other. Somewhere along the way, Joss let go of my arm, but I'm too focused on him to realize when.

"My Polaris," he says, and something in my chest misfires.

He lifts his hand like he might touch my chin again, but this time he hesitates, just long enough for my brain to completely short-circuit at the possibility of it. When his finger finally grazes my chin, it's light, playful even, nothing like the bold confidence from last night. It's soft. Careful. Like he's asking a question instead of assuming the answer.

That's somehow worse. Because now I'm hyper-aware of those honey-colored eyes, warm and bright and unfair.

Honey. Seriously?

I thought sage green and I were locked in for life. Apparently, the second a boy with honey eyes looks at me gently, I fold like a lawn chair.

"Polaris? her name is Remi, and why are you touching..." Maddie's words are cut short.

Joss pulls her back a few steps and whispers something in Maddie's ear that has her eyes wide and her jaw slack.

I look back at Zane, this time his smirk reaches his ears, and it blooms right before me into a full-blown smile. The kind of smile that you can't look away from, it's laced with charm and danger, just like Papà said.

"Olive oil, that's what you are." My breath staggers. "Please don't ask what that means." I'm hemorrhaging words.

Joss steps into my peripheral, and I've never been more thankful for her interruptions than I am in this moment. I'll be sure to tell Papà that next time he complains about her not knocking or using the back door.

"So I hate to break this up, but I'm starving." She directs her attention to Zane. "Hi, I am Remi's best friend. You should totally sit with us for lunch."

Of course she would. Subtlety has never been Joss's thing.

Zane's eyes flicker past her, landing right back on me. For a second, the whole cafeteria fades. My stomach flips because it feels like he's asking me what he should say without opening his mouth. I can see the skin on his jaw tighten as he's deciding what to do.

"Appreciate it." He looks to her, and then back to me. "But I've got something I need to take care of today."

Joss tilts her head, suspicious. "Weird," She draws the word out, then grins. "Well, okay, meet you over there, Rem." She winks, giving us a look over her shoulder that I can't quite decipher.

I can feel his eyes on me. I'm bracing myself for the letdown. Who am I? I'm not the girl who is disappointed, that means I care, and that's not in the plan. Caring about someone is so far away from the plan. I think I need a new plan.

"Rain check?" His face relaxes, voice low, like he wants me to be the only one who hears it.

He blinks, grabs my hand, and softly begins to rub back and forth with his thumb. Clearly, I'm going to need a new plan. The old plan is in the trash can… on fire. The way his thumb moves against my skin sends a tiny spark racing straight through me, making me feel it somewhere deep in my chest.

"Remi, are you coming?" Joss stands next to me, holding a tray of food.

I really dislike her interruptions again. I exhale the air caught in my chest, but by the time I look back at him, he's walking away. I'm left with the sound of Joss whispering, "This is going to be fun."

Zane

I hated leaving her in that moment, but it's too soon for me to face the firing squad of her friends right now. Especially since the blonde one, I can't think of her name, just hit me. I didn't like the way her eyes skimmed over me, like I was a game and she wanted to play. A toy on a shelf. Here one minute and gone the next, it left me feeling disposable. Maybe she hasn't told them about me. That has me questioning everything. I know it's sudden. It just feels right. She feels warm, and what I imagine comfort would feel like, the kind you find in a loving home.

My parents neglected to show me comfort and warmth. They showed me the opposite. Cold and empty were more their

style. I was five when they finally left for good. Leaving
Greyson, my brother, who was seventeen, to care for not only
himself, but his little brother, too. We kept it a secret until he
turned eighteen and became my legal guardian. That was the
day I learned I was forgettable. Easy to walk away from. Easy to
leave behind.

The rest of the school day drags, each class blurring together
while my mind circles the same place it keeps drifting to…her. I
already know I'm stopping by the counselor's office tomorrow
to try to get my schedule changed. I want to see more of her.
And tonight, I'll actually get the chance.

I picked up food for Mrs. Ethridge yesterday before helping
her load supplies at the hardware store in town. Mr. Moretti
somehow recognized me as Remi's friend and invited me over
for dinner tonight. A real dinner, something I'm not sure I ever
had. Greyson did his best, but tv dinners were usually on the
menu. A family around a table, though, that's something new.

My palms are slick with nerves as I reach her steps. I ring
the doorbell and suck in as much air as I can. Acceptance aches
heavier than I expected.

"Hi, it's so nice to see you again." Mrs. Moretti says as she's
pulling me in for a hug.

She kisses one cheek, then the other, warm and familiar, a
true Italian greeting. Mr. Moretti appears beside her almost
instantly, his hand settling on the small of her back as it belongs
there. That, right there, is what a real union looks like. He leans

in and greets me the same way she did, the gesture surprisingly natural.

"I've heard Italians make strangers feel like family. Guess that makes me the lucky one tonight." I say nervously, extending my hand in front of me, revealing the flowers I brought. "For you, Mrs. Moretti."

A small gasp escapes Mrs. Moretti.

"Ah, bello, you didn't have to bring me flowers… but of course, I'll accept. They're beautiful. Please call me Elena, and this is Domenico." She pats his chest and smiles up at him. "Nico is fine." She lifts one shoulder, grabs the flowers, and saunters away.

"Well, Prince Charming, follow me into the heart of the house, il cuore della casa." he throws his head back, and his hands are stretched out wide. As if he's in the kitchen, welcoming me in.

I follow him through the house and into the kitchen, that's where I see her. My Polaris kneading dough with both hands covered in powder. She softly hums to whatever Italian music is playing in the background. Her shoulders relaxed, swaying to the beat, hair in a messy pile on top of her head.

"Teroso, say hello to our guest," Nico calls out as we fully enter the kitchen.

It isn't even a sound, it's the way her chest visibly tightens, the way her lips part as though the air itself betrayed her. I hear it anyway. Her face was a mixture of shock and terror. With a hint of surprise. It makes me lift the corner of my lip. Heat dancing across her cheeks in a way that accentuates her freckles.

"Nice to see you, Remi." I take a deliberate step towards her.

One more step and I reach for her. She is still frozen in place. I run my hand from the side of her ribcage towards her spine. She takes a sharp inhale. I lean in to kiss her cheek, just like her parents did to me moments ago. Her signature scent blankets me in coffee and basil. I can't help the quiet breath that slips from my lips.

A pan clanks in the sink behind me, and I instinctively take a step back. Her mouth is agape, and her eyebrows are raised. Her flour and dough-covered hands haven't moved. She didn't expect me to be here. Her eye twitches, and a smile begins to appear. She closes the space between us.

"Zane," She reaches her arms around my waist and pulls me back in for a hug of her own. "I didn't know you were the guest for tonight's dinner!" She says over my shoulder, to where Elena is standing.

When she pulls back, she pinches her lips between her teeth, her cheeks are the perfect shade of pink. She's nervous, but excited. I can tell by the way her walk is slightly elevated and bouncy that she's walking on the tips of her bare feet. Her jeans, which she wore to school, have been traded for a soft, matching top and bottom. She looks comfortable. Too comfortable to notice how she's completely undoing me, just by being her.

"How can I help?" I hear myself say

But when I do everything in the kitchen, it freezes. No more dishes clanking, no more humming from Nico, Elena, and Remi are stopped cold in their tracks.

"Guests don't cook in my cucina." Nico is the one who breaks the silence.

I look at Remi, and she is trying to conceal a smile. She darts her eyes in my direction and back at the dough she's kneading.

"Um, sit here, Zane. I'm almost done with the dough." She speaks through the smile plastered on her face.

I watch in utter silence as they flow, like a dance they've practiced their entire lives. It feels like I'm seeing the inside of a secret. Nico meant it when he said the heart of the kitchen. The way they move in tandem, not running into one another but moving around the kitchen as if it's choreographed, and they've been in training their entire lives. The smells of garlic, tomatoes, basil, oregano, and love sift through the air so beautifully. I wouldn't fit in very well at this dance. Not because I can't dance, but because I don't know the first thing about cooking.

"Hi," Remi says, appearing before me, drying her hands off on a kitchen towel. "Do you want a tour?" She tosses the towel onto the counter. "I'm done with my part." She looks up at me, smiling.

She's so breathtakingly beautiful.

"I'd love one, thank you." It comes out as a whisper.

I've never stepped into a house that felt this alive. Every corner carries a piece of someone's hand, someone's memory. You can see Elena's mother in the details, the way the colors flow into each other, the way light bends through the windows like it was invited in.

Remi leads me through the house, and she touches everything she loves, as if her fingertips keep the memories awake. Her hand trails across the table behind the couch, lined with little trinkets she tells me Nonna carried back from Italy. She stops at the mantel, lifts a frame, and presses it against her chest like it might disappear if she lets go.

Her stormy gray eyes pull me into the picture before I even see it. Three generations around a kitchen table, mugs in their hands, steam curling up between their smiles. She whispers it's her favorite caffè latte, of course. I'm encapsulated by the story of her Nonna, Elena, and her child, Remi. She tells it as if this is her favorite memory.

In that moment, I feel it, all the things I never had in one room. The weight of belonging. The ache of home. It doesn't make me sad, it excites me. Maybe I can have this one day too.

"Remilia, A tavola! Dinner's ready!" Nico calls from the kitchen. Remi exhales and sets the picture back onto the mantle.

"Remilia?" I close my eyes as I savor her name on my lips. I open my eyes, and I'm instantly locked into the eyes of the girl who holds so much of me already. I reach for her elbow and drag my hand down towards her hand. Slow, deliberate.

She inhales sharply, the sound small but cutting through the hum of the house like it's meant only for me. Her skin warms under my touch, and I swear I feel the shiver run through her before she even realizes it herself.

Her lips part as if to speak, but nothing comes. Instead, her gaze drops to our almost entwined hands, and then back up, braver this time. Her eyes squint slightly, a challenge flickers, curiosity too.

I lean in just enough that only she can hear me.

"It fits you," I murmur, letting the name roll again in my head like a secret I wasn't meant to know. "Remilia."

Her lips twitch into the ghost of a smile, caught between nerves and something heavier. She doesn't pull away. She doesn't want to. I feel a tilt in my chest. Like, my world was a little more anchored towards hers. The noise of her family's kitchen fades, and it's just the two of us.

She raises her eyebrows ever so slightly. I can see the moment she lets curiosity win. She laces her fingers with mine, squares her shoulders, and suddenly I'm being led towards the kitchen. My north star, pulling me.

Remi gives my hand a tight squeeze as she looks over her shoulder right before we enter the kitchen. She lets go, but the smile she gives me as she tucks her hair behind her ear feels like the main course for tonight.

Nine

Zane

I can feel my heart beating in my stomach. Is it because the food smells amazing, or am I hungry for more stolen moments with my Polaris? The air is fragrant with garlic and tomatoes, basil curling along the edges like incense. Tonight explains why she smells of basil and coffee all of the time. My newest favorite combination. Laughter drifts over the clatter of pans, and I can't tell if it belongs to her mother or her father. Probably both.

They're doing their dance again, moving around each other without interference. Elena slides a pan across the counter just as Nico catches it without looking, humming under his breath. She tosses him a smile that carries history, and he answers with a wink, never missing a beat. Their flow is practiced, easy, full of something I've never had, never even seen, but suddenly ache so bad for.

Then there's Remi… no, Remilia, slipping so seamlessly into their dance. Falling right into place as though she was born in this very kitchen. I watch in silent awe as they flow. Nico was right about this being the heart of the house. I wonder if it's possible to feel both like a guest and like I've stumbled home in the same breath. Do they make everyone feel this welcomed, this apart, without actually being apart?

Elena notices me first. She brushes flour from her hands and gestures toward the table, her smile the kind that leaves no room for hesitation.

"Sit, bello. Guests don't stand in my cucina."

Nico shouts something to Remi, using her full name, and my chest tightens so sharply that I have to close my eyes. The name sounds so angelic. Something so soft that in a way it doesn't feel real. She's Remi to me, feisty and witty, but here, she's Remilia, stitched into every corner of this house. It sounds like something you'd say forever. Like a name you'd use in a future you could only hope to have. The kind of future that would feel like a blessing just to imagine. If I'm being honest, I'm scared to picture it. Only because some part of me already wants it.

There is a sudden burst of laughter behind me, and then the plates clatter onto the table around me. The smell of garlic and oil rising from the bowls as they're passed invades my nostrils in the best way possible. I've never seen a family eat like this, never seen food treated like a language. Let alone a family that eats together at a table. Domenico heaves the pasta bowl toward me, eyes crinkling.

"Eat, ragazzo. You're too thin. My wife feeds everyone until they burst, don't offend her by refusing." He tips his chin down, a dare I've come to recognize in his eyes.

Elena swats him with the wooden spoon, laughter spilling out of her.

"Domenico, let him breathe. He'll eat."

Remi rolls her eyes, saying something under her breath I can't quite make out. I'm almost certain her mother notices the way I look at her, because her lips twitch with the faintest knowing smirk. It's adoration. That's the look she's seeing.

The table dance they're doing has sped up a bit from the cooking dance. I'm starting to get a little overwhelmed. Bowls of pasta being passed over my plate, forks clanking, and ice being scooped into cups. It's flooding my nervous system, in the best way possible. The problem is, I don't know the dance they're doing, or how any other table works. Looking down at my plate, feeling a little insecure, I see Remi's slender hands scoop the pasta onto it. I can't hide my smile.

Nico leans forward, putting another scoop of pasta into my bowl. "Eat ragazzo, you need strength if you're going to survive around here."

"Papà," Remi groans. Pressing the same slender hand she just served me with onto her forehead. "You can't just say things like that, Papà."

"Why not?" He says with a pointed glare. "It's true, no?" Nico uses both hands to point at me. "Look at him teroso, the wind will knock him over."

It's Elena's turn to chime in, "Ignore him, Zane. He's been saying the same thing about Remi since she could walk." She says as she swats Nico on the arm.

I look over at Remi, who is directly next to me, and she's still rubbing the palm of her hand into her head. I gently move my hand to her knee under the table and give her a slight squeeze. She peeks out from under her palm at me, and I give her a 'You okay?' Puzzled look. Her eyebrows shoot towards each other, and she gives her head a little shake.

It's our own special way of speaking where no one else can hear the conversation. It feels familiar, remembered almost, even though I don't think we've ever confirmed what we interpret to be true. I stare at her for a second longer and then return to take a bite of the best pasta I have ever eaten.

"Hmm, this is good," I say with my mouth still stuffed with food. "What's in this?"

"That's my Nonna's Sunday sauce!" Remi announces with a smile.

"You'll have to marry her to get that recipe, bello," Elena says with a raised eyebrow.

I look at Nico, and his face has dropped, his eyes focused on the dish in front of him. His fork has stopped moving, and it looks like he has stopped breathing, too. He lifts his chin, and his face is unreadable. When I finally swallow the pasta that's in my mouth, I look up to meet Nico's unreadable eyes.

"Well, if the pasta's this good, I can't say the offer doesn't tempt me," I say with a smirk.

He doesn't seem to think it's funny, I can tell by the way his eyebrows are knitted together forming a scowl.

"Hey!" I declare with my hands raised, "I'm only here for the pasta tonight, Mr. Moretti." I say playfully.

Nico cracks a smile and stabs his pasta, his eyes never leaving mine as he chews. Elena pours him a little more wine, rubs his arm, and whispers something in Italian that I cannot understand. The words seem to instantly untie the tension in his chest, and he leans over, pressing his forehead to hers. They share a moment, and then he offers me a peace offering by passing me the bread.

"The rosemary," he says, tapping the crust. "I grow it fresh in my garden," Nico says, looking deep in thought. "Because my mother always told me…" his voice softens to a whisper as he's lost in his own memories.

Elena's voice cuts through the silence, smiling, "Un pane senza rosmarino è come una casa senza amore."

Remi leans in closer to me, whispering. "Bread without rosemary is like a house without love." Her eyes were still locked on her parents.

I don't understand Italian, but I don't have to. The way Remi smiles at the words, like they're stitched into her bones, tells me everything. Nonna was the love that filled the kitchen, her traces are everywhere. I can recognize that, I don't know it personally, but I'd like to.

Elena tilts her head, eyes soft but searching. "So, Zane, what brings you to Copperridge?"

I set my fork down, buying time with a sip of water. "My aunt lives here. Figured it was time for a change of scenery."

This is the moment I was dreading, the place in the conversation where the past presses in and I can't pretend it's simple.

"And before that?" Domenico asks, not unkindly, just curious. His hands rest heavily on the table like he already knows the answer won't be simple.

I toy with the edge of my napkin, while my other hand rubs back and forth on my thigh. I inhale and decide to be open, they've opened their home to me and shown me nothing but love. The least I can give is my truths.

"I lived with my older brother for the majority of my life. He's having a baby, and I felt it was a perfect time to give them the space that they will need with a new baby coming." I glanced at Remi, her stormy eyes fixed on me softly.

Elena's voice softens. "Do you miss your home?"

I give her the truth I never say out loud. "I don't miss places. I miss the idea of them." I toy with the napkin again. "I've never had a family in the sense of mother and father, that's foreign to me. My parents left me with my brother when I was five. He did his best, but he was seventeen. Home was always a fairytale."

The silence is heavy but somehow feels non-judgmental. I risk a look towards Remi, her storm-gray eyes are softer than I've ever seen them, like she's carrying the weight for me. She doesn't say anything, just presses her knee against mine again, steady and certain. It's enough.

"Family is about the ones who stay, Zane. Not the ones who leave." Nico breaks the silence.

My eyes meet his, seeing the softness, then they flick back to Remi. I just laid all my truths down on this table, and I don't want it to change her view of me. Her eyes find mine, and I can feel the warmth pouring from them. My body stiffens at the unexpected touch. She grabs my hand under the table and gives me a tight squeeze. She's comforting me.

Elena clears her throat softly, a smile tugging at her lips. "Then tonight, you're family. And around here, no one leaves without leftovers. I'll make you a plate to go, and you can help Remi do the dishes. Si?"

Unable to form words, I give Elena a nod, turning my attention back to Remi. I let out the breath I was unconsciously holding. She instantly bites down on her lip and tucks her stray hairs behind her ear. I make her nervous.

"Come on," She says with a scrunch of her nose.

I'd follow her anywhere.

Remi

The air outside is cooler, softer, and it feels good against my cheeks after the heat of the kitchen. I lean against the porch railing, still hearing Papà's laugh echo through the walls, still tasting Nonna's sauce on my tongue.

But mostly, I hear him.

"Home was always a fairytale."

It loops in my head, over and over. I've known him for four days, and yet that one sentence feels like he handed me the most fragile part of himself. I don't know if I should protect it or run from it. It's way too early in this, whatever this is, for my heart to be doing backflips like it has been doing since he delivered that line.

The screen door creaks, and I don't have to turn to know it's him. He was saying goodbye to my parents when I stepped out here. I'm sitting on the porch swing, and he's leaning against the railing, staring at me like he's about to lose a heart he doesn't know he already owns.

I freeze.

When did that switch flip? When did I give him anything?

I'm not the girl who believes love is something meant for her, and definitely not the "here, take my heart" type after four days.

"You don't have to look at me like that." He pins me in place with a sad look.

Confused, I looked back at him, "Like what?"

"Like I've said too much." He exhales, his chest deflates a bit.

How long has he been holding that in? I don't think he's said too much. I want to know more. I want to know everything he hasn't had, so I can give it to him. I want to fill those empty spaces with nothing but good memories.

"You didn't say too much." My voice is steadier than the one I hear in my head.

His eyes lift to mine, sharp and searching. It's like he's waiting for me to flinch, to pull back, to run away and hide. All I want to do is run towards him.

"Zane, I know we haven't known each other that long, but you don't have to carry the things you carry alone, it's probably a lot heavier than it looks." Pausing, I try to steady my breath. I need to convey confidence right now, and the only thing I can think of is when I decided to care so much about him. "But it doesn't scare me, Zane." I'm standing now, scratch that, I'm walking towards him.

His guarded edges soften just a bit. For a split second, he looks younger, almost unsure. I know he's not used to being chosen, not like this. Relief slips through the cracks, but fear hangs right behind it, fear of believing me, fear of wanting this, fear of losing something he never thought he'd get to have. It's all there in his eyes, uncertainty and hope tangled together, and it hits me how badly he wants to trust this… to trust *me.*

"If anything, it makes me want to stay, Zane." I hear myself admit.

I'm in his space now, laying my hand lightly on his chest. I can't tear my eyes from where my hand is touching his. Blinking slowly, I look up at him. His eyes, much softer, the wall he had up is down, and I'm lost in the silent plea I see behind them.

"Remi." There's a tremor in the way he says it, like he's crying out, asking for help. "No one has ever stayed."

I'm searching his eyes just as he's searching mine. His hand is covering my hand on his chest. I can feel his heart begin to race; he's scared and nervous. How can I make him see that I can be an anchor for him, even if it's not romantically? Even if he just needs a friend, a place that feels like home.

"That's okay, Zane. There's a first time for everything. Lucky for you, I'm stubborn, and I don't scare easily."

He lets out the smallest of breathy laughs. His eyes roam the porch around us before settling back onto me. I can feel his breath hitch in his chest. His heart rate picks up again, and his eyes search my face. I know the wind is blowing the porch swing behind me, I can hear it squeaking, but the only thing I can focus on is him.

He tucks his lip into his mouth and releases it quickly. Like he's trying to say something, or hold something back, I can't tell which. He leans in and places his forehead onto mine, like my parents do all the time. His eyes close, and he drops his shoulders as he releases the tension in his chest.

Zane squeezes my hand that's on his chest.

"Remi?" It's almost a whisper.

"Im right here." I match his whisper.

"Thank you for tonight, I've never experienced anything like it."

I open my eyes to look at him, but his eyes are still closed. His forehead resting against mine still, he's so close. I get a good look at his full lips and even fuller set of eyelashes, and a pang of jealousy hits me. Seriously? Why can't I have those?

"I'd better get this food back to my aunt." He says as he lifts his head.

No.

My intrusive thoughts make me want to stomp my feet and beg him to stay a little while longer.

"Okay" is all I can manage to say, chewing the inside of my lip, trying not to let my disappointment show.

"Will you save me a seat at lunch on Monday?" He asks as he moves my hand from his chest to down by his side, still holding it, fingers intertwined this time.

I kicked a non-existent rock, trying not to throw a fit, but too scared to ask him to stay.

"Yeah, I can do that." It's almost a whisper.

He lets my hand go and is halfway down the steps when he stops and looks back up at me. The heaviness he wore moments ago is gone, replaced by something lighter, maybe even playful.

"Oh, and Remi, can you please make sure I'm nowhere near the blonde who has the pick me vibes?" With his eyebrows pinched together.

I chuckle and am shaking my head when I say, "Yeah, Zane, I can do that."

He brings his thumb up to his lip and pushes it to the side, it's what he does when he's thinking. I've witnessed him do it a few times over the last few days.

"Goodnight, Remilia," he says softly with a smirk.

He walks away, leaving the word echoing after him like a thread tugging at the edge of my heart.

Remilia.

He said it quietly, like a secret. Like a promise. Like a name with a future stitched inside it. The porch settles into silence, but the moment stays playing on a loop in my mind. I close my eyes for a second, letting the night wrap around me.

Four days, I remind myself.

It's only been four days.

Jen

☾

Remi

I woke in the dark, the dream's taste still lingering, matching the headache most likely brought on by it. Dreams of Nonna always follow with a lingering migraine, it's like she's trying to get in my head, literally. I let out a heavy breath and unwrap myself from this blanket cocoon. Reaching for what I always reach for In the dead of night, the dark blue box under my bed.

It was my Nonna, my grandpa, Nonno Giuseppe, who made it for her when they were dating back in Italy. I never met him, but he gave me something... my god-awful middle name. I mean, seriously, my mammà's hormones must've been going wild if she thought it would be acceptable to name me Remilia Giuseppina. Reaching for the lamp on my nightstand, I look like I won't be going back to sleep anytime soon.

Nonno must've thought she hung the moon and the stars because he took his time carving crescent moons and stars all over this box. Blue and gold, Nonna's favorite colors. Head over heels, those two, or so I'm told.

Opening the box is like a blast from my own past: letters from fourteen-year-old me, written to a boy I only ever met in my dreams in the dead of night. Letters plagued with embarrassment from a sleepover from hell, the day I stopped writing to L. Holding these letters always feels like I'm opening a door I had slammed shut for so long.

I trace my fingers over the folded edges of the letters. I must've been writing passionately because I can feel the indentations from this side. Always blue ink, his favorite color. Shaking myself out of the spell that L always put me in, I unfold one and begin to read.

Dear L,

Last night you showed up in my dream again. We snuck out to the swings at the park, the whole town asleep, but the crickets were wide awake. You pushed me higher and higher until the ground blurred, and I swore I could see the whole world from up there.

You said, "If you jump, I'll catch you."

And I believed you. So I let go.

The next thing I knew, we were running through the dark streets barefoot, laughing so hard it hurt. It felt like we could go anywhere, do anything.

*When I woke up, the grass stains were gone, and my feet were clean,
but the feeling stayed. Maybe that's the magic of you, you only exist
in dreams, but you feel more real than the day ever does.*

Love,

R

Fourteen-year-old Remi was down bad for a boy she met in
her dreams. I tell myself one is enough. One trip down memory
lane, and then back to bed. I've never really been good at
stopping where I should, though. My eyes land on another
envelope, and before I can talk myself out of it, I'm reading
again.

Dear L,

*In my dream last night, we sat on the porch swing long after everyone
else had gone home. The sky was dark, but the air felt like sunshine.*

*You leaned back on the chains and said, "Home isn't real. It's just a
fairytale people tell, so they feel safe."*

*I didn't know what to say to that, so I just picked the paint off the
armrest and listened.*

*Somehow, the way you said it made me want to believe you were
wrong... even if you sounded so sure.*

Love,

R

My stomach drops. The page trembles in my hands, though the air in my room is perfectly still. Those words "home is a fairytale" I just heard last night. From Zane. His voice still echoes in my head, low and tired, like he'd carried the thought around for far too long.

I blink hard and reread the line. Once, twice, three times. There's no mistake. Fourteen-year-old me wrote down his words years before I ever knew him. It's not word-for-word, but those are his words, aren't they?

The thought should scare me, or at least make me laugh at how ridiculous it sounds. Instead, I just sit there, the paper soft between my fingers, the silence stretching around me. The words feel like they've been waiting all this time, tucked away in the box until I was ready to hear them again.

I don't close the letter right away. I let it rest in my lap, my thumb brushing over the ink as if it might smudge onto me, become part of me. It doesn't. It just stays there, steady and unshakable, daring me to wonder what it means.

I must have fallen asleep reading it over and over again. The morning comes with the letter open on my lap. My eyes are too tired to keep rereading, but my mind hasn't stopped circling the words. *Home isn't real. It's just a fairytale.*

By the time I'm ready for the day to begin, the box is back under my bed, tucked away as if nothing happened. The weight of the words on the page stays with me, though. It follows me through breakfast, through the hollow small talk with Mammà, through the ache behind my temples that refuses to fade.

So when Joss texts about trivia night at the Copper Café, I don't argue. Maybe noise and laughter will drown it out. If that doesn't work, the caffeine will. Maybe I just don't want to be alone with that echo in my head. A distraction is exactly what I need.

I push open the café door, and the air smells like espresso and cinnamon sugar. It's warm in here today, a change of pace from the usual cold draft. Trivia nights are usually pretty slim, but today the room is crowded with voices. Doing my usual scan of the place, I'm instantly drawn to the side we never sit on, the side where Joss always gets distracted with tiny animals she swears she can see on the burn orange textured wall. That's where I find a boy with honey colored eyes, sitting with someone I don't know.

I'm quick to look away, pretending like I didn't see him. His focus was on the boy he was sitting with. I do a quick scan of the other side of the cafe, my side, to find Joss and Maddie picking up their coffee, and what looks like mine. I make a beeline for them. Please let tonight bring on a distraction.

We grab a table nearby, and before the caffeine hits, I'm flooded with questions about how dinner with my parents and Zane went. Even though I spent most of my morning replying to the group chat, answering what I thought were all the questions they had. Boy, was I wrong.

I'm saved by the preverbal bell when Ms. Whitlock interrupts all the questions to go over the rules. I can't help myself, I feel my body being pulled to where Zane sits against the wall. I take another long sip of my cafe latte before I give in and look his way. His eyes are already fixed on me softly, that must be the gravity he keeps talking about. My eyes stay locked on his until Joss nudges me, pulling me back to reality.

Ms. Whitlock tells us to pair up in teams, and before I can register what's happening, we get pushed out of our corner and right into the middle of the cafe. At the same time, Zane and his friend come barreling through.

"Hey, Remi." He greets me and leans in for a kiss on the cheek, the way my parents taught him.

I can't lie, it makes me blush.

"Hey, you," I say, giving him a kiss of my own. "You come to join the reigning champs?" I spit out, with a bit more sass than intended.

"Something like that." He retorts. We all take our seats just as Ms. Whitlock starts with her first question.

Zane is sitting across from me, which is great because I get a front-row seat to the way he runs his fingers through his hair when he gets stressed. I like the way he writes his answers down and then leans back in his chair, eyes fixed on me. Giving me all of his attention. I tend to take longer than I need to with my answers to avoid eye contact. Let's be honest, it feels kinda nice to be under the weight of his gaze.

We're on our second round of trivia when Joss and Maddie lean in and ask me, both whispering at the same time.

"Who's the guy with Zane?" Maddie asks, her brows raised.

I shake my head. "I have no idea. I've never seen him around."

"He hasn't stopped talking since he sat down," Joss mutters, rolling her eyes.

She's right about that, that boy has not stopped talking, whether he is answering the trivia question or commenting on someone else's answer. He's giving Joss a run for her money, and no room to speak. Which is very difficult to do.

"Loudest voice in the room and not even cute enough to get away with it." She says when I don't respond.

Across the table, the guy leans back in his chair, grinning like he caught every word.

"That's debatable," he says, pointing his pen at Joss. "And for the record, you'd be losing without me." I can't help but laugh.

Joss groans. "Oh, perfect. He's cocky, too."

Zane doesn't even look up from scribbling the answer. "He's my cousin. Eli."

"Surprise," Eli says, lifting his coffee cup in a mock-toast. "Don't worry, I only crash trivia nights when I'm feeling generous." He winks at Joss

"Generous?" Joss snorts. "Pretty sure the only thing you're giving us is a headache."

Maddie hides a laugh, her shoulders shaking. I glance between the three of them, trying to piece together how this stranger slid into our night like he's always belonged here. Zane seems to keep everyone at arm's length, so seeing him with Eli is new. Who am I kidding? All of this is new. There is a looseness to Zane tonight, a side he hasn't shown me yet.

I'm not sure whether I should be grateful for this side of him or annoyed that I wasn't the one who could bring it out of him. The game keeps rolling, questions blurring with Eli's loud commentary and Joss's constant bickering, but I can't stop stealing glances at Zane. Most of the time, he's looking back.

Trivia winds down, and everyone starts gathering their things. Eli announces he's staying to help the barista close up, "Earning his keep," he says with a wink. Which leaves Zane standing beside me in the doorway, hands shoved in his pockets.

"Did you drive tonight?" Zane leans closer to me as he asks the question.

"No, I needed fresh air, so I walked," I whisper back.

"I'll walk you," he says, like it's not even a question.

The night air is cooler than I expect when we step outside, the laughter and music of the café muffled as the door swings shut behind us. For a moment, neither of us says anything. Our footsteps fall in sync on the sidewalk, the rhythm steady, and this feels nice.

I wait for him to fill the quiet, stealing glances his way, thinking he will break the silence, but he doesn't. Zane walks with his hands shoved deep into his pockets, eyes on the road ahead. Not tense, exactly. Just... quiet. Like the noise of the café drained him, and this is what's left.

It should feel awkward, but it doesn't. The quiet stretches, settling around us like something fragile, and I'm almost afraid to break it, but I do it anyway.

"Do you know why the town is named Copperridge?" I chew nervously on my lip.

He cocks his head to the side and shakes his head no. My heart sinks a little, I was fully expecting to hear his voice.

"Okay," I raise my eyebrows, "Would you like to know Zane?" I ask, slightly annoyed.

He tucks his lips into each other, takes one hand out of his pocket, and rubs it through his luxurious waves. He smirks, finally glancing over at me.

"You're not gonna let me get away with silence, are you?"

My grin is big. "Not a chance," I shoot back, though my cheeks heat under his attention. "So... Do you want to know or not?"

"Fine," he says, stretching the word out as it costs him something. "Educate me."

I huff, but can't help smiling as I bite my lip. "Copperridge got its name because the sunsets hit the hills just right. Makes the whole ridge glow like burnished copper. My Nonna used to say it was the town's only treasure."

Zane's eyes flick toward me, thoughtful now. "Not it's only treasure."

The way he says it makes my stomach flutter. I look away quickly, pretending to focus on the cracks in the sidewalk, because if I look at him too long, I'll forget to breathe. Okay, Remi, you've got this.

"How about I show you, I'll grab my car and be right over, okay?" Silently praying he will say yes.

"No way, Remi," he says, pulling out his keys and shaking them slightly in the air for me to see. "We can take my truck."

It's a good thing we didn't make it far. We spin on our heels and walk back towards the coffee shop, where he left his truck. A part of me wonders why he didn't just offer to drive me home. Then again, I left my car parked outside of his house overnight just to spend more time with him, who am I to judge?

Once we get close to his truck, he picks up the pace to get in front of me, opening the door and waiting until I climb inside to shut it.

"Let me grab something from the house first. Then you can tell me how to get there, okay?" he doesn't wait for my response, just puts the truck in reverse and drives.

When we park at his house, I get the chance to breathe, finally. A moment to replay what he said without him watching my face like it's a puzzle he can solve.

Not only is it our treasure.

The words hit me again, harder now that he's not sitting beside me. My dad calls me *tesoro* every morning like it's just a fact, like it's stitched into who I am. Nonna said that Copperridge had only one treasure: the ridge glowing at sunset.

But Zane... Zane said it as if he meant something entirely different. Like he meant *me,* like I was the treasure. And that thought? Yeah, that sends a quiet panic rattling through my ribs. Because I'm not the girl people treasure. I'm not the girl anyone looks at and thinks, Y*up, she's gold.* I'm definitely not the girl who falls apart over one boy's soft voice and one sentence that shouldn't feel like a confession.

The truth is, I liked the way he said it. I liked it way too much. I need some fresh air, so I open the door to get out. I need to pace a bit and walk off some of this nervous energy.

Before I can unpack it any further or walk off the nervous energy, the front door swings open, and he jogs back toward the truck, a bag slung over his shoulder. Casual like he didn't just drop four words that have been echoing in my mind ever since.

Who is this boy, and where did he come from? His light-wash jeans hug his hips and thighs, and his black hoodie matches those black combat boots he's always wearing. He walks past me, tosses the bag in the bed of the truck, and then pauses

"You okay?" I ask anxiously.

Instead of words, he pins me with a stare and stalks his way towards me. He reaches for my hands and pulls them down to his side, which in turn pulls me off the cool door and into his space.

"Thank you." I can barely hear him over how fast my heart is beating. "Sometimes big crowds can really put me in a funk. Thank you for dragging me back out." He says as he presses his forehead to mine.

I can't think, can't breathe, can't do anything except whisper, "We should go before we miss it." Because what else do you say when your whole body is buzzing like this?

His forehead lingers a beat longer before he picks up his head and meets my eyes. He holds there for a second, searching for something. I'm so focused on his eyes that I almost miss the twitch of his hand, like he is trying to be still, but he just can't. His eyes drop to my mouth, and on instinct, I wet my lips, his eyes instantly pop back up to my eyes. Something flares in his eyes, like he's trying to hold onto what little control he has.

Reaching behind me, he pulls the door open.

"Get in, Remi, sit in the middle," he says in a low tone, more frustrated with himself than with me.

Zane drives for about ten minutes until we reach the outskirts of town. I'm sitting close enough to smell the cedar wood and the faintest scent of sweetness clinging to him. His thigh pressed solid right next against mine, with his hand laid on my leg, letting his fingers trace an infinity symbol on my skin.

Thank God I chose today of all days to wear shorts.

"Pull over here," I say, a little too breathy.

Zane moves his hand to put the truck in park, and I instantly miss the warmth against my skin.

We climb out, and the ridge stretches wide before us, the town below awash in copper and rose. The sunset looks like it's on fire, every cloud edged in gold. I lean back against the hood, the metal warm against my spine, and let the view overwhelm me.

Zane doesn't really look at the sky. Instead, steady and unreadable. He pushes off the truck and comes to stand close, too close, until I can feel the heat rolling off him. On instinct, I turn my body to face his.

His hand brushes mine, slow at first, then when I don't pull away. My breath stumbles, my eyes still locked on his. There's something there, beneath the surface, the same blaze I saw in his eyes before we got into the truck.

"Remi…" My name falls from his lips like a secret, barely there.

Suddenly, the space between us is gone. I'm not sure if it was him or me who closed the gap. His rough hand finds my neck, his thumb moving slowly back and forth on my cheek. Yes, and pulls his lips together.

His eyes open, and there's a question there, an unspoken one. I want to scream and tell him my answer is yes. But I'm frozen in this moment, I look down where his lips are still tucked in, like he's trying his best to restrain himself, that's what breaks me.

I lean in first, closing the last inch of space. His lips part against mine, and the restraint shatters. Zane nudges my nose with his, and the second I feel his heavy breathing against my skin, I'm done for. The kiss is cautious at first, careful, like he's afraid to push too far, but it deepens when he realizes I'm not pulling away. My body melts into his. His hands tighten against either side of my jaw, the rough pads of his fingers grounding me even as the rest of me feels like it might float away.

It's over too soon, just long enough for me to know I'll never be the same again. He pulls back, forehead resting on mine, breath unsteady. My fingers curl into the sides of his hoodie, pulling him back into my body, holding on like I can keep the world from moving on.

"Remi…" again he whispers, like my name is the only thing he's sure of.

I don't trust my voice, so I just stay there, holding the moment between us. Hoping this moment lingers long enough to carry us into what comes next.

Eleven

☾

Remi

I haven't seen Zane since the night at trivia, the night that changed everything. Kissing him was a dream I never wanted to wake up from. The way he touched me, so steady, so certain, yet somehow tender, as if he pressed too hard, I'd crumble in his hands.

Since then, nothing. Sunday came and went, and he was nowhere to be found. Now it's Monday, and he's not at school either. I don't have any classes with him, but last week he asked me to save him a seat at lunch today. I don't understand why I care, but I do.

"You okay?" Joss pulls me out of my thoughts.

"Yeah, I'm good, just making a mental checklist, you know," I say with a shrug.

"Sooo totally daydreaming of Zane!" She sings his name and nudges me with her shoulder. I treat her to an eye roll. Why is she always right?

"After you left trivia night, that guy with Zane stuck around." She says as if she hasn't been replaying his face in her head all weekend.

"Let's not pretend you don't remember his name," I say, concealing my sarcasm.

"Anyway," She blows me off. "Ask Zane if he will be back for the fall festival, would ya? We could all go together, you know, as a friend group." Joss is trying so hard to be nonchalant, but I fortunately see right through it.

"Okay, Joss, I'll do that just for you." I laugh and grab my things.

I totally forgot about the fall festival, it's the number one thing to do this time of year. Live music, carnival rides, food on top of food. There's no way I can make it through without the fried Oreos, and everyone in town knows I'm going home with the biggest bag of kettle corn. It's my absolute favorite.

The bell rings to go home, but the headache it brought on carried the ringing all the way home. I find myself standing in the driveway, flinging my keys back and forth in my hands, staring at three houses down. Before my brain is aware that my body has made a decision, I start walking, and I don't stop until I'm in front of his house. My hands are shaking and clammy as I ring the doorbell. I spin around and turn my back to the door, needing to calm my nerves before I face the boy my lips were attached to only days ago.

Suddenly, I hear Zane's voice, but when I turn around, he's not there. Am I hearing things? My head tilts to the side. There's no way I'm dreaming this up.

"Remi, im talking to you on the doorbell camera." I hear his voice again.

"Oh, uhm, okay," I say nervously, scratching my head.

"Pull out your phone." He must be somewhere kind of far because I can only hear every other word he's saying, but I pull out my phone anyway.

He gives me his phone number, which I add to my phone. What am I supposed to do with it? I stand there for just a second, looking down at my phone and back towards the camera.

"Don't just stand there, stunned, Moretti, call me. I want to hear your voice." He says with a chuckle.

"You wish, Zane." And I turn on my heels. There's no way my nerves will allow me to call him.

"C'mon, I want to hear your voice." He says in a much softer tone that softness is what undoes me, and I stop in my tracks.

Right there on the porch, I'm sure he is still watching. I pick up my phone and send him a text as I walk home.

Remi: Just making sure you're okay. I didn't see you at lunch.

His reply is instant, and I can't help but smile.

Zane: I said I wanted to hear your voice.

Remi: Too bad, I wanted to see your face. Neither of us is going to get what we want.

Zane: I'm almost home. Turn around. Wait for me.

Remi: You miss me or something?

Zane: Remi, I've missed you for eighteen years. I don't want to miss you anymore. Please, turn around, wait for me.

The whirlwind that is Zane is consuming me, literally. I'm instantly turning on my heels and heading back to his house. I smile and shake my head.

Remi: Eighteen years is a long time, loverboy. I guess we'd better not waste anymore of it.

Zane: Then stop making me wait, let me make up for it. I'm here.

What am I supposed to do with that? I instantly screenshot it, send it to Joss, and I'm on my way back to him. He is leaning on the back of the truck when I look up, and the moment our eyes meet, he pushes off the truck, wearing that smirk I love to see. He doesn't say anything, just reaches for me, grabs the opening of my cardigan, and pulls me in for a hug. This hug feels different than any hug I've gotten before.

I haven't had many hugs from boys before, though, so im not really saying much. This one lingers, this hug feels very intimate. His arms are wrapped around me with just the right amount of pressure. He pulls back slightly and moves his hands to the back of my neck, his thumbs stroking my cheeks back and forth. He looks down at my lips and then back to my eyes.

"I've missed you." He says, still searching for something behind my eyes. "You're beautiful, so beautiful I don't know why I haven't made that known sooner. The first day I saw you, these stormy eyes pulled me in, and I haven't been able to look away since." Still stroking my cheeks back and forth.

I reach my arms up to his wrists, and I tilt my head down, pushing out the air he just caused to get caught in my throat.

"Zane," I say, breathlessly. "You make it hard to think. Hard to breathe too if I'm being honest."

I look back up at him, and he's smiling, and this time it reaches his eyes. My body chooses that moment to betray me, my stomach growls so loudly I'm certain the whole block heard it.

"You're hungry, let me make you something to eat." He grabs my hands and pulls me around to the front door.

I've never been inside Zane's house before. Will his aunt be home? I'm not ready to be alone with him, but I am ready to meet his family. I mean, why not? He has met mine. Okay, breathe, Remi. You're spiraling.

"Breathe, Remi. I can hear you panicking." He chuckles.

Snapping my head up. How the heck did he know I was back here freaking out? He opens the door and pulls me through it. He looks at me and smiles, reaches for the door behind me, and closes it.

"Zane, is that you, honey?" I hear a woman's voice, back to panicking.

"Yes, Aunt Cami, it's me." He says, grinning. "I have someone I want you to meet."

She says something back to him, but my heart beating in my ears is too loud for me to hear anything else. Zane pulls me through the front hallway into the kitchen. I can't see much because he's taller than me, and his broad shoulders are blocking my view of everything else. I can tell you the color of the floor, that's it, though. It's a rich, warm brown.

"Aunt Cami, this is Remi. Remi, this is my Aunt Camille." Zane steps out of the way, and I finally lay my eyes on the woman on the other side of the voice.

She's beautiful. Her shoulder-length blonde waves flow so effortlessly and complement her high cheekbones. She is eye level with me, so she's probably five foot two or so. Her lips are full just like Zane's, but her smile is radiant and lights up her face. She's coming my way, wearing that smile with her arms out to greet me.

"Hi Remi, I was wondering when I was finally going to meet you, you're more beautiful than he described."

She grabs me and wraps me in for the warmest hug. It instantly takes me back to Nonna. She always made me feel warm and loved when she hugged me. I close my eyes and let myself get lost in Aunt Camille's hug.

When she pulls back, she's still wearing that smile.

"Are you hungry, sweet girl?" She asks, still squeezing my shoulders a bit.

"Yes, actually, I am." I match her smile. "It's so nice to meet you, Camille."

"I was already making Zane's favorite sandwich, so I'll just make two instead. Oh, and Remi." She pauses and looks up at me tenderly, "Please make yourself at home, and call me Cami."

I walk over to the bar, where Zane is now sitting, telling Cami how today's helping Eli went. I guess I now know where he went. He reaches down under the bar and pulls my bar stool closer to his. When I reach a spot pleasing to him, he places his hand on my leg as he finishes telling her the story of his day. I notice the way her eyes light up as he talks about helping Eli. Cami is still preparing the sandwich, but she's giving Zane her full attention.

"You want a tour?" He asks me quietly.

His question jolted me. I was so wrapped up in listening to them that I forgot I was sitting at the bar in his kitchen. I nod and let him lead me by the hand through the house. I can feel the love here, there are books and paintings everywhere. Every time he stops me in front of a painting or a bookshelf, he pulls me in front of him, pointing out his favorites from just behind my shoulder.

Zane tells me his Aunt Cami is an artist and an art collector. He points out the ones she's painted, the ones she's had to move heaven and earth to find. The ones he tells me she has painted are by far my favorite. He leads me by the hand into the hallway and pauses before opening the next door. His shoulders stiffen, and I see him chew on the inside of his lip.

"Hey, you don't have to show me your room. I'm perfectly fine with sitting at the bar and talking to your Aunt Cami some more." I squeeze his hand and give him a little tug back in the direction of the kitchen.

"No," he says firmly. "It's not that I don't want you to see my room, it's just.." He pauses, and his voice gets a little quieter. "It's just the place where my walls come down." He releases the air from his lips, as if that was a lot for him to confess.

"I get it, take your time," I say gently to him, rubbing my thumb back and forth on his hand to offer him some comfort.

He looks down at my thumb and pushes the door open. I instantly let go of his hand and step inside.

"Zane, it's so artsy in here, I love it." I take my time looking around the room, drinking it all in. "It's the perfect combo of moody and comfort. Omg Elena Moretti would die to be in here. Did you do this yourself?" My voice is coming out rushed, but I can't help it, I'm obsessed with his room.

He is leaning against the door frame, his lips tilted in a half-smile, when I look back at him. I continue to walk around and look at the art, the books, the..

"You play guitar?" My head snaps in his direction.

His eyebrows pull together in the middle, he pushes off the door frame, and pins me with a stare.

"Are you serious?" His chin tips down when he asks me.

"Yes, I'm serious, that's so cool." I shrug back at him

Why is he being so weird? Maybe he doesn't want me to ask questions yet. Maybe I'm just here to observe.

"Remi, the night after we first met, I was playing the guitar. I walked you home, and we played a game of 21 questions. You don't remember that?"

Oh crap, did I forget? I'm losing it, I've been so forgetful lately. Just this morning, my mother scolded me about leaving my laundry in the washer.

"Oh, yeah, uh, I guess you were, weren't you?" I spin back around and pretend to look at one of the books on his shelf.

I can feel him getting closer. He snakes his hands around my waist and plants a kiss on the side of my jaw. Instinctually, I lean into it, into him.

"Am I that easy to forget, Remi?" He asks, a certain sadness to his tone.

I whip my body around on instinct, that question was laced with insecurities and I didn't mean for that to happen. I wrap my hands around his neck and lean back so I can look him in his eyes.

"You're not easy to forget at all, Zane. I've been trying to get you to stop taking up space in my mind since the day I met you." I pause and look deep into his eyes. "It hasn't happened yet." I twirl his short waves through my fingers, as my body betrays me once again, but I announce that I'm still hungry.

"C'mon, Polaris, those sandwiches should be done by now." He grabs my hand and leads me towards the kitchen.

I pause to close his door, taking it all in one last time. Did I really forget that he played the guitar? I couldn't have forgotten a moment like that, could I? I shut the door and bring my hand up to my eyes, my head is beginning to throb. Not this again.

Twelve

(

Remi

The storm rolls in before the sun is even up, a low rumble that rattles the windows and makes my head throb even more. I press the heel of my hand against my temple, like that might keep the migraine from splitting me open again, but it doesn't do much.

Downstairs, voices slowly rise, overpowering the storm, my parents. It sounds like they're arguing. Their fight carries through the walls, sharp edges of Italian and English tangled together, louder than the thunder. I throw the blanket over my head, wishing for silence, wishing for anything but this. I knew there was tension between the two last night at dinner.

"I didn't know pouring vino at Nonna's would be all this marriage consisted of, Nico." My mother's voice cracks like thunder.

Thunder shakes the house, and I think maybe the storm outside is jealous, it's not the loudest thing in Copperridge right now. I drag myself to the window and stare out, focusing all my energy on two raindrops trailing down my windowpane. Distracting my mind from the fight downstairs and this pounding headache I still have, I turn the raindrops into a race. Who makes it to the bottom first? Can the droplets dodge the other droplets on the pane?

Annoyed with it all, I decide a hot shower with the music blasting is the way to go. I let the bathroom billow with steam as I search for the perfect song to fit my mood. Pressing play on my phone, I toss it on the counter, tie my hair in a high bun, and finally let the air out of my lungs. Hoping that when I exhale, my day will get progressively better. Olivia Rodrigo's Brutal plays on repeat until I'm drying my body and dousing myself in my favorite vanilla body butter.

There is silence downstairs when I come out of the shower. Maybe this is why I've always feared love, always feared companionship. One minute it's fields of daisies, the next it's silence. One minute, Nonna was happy and in love, and the next, she was in utter heartbreak, missing her best friend. I take the silence as my cue to grab the keys to my car and head to Nonna's for my shift.

I open the door to Nonna's, and my entire body shifts into a better mood, like someone flipped a switch inside me. This place has always felt like a second heartbeat, a home inside a home. Just stepping inside makes my shoulders drop, and my chest loosen in a way it hasn't all day.

"Hi, Nonna," I whisper to the air, already grinning as my lips tug upward without permission.

Nonna's is always busier on stormy days, people packed shoulder to shoulder in the booths, umbrellas dripping, voices loud enough to make the old windows shake. I tie on my apron and squeeze behind the counter where Rachel, my Papà's manager, is already moving like she owns the place. She's balancing two cappuccinos in one hand and calling out an order in Italian with the other. Rachel has worked for my parents for so long that she's invited over every year for Christmas.

"There she is!" she shouts over the clatter of dishes, grinning at me. "Thought the rain swallowed you whole."

"Close," my eyebrows shoot up towards my hairline, grabbing a stack of menus. "Storm. Migraine. Parents arguing." I roll my eyes.

Rachel winces, but only for a second. She leans in just long enough to bump her shoulder against mine. "At least here, we have fresh garlic bread every 26 minutes," she wraps her coffee-filled hands around my shoulder. "Your friends are in the corner asking for you." And then she's gone, shouting more orders in Italian.

I grab the silverware and the napkins and head over to where Joss and Maddie are seated. If they're here to talk my ear off and get free food, they might as well help me roll the silverware.

"Where have you been, Remi? We've been waiting for like 20 minutes." Joss is talking at me and not to me.

My eyes are wide, and I'm staring blankly at her. This headache, the storm, and now Joss's attitude, I thought this day was going to turn around.

"Hey, Remi," Maddie speaks softly. "You doing okay, Rem? Haven't seen you or talked to you, and you look a little.. uh off, I guess." She grabs the silverware and begins separating it.

I fill the girls in on how my morning started, with my parents and Mother Nature fighting for attention. Joss gives me a pathetic smile, she doesn't really understand the two-parent household and how sometimes it can be a lot to handle. Maddie's face scrunches up like she's maybe running from the same problem today.

"Well, Joss decided to go full on FBI and stalk Eli's Instagram." Her eyes are big like she's got juicy news.

I look at Joss and pin her with a 'you haven't told me any of this' glare.

"You've been occupied, okay." She says, her hands up in the air signaling a white flag. "He's cute, okay, I had to look and see what he was about." She singsongs.

She singsongs. Then proceeds to tell us all about *Eli Navarro*. Turns out he's in a band, he works at a hardware store, he's nineteen, and lives one town over in Briarwood. By the end of the conversation, I feel like I know everything about him. I mean, how she found out that his favorite food was fried catfish, I'll never know, or ask.

"So, I was totally thrown off guard and jealous at first, but I really am happy for you, Remi." Maddie grabs my arm and gives it a squeeze.

"What?" I stare back at her quizzically. "What are you even talking about, Maddie?"

"Oh, uh. I'm talking about you and Zane. He's clearly only got eyes for you. He won't even look other girls in the eyes when they're speaking to him. I have him in biology for the third hour, and Jenny Carver is always trying to get his attention." She lifts her shoulder as she rolls the last set of silverware. "Zane never even looks up at her. It's got to be embarrassing for her. I mean, to be ignored like that." She finally looks up at me. "I'm happy you're happy, Remilia."

On instinct, Joss and I lock eyes and burst into laughter. I get up and go around the table to give Maddie a tight squeeze.

"Oh, Maddie, it's been so long since you've been this version of yourself. I know your parents' being gone all the time takes a toll on you, but I'm so glad you came back around to... well, you." I say, and I pull her in.

"Here's your food, girls." Rachel's voice breaks the love fest. "Oh, thank you so much for finishing all the silverware. This storm doesn't seem to want to quit for good, and we're about to get a whole lot busier. Speaking of, Remi I need you on bread duty, table seven is almost out, and I need to man the bar."

"Well, you guys enjoy your pasta. Joss, just follow him, he can probably already see you viewed his profile. Don't be weird," I pin her with a look. " It's weird, tell her Maddie."

I wave my hand in the air, hoping that Maddie can talk some sense into Joss. I'll check on you guys in a few. I blow them a kiss and walk towards the bread station. Those two are a full-time job.

I think I had to bring the girls about three loaves of bread, and each time I did, Joss would tell me something new she found out about Eli. I decided to take my fifteen-minute break out back instead of at the table with the girls. As soon as the door opens, I'm reminded of the storm outside. Wind and rain everywhere, I won't be out here long. Pulling out my phone, my finger lingers over Zane's contact.

My finger lingers for far too long. My mind drifts to him, to our kiss, and my stomach does that flip thing. Has anyone ever studied whether butterflies in your stomach are actually your body's early-warning system instead of some cute romantic metaphor? Because mine feel suspiciously like danger signs wrapped in glitter.

Before I can spiral any further, I get an email from the last college I applied to. Great job, universe. Nothing snaps you out of a daydream about a boy like a reminder that the future is knocking. I tuck my phone back into my apron and head back into Nonna's.

After my shift, I head straight home, in desperate need of my bed to sleep the rest of this migraine off. The Tylenol I've been popping like candy isn't even taking the edge off anymore. I open the door to the house, and the only thing I hear is how loud it is.

Walking into the house, I know the fight isn't over, I can still feel the tension in the air. There's no music, no smell of garlic, no singing, no speaking passionately about absolutely anything, just silence. This is the aftermath of the storm, and I'm not talking about the one that's still going on outside. My parents are on opposite sides of the couch, which for them might as well be the opposite sides of the country. I slip past them and head straight for my room.

The first thing I do is turn on my lamp, the warm yellow light isn't harsh enough to irritate my migraine further, but it also sets the mood and turns the walls of my room a honey color. Almost the exact same color of Zane's eyes. I crawl into bed and cocoon myself in my comforter. My mind on exhale takes me to Nonna's box under my bed. I reach down and run my fingers over the carved moon and stars on the box.

I miss you, Nonna.

I bring the box onto my lap and get lost in the memory of when my Nonna gave it to me. 'Hide your treasures in here, Qui dentro, il cuore trova riposo.'

"In here, the heart finds rest," I whisper to myself.

I ease the lid open and dig for a letter at the bottom. Running my fingers over the indentations, I take my time and carefully open up a letter to a boy I only ever met in my dreams.

Dear L,

Last night we ended up sitting on the swings at the park again, but this time you brought sandwiches. Nothing fancy, just two crumpled paper bags from the gas station down the street. We sat there with the chains creaking and the crickets screaming, unwrapping sandwiches that tasted more like mustard than meat.

You made a face at yours and said, "This is terrible," but kept eating anyway. I laughed so hard I almost dropped mine, and you said that was the point, food isn't about the taste, it's about who you share it with.

I don't even remember finishing mine, but I remember the way you kicked at the dirt with your sneakers, like the whole world could wait while we sat there with our bad sandwiches and better company.

Love,

R

I take my time folding the letter back up, thinking of how fourteen-year-old Remi must have felt eating a sandwich on the swings with the boy of her dreams, literally. For the first time today, the tightness in my head eases up. I pack up the box and place it gently on the floor next to my bed. I'm re-wrapping myself in my comforter when my phone buzzes on my nightstand. It's probably Joss telling me she got caught snooping on Eli. Smiling to myself, I reach for my phone only to see a text from Zane.

Zane: Feels weird not to see you today.

Remi: Yeah, don't let it happen again.

Zane: lol

Zane: Then come with me to Briarwood tomorrow. Eli's band is playing.

Remi: Can the girls come too?

Zane: Yeah. Pick you up at 10.

I grin at the screen, feeling my cheeks heat. I sent a quick text to Maddie and Joss with the plan for tomorrow. Joss replies with the big eye emoji. I shake my head. That girl is trouble.

Remi: See you at 10, Zane.

Rolling myself back up and settling in, I notice soft music coming from the kitchen. That makes me smile. The raindrops are quieter now, much quieter. It seems like all is well in the Moretti home again, and suddenly, ten a.m. is the only thing I can think about.

Thirteen

☾

Remi

"That's the third outfit you've put on Remi. Pick one already. It's just a music festival in the park." Maddie scoffs.

"Tell me again why I invited you two over early to help me get ready, if you're not going to help me get ready." I give her an eye roll as I head back into the closet.

I know this isn't my wedding day, but I have been to a million concerts. Every outfit feels like a decision I don't know how to make, though.

"Do you think this bright orange shirt will make Eli notice me from the stage?" Joss cocks her head to the side and plays with her hair in the mirror.

I come out of the closet in a plain black tank top and my favorite light wash jeans. This will have to work for today, I'm over it already. I sit on the edge of my bed and lace up my high-top black Converse while Maddie and Joss are gushing over Eli and his bandmates in the background.

The door pops open, and my jaw instantly relaxes as I see my mammà standing there with four large to-go cups of coffee. My shoulders slump as I inhale the scent of my favorite drink, and I make my way over to where she's standing. She gives me a knowing look and wraps one of her coffee-filled arms around me.

"I made yours extra strong teroso." She rubs my back gently. "You're going to need it with these two." She chuckles.

When I pull back, she hands me the tray of coffees. The girls run up behind me and grab the ones with their names on them, kiss my mammà on the cheek, and head downstairs.

"I made one for Zane as well. I don't know what he likes, so I made him your favorite." She curls my hair around her fingers. "This is nice, I like what you've done with your hair, Remi." She smiles gently. "I have the perfect shade of lipstick for you, come." And she drags me down the hall into her room.

She sits me at her vanity and starts rummaging through her drawers. My mother is always put together, she takes pride in looking her best. It's something I admire about her, it's never over-the-top, but it's always perfection.

"Bellissima, a touch of color, not too much, just enough to make your eyes pop." She says as she applies the lipstick for me, holding my chin so gently. "Beautiful, I knew this one would be perfect for you! Here," handing the lipstick to me, "It's yours now, it will never look this good on me." I take the gold lipstick tube and inspect it.

"Mammà, this is your favorite one, I can't take this."

I knew this tube looked familiar, but it was the name that told me it was her favorite. Every time my parents get dressed up fancy, she does her makeup, applies this particular Charlotte Tilbury lipstick, and my dad always calls her his 'super model'.

"It's yours now, bellissima. Now go, your friends are waiting." She waves me off.

It's moments like these that remind me how much my mother knows me. Giving me a shade of lipstick that makes me look a little braver than I feel.

"Thank you Mammà." I plant a kiss on her cheek, and I head out the door.

The girls are waiting on the porch swing when I open the door, giving me a mischievous smile over the rim of their coffee cups.

"What are you two planning?" I ask anxiously.

Before the girls can answer, Zane opens the door to his truck. On command, the girls stand up and head towards the truck. Just the sight of him has me stunned. His jaw is so sharp, I just want to run my finger across it. I bring my finger up to my jaw and run my finger across mine, feeling the sensation he would feel if I had the guts to reach up and do it.

"You okay?" Zane asks, snapping me out of the trance I was in.

"Yes, more than okay actually. Uhm, my mammà made you a caffè latte the Nonna way, my favorite." I hand him the coffee and finally bring my eyes to meet him.

"Honey," my eyes balloon, I can't believe I just said that out loud. My throat bobs as I swallow down my embarrassment.

"Honey, huh?" Zane's smirk appears, slow at first. I watch as the smile lifts his cheek up towards his eye.

"Careful, Remi, might start expecting you to sweet-talk me more often." His smirk grows, but he tries to mask it by taking a drink.

Heat prickles up my spine, coloring my face scarlet. Humiliation and anxiety tangle inside me, and for a second, I desperately wish I could melt into the porch and vanish.

"I was talking about the color of your eyes, I just didn't mean to say it out loud." My words are laced with humiliation.

Zane spins on his heels and starts walking towards the truck. "Come on, *honey,* we're going to be late." He announces over his shoulder, trying to contain his laughter.

"Ugh," I groan, "You're never going to forget I said that, are you?" I drag my hands down my face, careful enough not to smear my lipstick.

"Not a chance," his eyebrows shooting up towards his hair, which looks super shiny today.

He opens the door for me as I scoot in. I shoot a look at the girls in the back, looking at something on Joss' phone, most likely a picture of her newest obsession, Eli.

Zane gets in and closes the door, still holding onto the grin that is bordering on a full-blown smile at this point. I bring my fingers up to my temple and rub. This coffee had better fix this headache and this day. I can't believe I just let that slip out. I'm usually more poised than that, at least on the outside.

Twenty-ish minutes later, we're pulling up to a park that's overflowing with energy. People everywhere, food trucks, vendors selling things, photo booths, and a huge stage with speakers surrounding it. Zane and Eli spot each other almost immediately, his guitar slung over his shoulder.

"Eli, what's up, man? You remember Remi, Joss, and Maddie, don't ya?" Zane greets his cousin with a half-hug, half-back pat thing that men always do. Eli clears his throat and pins Joss with a stare.

"How could I forget?" Eli retorts, sounding slightly annoyed at first. His expression softens as he looks at me. He steps forward and pulls me into a friendly, playful hug, the kind an older brother would give a baby sister he hasn't seen in a while.

"Um, hi Eli. We are excited to hear you play." I say, trying to break free from his grasp. Zane is smiling, shaking his head.

"No hug for us?" Joss throws her hands on her hips and gives Eli a flirtatious smile. Maddie was standing tall behind her, but looking somewhere else. Joss nudges Maddie with an elbow.

"Yeah, hi to you too, Eli." Maddie finally brings her gaze to the group.

"Look, we are going on in about twenty, I've got to get to the band. I'll find you after." He looks to Zane as he is slowly backpedalling towards the stage.

Zane and I give each other a look, and if I had to ask him, he would probably say he's thinking the same thing that I am.

I'd run away from them, too.

"He is sassy today," Joss announces to the group. "Anyway, let's go find a good spot up close to lay out our blanket." She's already heading towards the stage, expecting us to follow, and we all do.

When we are finally sitting, Zane reaches over and twirls one of my curls around his finger. My breath hitches in my chest. He's staring at my hair, looping it over and over again in his hands.

"I like your hair like this. Your waves are pretty, too, but the curls make your hair so shiny. Like Honey," He says, meeting my eyes.

"I knew you wouldn't let it go," I say, swatting his hand out of my hair.

"Im being serious, it's nice like this. Don't be surprised if I can't keep my hands out of it today." He pushes his lips to the side. At the same time, his eyes drop slowly down towards my lips, where they settle for a few beats and snap back up to meet my eyes again.

"Do you like it?" I hear myself ask self-consciously, "It's a new lipstick." I pull my lips in nervously, waiting for his reply.

"I love it actually," his tongue coming out slightly to wet his lips. "Makes the flecks of green and blue pop in those stormy eyes of yours."

His eyes feel like they're penetrating my soul with the way he's staring at me right now. We stay as such, eyes locked onto each other, until the band is introduced. Music thumps from the speakers, and it just so happens to match the beat that my heart is giving off right now. Zane pulls me closer towards him and wraps his arm around my waist, both of us swaying back and forth to the music. As close as I am now, I can't help but want to be closer. He must be thinking the same thing because I hear him say "screw it" under his breath as he moves to pick me up and set me between his legs.

I'm so glad he can't see my face right now, because I know my eyes are bugged wide, and my cheeks are tomato sauce red. It takes me a second to relax my body into his. His arms rest on his knees, and my back rests on his chest. This feels good, a little too good. I never want to be anywhere else.

Eli's band finishes up about the same time Joss starts complaining about starving to death. She's so dramatic, but I'm with her on this one, my nose is flooded with different scents from the food trucks behind us. They have everything from chicken on a stick to Indian tacos. The girls decide on hamburgers, but there is no way I'm passing up the nacho stand, cheese, and jalapeños. That's an automatic yes, from me.

We meet up at the lemonade stand, where Maddie is contemplating between two flavors, blueberry and pomegranate. She's flirting with him to try to get both for the price of one. I stand there for about forty-two more seconds before I cut in.

"Girl, come on. We will take both of those and a cherry lemonade, please and thank you." Before she tries to rebut, I swipe my card and move out of the way.

"It wasn't about the money, Remi. I wanted both, and I liked his banter." She flips her hair over her shoulder, looking back at the guy making our lemonades.

"My nacho cheese is going to get cold, plus I wanted to try both flavors too." I lie, I don't want to tell her that I'm reaching the point of hangry. The lemonade man tells us our drinks are ready, and I beat Maddie over to grab them.

"Thanks, and my friend thinks you're hot. Look her up on Instagram, name's Maddie with three e's, you can't miss it." I grab my lemonade and turn to Maddie, whose jaw is on the ground. "Thank me later, sis," and I blow her a kiss.

We all sit down at the picnic tables to eat, and immediately Joss and Eli are at each other's throats.

"Ugh, who puts pickles *under* the cheese? That's just disrespectful." Joss unwraps her burger and immediately groans.

Eli takes a massive bite of his own and talks around it. "Only a psychopath takes the pickles off in the first place."

My eyes go wide as I look over at Zane, who is shaking his head as he mouths, " Here *we go again.*

Joss glares. "I like pickles, I just don't like them soggy and smothered in fake cheese."

"Then you're eating it wrong. The pickle-to-cheese ratio is sacred. You can't just rearrange it." Eli waves his burger like it's a gavel.

Joss huffs, pulling her bun apart to flick a pickle slice onto his wrapper. "There, balance was restored. Congratulations, you're the proud owner of two extra pickles."

Eli doesn't even blink. He pops them straight into his mouth and grins. "Thanks. Tastes like victory."

Maddie snorts into her lemonade. "I swear, you two could fight over oxygen." Her phone vibrates on the table, and she looks up at me and smiles. "Looks like I just got a new follower on Instagram, thanks, Rem," she winks.

"You want a bite?" I look over to Zane, who didn't order anything. His eyes meet mine, a sweet smile on his face.

"Thank you," he says, tucking my curled hair behind my ear. "But I'm still full from breakfast." His eyes drop to my lips, and I can't help but do the same to him. He brings his thumb up to my lips and smiles as he wipes the nacho cheese from my face.

No one should be allowed to look at me like that with nacho cheese on my face.

"Embarrassing thing number two, great." I set the chip down and push my food back. He lets out a quiet chuckle and scoots my food back towards me.

"Adorable," he pauses, "both things you call embarrassing, I call adorable. Now eat, you get grumpy if you don't." He smiles.

"Are you having fun?" I ask, shoving a chip into my mouth. Thankful he pushed my food back towards me, these nachos are amazing.

"The music is nice." He says as he runs his fingers through his waves. His eyes are on the crowd now. "I just don't enjoy crowds." Eyes meeting mine again.

"So you're basically a hermit crab," I say proudly, chewing on another bite of my nachos. He smirks and stands up, stepping one foot over the picnic bench and sitting back down, facing me.

"No," he pulls my body closer towards his, then pulls my nachos in front of me. "Im just used to the quiet."

I put my chip down and wipe my mouth, making sure there's no cheese this time. I drop my napkin onto the table and pin Zane with a stare. "You do realize I'm Italian, right? Quiet isn't in our DNA."

His eyes drop as his finger hooks onto my belt loop, and he begins toying with it nervously. "I survived dinner with the Morettis," he pauses before meeting my gaze, his eyes are soft. "I think I can learn to love the broken volume in which you guys operate."

I open my mouth to fire back, but nothing comes out. He's still tugging gently at my belt loop, eyes locked on mine, and I don't remember what joke I was about to make. All I can do is stare, hoping he can't see how fast my heart is beating.

I turn away from the heat in his eyes and grab another chip. I raise my eyebrow, knowing the dare that's on the tip of my tongue. I look back at him, the same heat in his eyes.

"Love, huh?" I say, popping the chip into my mouth.

Joss slaps the table, making everyone jump. "Eli, I swear if you put mustard on a burger one more time, we're done as friends."

The whole table groans as Eli piles more mustard onto his burger. The argument explodes again, pulling everyone back into the chaos. Everyone except me, my focus is still fixated on the slow drag of Zane's finger trailing up and down my belt loop. We stay that way until the sun begins to set, casting a copper hue over everything. Today was supposed to be nothing, a random Sunday at a music festival, but it's turned into a day I know I won't forget.

Something in me is shifting, and I don't think I want it to stop.

Fourteen

☾

Remi

Zane parked at his house, and we walked the rest of the way. Maddie and Joss went their separate way, probably up to no good. The night turned colder than I expected, and the tank top I chose to wear was not a good choice at all. I tried my best to tough it out, but it's Zane, and he noticed anyway. One minute he was walking next to me, and the next minute he was pulling his hoodie over my head. It swallowed me, I mean, my knees were to my knees, but it was so warm I didn't complain. The scent of him clung to the fabric, cedar and a hint of sweetness.

When we got to my door, he didn't say much. Zane isn't big with his words anyway. He speaks through movement, through touch, and he speaks with his eyes. Which is what he's doing right now, he lifts my chin with one hand and wraps the other around my waist, drawing me into him. The sigh that leaves him speaks louder than any words he could say out loud.

Zane shifts his hand from under my chin to the back of my neck, pulls me in, and brings my forehead to his lips. He kisses me there, soft and lingering. I can't be sure what he means by it, but it feels like he's asking for forever. My response is easy, I wrap my arms around his waist and lean my head into his kiss.

"Goodnight, Zane. Text me when you get home." I say into his chest. He pulls back slightly, hand still on the back of my neck.

"Goodnight, Remilia." He uses my full first name as he places another gentle kiss on the side of my head.

I stand there stunned, his footsteps fading. *Remilia.* My full name, the one I've spent years rolling my eyes at, hating even. No one says it like that, like it's something worth tasting slowly. Tonight, I don't hate it; I think I might finally love it.

Long after Zane has gone home, I'm still replaying the way he said my name, *Remilia,* over and over again in my head. Wrapped up in his hoodie, I have the urge to reach for Nonna's box. Fourteen-year-old Remi would spit noodles out of her nose if she knew how gone I was over this boy already.

I run my fingers over Nonna's box, feeling the texture of the carved moon and stars. What would she say about Zane? Would she like him? I already know the answer to that. Nonna would've liked him the moment he asked if he could help in the kitchen. Of course, she would've said a few choice Italian words followed by no, but she would've liked him.

I lift the lid and sift through the letters, finding one I haven't read yet. Folded with intention, I carefully open it.

I quickly fold the letter back up. Fourteen-year-old me probably daydreamed of that moment for weeks after. I want to laugh at her, but I can't because swaying back and forth today at the music festival with Zane will probably be on replay for the weeks to come.

L only existed in my dreams, but Zane? Zane Carter is real. He walked me home, gave me his hoodie, kissed my forehead, and said my name as if it were an exquisite Italian dish to be savored. I gently fold the letter and place it back into the blue box, just as my phone lights up.

Zane: Made it home.

Zane: Goodnight, Remilia.

Remi: Stop making me smile at my phone like an idiot, Zane.

Remi: Thanks for the hoodie, btw.

Zane: Keep it. Looks better on you anyway.

Great, I'm smiling at my phone again.

Remi: Goodnight, Zane.

Monday mornings suck less when I wake up to the scent of Zane, still wrapped in his hoodie. I pull the neckline over my nose and inhale, breathing him in one more time before I have to get out of this bed.

At school, Joss and Maddie are huddled up at my locker, steam coming out of their coffee cups. The second I walk closer, I already know they're up to something. They look like they're already up to something, ugh, it's too early for this.

"Don't start," I say, opening my locker and shoving my books inside.

"We aren't saying anything." Maddie's words were laced with humor.

"Yet," Joss adds with a raised eyebrow.

Before I can respond, something inside of me pulls my attention to the doors I just walked through. I can feel his presence before my eyes even meet his. Zane is here. I take him in from head to toe before I snap my head back in the direction of my locker. On inhale, I close my eyes, thinking of the maroon fitted shirt he's wearing, the way it hugs his shoulders and biceps should be illegal. Paired with jeans and his normal combat boots, with his backpack slung over one shoulder, I can't make myself look back over at him.

"Morning," Zane announces with a soothing timbre.

A shiver runs up my spine. I breathe in and am instantly taken back to the hoodie he gave me last night. Cedar and sweetness, I can't help but smile. I lift my head, still unable to turn his way.

"Good morning," I say, concealing my smile.

I can feel his warmth behind me. He steps closer and leans over to whisper something in my ear. His breath cascading over my cheek makes me close my eyes and savor the moment.

"Save me a seat at lunch, Polaris."

Then he does something I didn't think we were ready for. He pulls my back into his chest by wrapping his arm around my stomach, and he plants a kiss on my cheek. What feels like a simple press of the lips to my cheek feels an awful lot like an announcement to the world, like a claim, or even a promise.

I don't even get a chance to tell him yes, he unwraps himself from my waist, and when I turn around, he's gone. Turning around was a mistake, though. Everyone has stopped what they're doing, and all eyes are on me. On instinct, I turn myself around back to my locker and wait for the commotion to pick up again.

"Well, that wasn't on my bingo card for a Monday morning at Copperridge High," Maddie says, eyes ballooned, like everyone else.

"Do we clap or…." Joss retorts, and we all start laughing. Commotion picks back up, and it looks like everyone has stopped looking at me.

"C'mon, let's go." I close my locker, square my shoulders, and head towards first period.

Crap, I'd better text my mom and tell her not to go to the post office today. I pull out my phone and shoot a quick text to my mom.

Remi: Mom! Whatever you do, don't go see Mrs. Callahan at the post office today. I'll tell you all about it later. Zane kissed me…In front of the whole school.

I slip my phone back into my pocket without even waiting for her to reply. My first three classes consist of looks and questions from people I haven't spoken to all semester. It made for an awkward morning, but if there's one thing I'm good at, it's putting my head in the books and ignoring everything around me.

The bell rings for lunch, and on instinct, I return to my locker to walk in with the girls. I guess I just assumed that Zane would meet me here at my locker. He knows we do this every day, but he's not here. My heart sinks as low as my eyes do, staring at my shoes, I kick a make-believe rock around to keep myself from the 'maybe he has regrets' spiral I'm about to head towards. I barely hear Maddie ask Joss and me if we're ready to go.

"You coming, Remi?" Maddie asks quizzically. My lips twist in disappointment, and I nod as I follow the girls into the cafeteria.

My eyes are still on my feet when we walk through the obnoxiously large copper double doors. This would've been our first time eating lunch together. What happened between this morning and now? Maybe he had second thoughts. He hates crowds, maybe the whispers heard all over campus were too much for him.

"Hey," Zane is walking in my direction.

"Hey, yourself," I say, taking a break from chewing on the inside of my lip.

He looks at me like I'm holding the answers to a question he hasn't asked. His eyes look worried, probably the same shade of worry I'm wearing. Does he regret kissing me in front of the entire school? Is he about to tell me it was a mistake, that we're moving faster than my Papà does when he's about to burn the Sunday sauce?

My stomach drops. Does he regret kissing me in front of half the school? Is he about to tell me it meant nothing? Did I read everything wrong? That I'm… too much? People like me don't get moments like that without losing them just as fast.

"What's wrong?" he says, hooking his finger under my jaw and tilting my head gently to meet his eye-to-eye.

"I uh" I pause, inhaling, collecting my thoughts.

I swallow. Hard. Panic pricks beneath my skin, sharp and familiar.

"I thought since you didn't meet me at my locker, you might have some regrets about kissing me in front of the entire school." My eyes shift away from his. That confession was hard to get out, but the silence after I deliver it is even scarier.

"Remi," he says, caressing my cheek with his thumb.

"I just know you don't like crowds or people, and I'm not sure if you have regrets," blinking away unshed tears.

"I knew exactly what I was doing, Remi, and where I was standing when I did it. I have no regrets. I only saw you." His eyes soften a touch when he says it. "Let's eat…honey," his sarcasm breaking through as he turns on his heels, grabs my hand, and leads me toward the lunch line.

He doesn't like crowds, but he chose to do it anyway. He chose me anyway.

I let out a heavy sigh as I reach for my food, I'm glad he doesn't regret it. That had the potential to devastate me. That is the exact reason I hate feelings, and I hate boys. Except for him, I don't hate this boy. I'm too emotionally sick to even think of eating a full meal, so I settle for an apple. My Nonna would flip in her grave if I ate that lunchroom spaghetti anyway. I look over to Zane as I pay for my apple, only to find him looking back at me with one side of his lips lifted. The way his eyes are lit up right now tells me he is happy.

"Your turn to lead me, Polaris. Where do we sit?" He nods towards the sea of people.

Scrunching my nose up, "You know, Polaris means a lot more than just the north star..." I make sure to give him a side eye as we walk to the table where the girls are already seated.

"There's a submarine, as well as a missile." I turn to give him a stern look. "It's also a Marvel character, so I'll take it, it's cute, but if I start throwing metal at your head, remember this moment," I smirk and take my seat, staring at him the entire time.

"So..." he sets his tray down and follows with his body. "You'd rather me call you what.. *honey?*"

"Oh my gosh, Zane, whatever your middle name is, Carter, I'm never going to live that down, am I?" I slam my hand into my head and die of embarrassment once again.

My phone vibrates in my pocket, and I totally forgot about the text I sent to my mom. I pull my phone out of my back pocket and gasp, loud enough for the whole table to turn towards me and ask what's wrong.

"Uh, one sec, im not entirely sure." I panic.

Mammà: Did you mean to send that in the family group chat, Remi?

Papà: Of course, she didn't. School isn't for kissing boys, Remilia.

Mammà: She didn't kiss him, Nico. He kissed her.

Papà: Can't wait to hear all about it, from you BOTH. Tonight.. Dinner.

Mammà: ....

Remi: I'm running away. Don't look for me.

I slam my phone down onto the table and squeeze my eyes shut, covering my face with my hands.

"I can't believe I just did that," I say, pushing out the breath I was subconsciously holding in. I calm my nerves and finally decide to lift my head, and when I do, I see the entire table is still looking at me.

I look to Zane first, "Sorry, but you have to come over for dinner tonight."

Then I address the rest of the table. I tried to text my mom this morning after Zane kissed me. I reach for his hand under the table, unsure of how he will react to me airing out all that I'm about to air out.

"I accidentally sent it in the group chat with my mom and dad." Under the table, Zane's hand stiffens in mine. Like the word dinner magically became dangerous in his eyes. I'm too scared to look back at him; I can feel the uneasiness oozing off of him.

"Breath Rem, this is the stuff you'll look back and laugh at someday," Joss says with wide eyes, like she doesn't even believe what she's saying.

"Like when, because plotting my own death sounds good right about now." I look down at my phone and nervously start to chew on my lip again.

"Hey," Zane squeezes my hand under the table twice.

I drag my eyes up to him slowly, my heart beating so fast you think I had just run a marathon. With soft eyes and a set jaw, Zane tries his best to give me a small smile.

"You're fine. They're your parents, Remi. You were going to tell her anyway, now we just" he pauses." "We do it together. And if it makes you feel better..." his thumb brushes the back of my hand, "...I'm not going anywhere, ever. Dinner's fine."

I gulp down the lump in my throat. The way he said it, low, steady, like a promise, makes the noise around us fade. My heart rate slows, and even Joss's wide-eyed stare starts to blur at the edges.

"Okay" is all I can manage to say to that declaration.

I exhale one more ball of nervous energy, and I pick up my apple, still gripping Zane's hand under the table. I hold up the apple and think to myself, *here we go.* I shrug my shoulders and take a bite.

Fifteen

☾

Zane

It's only three houses down, but my feet feel heavier than usual. Nerves, probably. I've met the Morettis before. This time seems more important. Like a test I have to pass. I'm sure about her, one thousand percent. I just have to make them sure about me. Remi cares deeply for her family, they are her root system, and she is consumed by their love. It flows through her and spills over onto everyone in her life.

As far as family goes, I've only ever known my aunt Cami and my brother Greyson, who raised me. It wasn't the root system Remi had. Functional is what I'd call it, yeah, functional is the correct word. I was the afterthought, the accident that showed up when my parents were already halfway out the door.

I can hear the Italian music billowing out of the Morretis' house from the street. I pause, one foot on the sidewalk leading to their porch, and one foot still on the street. Maybe a lap around the block will help me shake the thought of a failed family before I have to go and face a perfect one. I've almost made my decision when the door swings open, and I see her.

Remi walks out with a book in her hand, her Copperridge high t-shirt falling from her slender shoulder. She's the definition of effortless beauty. Making my heart skip a beat without even trying. She stands in the door frame, pinned into place as soon as she sees me standing halfway on the street.

Her head cocks to the side, her grin wide.

"You're early. I was coming out to read before the chaos starts." She shuts the door behind her and walks to the edge of the porch, her feet bare, poking out of her black flowy pants.

"I don't like being late." My voice is stronger than the thoughts that just shook me.

Her laugh is quick and infectious, and my feet start moving again, this time with less weight and a quickened pace. She's always pulling me closer without even trying. My gravity.

She takes a step back when I reach my final step. Her smile grows, and her nose scrunches slightly before she reaches for my jacket and pulls me into her. Wrapping her arms around my neck and pulling me close, she breathes me in. When I exhale, I realize this is the first time since lunch that I have forgotten about the nerves.

I close my eyes and wrap my arms tighter around her waist. I straighten my back, which unintentionally lifts her small frame off the floor. We stay like that for a beat before I set her back on her feet. For a moment, everything and everyone ceases to exist around us. Just her and me, the world muted.

The creaking of the front door brings us back to reality.

"Remi," Her dad. His voice was colder than the night air. "Why don't you go inside and give your mother a hand, while I speak to Zane?"

She squeezes me a little tighter and whispers, "I'll see you inside." Her lips brush my neck as she speaks. But it's Nico, her papà, that holds my attention.

I turn to face him fully, spine straight. He doesn't say anything at first, just looks me over like he's measuring something I can't see.

"You're quiet," he finally says, arms folding. "That can be good. Means you listen more than you talk."

"Yes, sir," I answer, not knowing if he meant it as a question or a statement.

He nods once, slowly. "But quiet boys can also hide things. Remilia is my only daughter. She is…" He pauses, searching for the word, then presses a hand over his chest. "She is my heart. You understand?" He takes two short steps towards the edge of the porch.

"I do." My voice is steady, though my palms are sweating. Shifting my weight to stay in his line of sight, I want him to see me, to believe me, to trust me. "I'd never want to see her hurt. Nor do I have any intentions of being the one who does the hurting, ever."

His dark eyes hold mine, sharp, testing. Then a small smile flickers, just for a second. His eyebrows raised like Remi's. "Good. Because if you do…" He taps two fingers against the porch railing like it's a warning. He squares his shoulders to face me again. "You'll answer to me, ragazzo."

"I understand." As I nod my head up and down.

He studies me for another beat, then exhales, reaching for the door. "Come inside. Dinner's getting cold. And remember, around here, you eat what's on the table, and you talk loud enough to be heard."

"Yes, sir," I say again, following him in.

Inside, the kitchen is alive, pots bubbling on the stove, garlic and tomato thick in the air. Remi's mother, Elena, stands at the counter, slicing bread, and when she turns to see me trailing behind Papà, her face breaks into a smile.

"Zane," she says warmly, wiping her hands on a towel before coming closer. She doesn't hesitate, just takes my face in both her hands like I've belonged here forever and plants a quick kiss on each cheek.

I freeze for half a second, not used to this kind of welcome, but her easy laugh snaps me back to the present.

"Ah, you're stiff. Don't worry, we'll fix that with food."

I'm still frozen, body stiff, eyes wide. Her reaction is entirely different from her husband's.

"Mamma," Remi groans from across the kitchen, already stacking plates. My body relaxes when I hear her voice.

Her mom waves Remi off, eyes twinkling at me. "You're welcome here, Zane. Any boy who makes my daughter smile the way Remi's been smiling lately… Well, he eats at my table. And eats *a lot,* capito?" Elena drops her chin and pins me with a look.

"Uh, yes, ma'am," I manage, shoulders easing a fraction.

She pats my cheek once more, satisfied, then points toward the table. "Good. Sit, eat, and don't be shy with the bread. Nico, don't scare him off. I like him." She declares as she shrugs her shoulders.

Nico pulls out his chair and murmurs some Italian words under his breath. I look to Remi, who is seated at the table, motioning for me to come sit down beside her. I take my seat, and at the same time, Elena puts a plate in front of me. It looks delicious, smells even better, but it's portioned for two of me. This is all too overwhelming.

"Eat. Remi's Nonna used to say *love is best served on a plate,*" *her father, Nico,* announces.

My eyes go wide, and I wonder if they're the type of family to take offense if I don't finish all of this. I can feel my stomach expanding. I feel a soft touch on my arm, it's Remi.

"Hey," She says quietly, so quietly I almost miss it. "Just look at me, Zane, if you get lost in the noise, just look for me."

Before I have a chance to answer, Nico's voice crashes through Remi's calmness, pulling our attention back to the table.

"I told him that there's no way he can finish all that food. Would you guys stop trying to scare him? Basta già, eh?" She looks at me and softens, " I said enough already," translating for me.

I know a few Italian words, none of which she just said, but I know the way it sounds in her mouth. Like music, like something older than the two of us put together.

The Morettis laugh and wave her off, but I don't. I can't. Because for a second, forget the weight of her father's stare. All I can think is that I want to hear her say everything like that, my name, her secrets, maybe even her heart. That paired with her instinct to stand up for me. I don't say anything, but I tuck this moment somewhere deep inside. How calm and sure of herself she was as she spoke up for me. If I didn't know she was someone different, someone safe, that would've done it.

"Okay, okay, fine," it's Elena who breaks my trance.

"So.. Zane Carter. You're the boy who kissed my daughter in front of the entire school?" The room falls silent when Nico pins me to my chair with his question.

"Papà," Remi nearly spits her drink out.

"No, it's okay, Remi." My eyes are still on Mr. Moretti. "Yes, sir, I didn't plan on doing that, but I don't regret it."

Elena tries to hide her smile from behind her glass. Remi is on my right, face redder than the pasta that sits in front of us. Nico's mouth turns down as his shoulders rise and fall.

"Okay, Zane." Nico sets his fork down. Eyes sharp. "Who are you? Where is your family?"

I grip my napkin under the table, but my voice stays level.

"Honestly? I'm someone who's still figuring that out. But here's what I do know: I don't lie. I don't play games. I take care of the people I let close. I didn't grow up with a lot, but it taught me to value things other people overlook, like quiet moments, good food, someone who actually listens." I take a deep breath and share a little more about my family than I did last time.

"I've already told you a little bit about my family. My aunt Cami lives here in Copperridge. She's the one who makes sure I don't completely fall apart." Deep breath. "And my brother, Greyson, raised me. Did the best he could, even when it should've been my parents' job. They…" I pause, choosing my words carefully. "They weren't really built for raising a kid again. I was in the accident. They wanted out long before I even came along."

I glance at Remi, and her eyes soften, like she wants to shield me. Buoyed by her silent support, I continue.

"So yeah, I don't have a traditional family, I guess." Looking back at Nico, who is studying me intently. There's no pity in his eyes. That's good.

"Life deals everyone a different hand." He leans back in his chair, voice even. "But you learn fast when it's hard, maybe that's not such a bad thing. Someone who values honesty, who doesn't run, and someone who takes care of the people he loves." his eyes flick to Remi. "Those are good qualities to have, Zane." He picks his fork back up and twirls the pasta around it.

I look down at my plate. Untouched. I pick up my fork and push some of the pasta around before Nico's voice breaks the silence again.

"Last question and I'll leave you to your pasta." He folds his arms over his chest as my eyes meet his. "What do you want with my daughter?" He deadpans.

"You're not seriously going to interrogate him, are you, Papà?" Remi cuts in.

His emotionless tone is still there, just pointed at Remi now. "Yes, I am." His head snaps back to me.

On exhale, I try to find the right words to say. What do I want with Remi? Everything.

"Have you ever stepped out of a cold house and let your skin drink up the warmth from the sun? That is what Remi feels like." I turn my head to my right, meeting her eyes this time. "She's the warmth." Giving her a tight smile, I turn back to Nico. "I've never felt that in a person. I imagine that's what love feels like, though I'm not sure I've experienced it to know."

I pause, not sure how my next line will land, or if it should be said at all. It's my truth, so I'll say it anyway. "So what do I want from Remi? Everything. Or forever. Whichever she will give me."

Nico doesn't react right away. He's calm, calculated, and he's studying me. The seconds drag on, and the only noise is Elena's glass as she sets it back down onto the table, pools forming in her eyes.

"You talk like a poet." He says quietly. "But I hear more than what you're saying. A young man who knows what the cold feels like." He leans forward. "It's too soon for the forever talk, ragazzo, but for now you can have this." His arms stretch wide to his sides. "You're welcome in our home anytime, and for now, you can live in this moment and enjoy not being in the cold."

"Let's eat now, shall we?" Elena breaks the thickness in the air, placing her hand on Nico's shoulder. The silent conversation between the two has me wanting to look towards Remi, but the heaviness of what I just said holds me in my place.

"Yes, let's eat," Nico says, looking at Elena as the tension rolls off his body.

Beside me, I feel Remi shift, her knee brushing deliberately against mine. My head still hung low from the weight of what Nico just said, and I glanced nervously her way. She's chewing on the side of her lip, trying her hardest to conceal a smile. But I see it, and I match it.

Remi

Under the table, my knee leans into his, grounding him the way he's been grounding me all week. Papà's words are still echoing in my chest, heavier than I ever expected. No matter how hard I try, I can't stop the grin tugging at my lips.

Zane just survived Nico Moretti's test. And the best part? He did it in that quiet, steady way of his, like he didn't even know he was proving himself.

I wave my fork around dramatically, time to shift the air in here.

"Honestly, I'm shocked Zane has made it this far, none of the boys in town have ever come within a mile of sitting around this table."

Mammà covers her mouth with her napkin and laughs loud enough to fill the entire downstairs. Papà shifts in his seat and lets out a grunt, like he's trying not to laugh at himself. Zane cracks a smile as he shakes his head in disbelief.

"You've never given them any chance either, teroso," Papà announces at the table.

"Yeah, well." My shoulders lift to my ears.

The rest of dinner flows back into a natural rhythm. Mammà shooshing Papà, forks clanking against the plate, and bread being passed up and down the table.

Zane doesn't say much, but he doesn't need to; we Morettis are natural silence fillers. He listens, drinking in all of the stories, his eyes flicking from one person to the next. Every few minutes, his knee brushes against mine under the table, letting me know he's still here, still grounding himself in me when the room gets too loud.

Mammà sprinkles in questions about school, music, and his favorite foods, and each time he answers with his quiet honesty, which draws people into him. I'm proud of Papà, he doesn't interrogate him anymore, and he adds questions to Mammà's original questions. Trying to get to know Zane a bit more, gauge who he really is.

When dessert lands on the table, everyone is laughing like old friends, including Zane. Which settles something deep inside of me. Catching feelings for someone wasn't on my imaginary plan, like at all, but I have to say, it might be my highlight of the year.

Later, when the plates are stacked and the kitchen finally quiets, Zane and I slip out to the porch swing, my favorite place. The night air is cooler now, cicadas buzzing, the sky heavy with stars. We don't talk at first, the swing creaks as we rock back and forth, slow, like the whole town's asleep except us.

Finally, I break the silence. "The warmth, huh?" My voice comes out soft, teasing, but my heart thunders anyway. I nervously look over to him, trying to use my shoulder as my personal shield.

His eyes cut to mine, steady even in the dark. "Yeah, Remi, the warmth. That's what you feel like to me." He pushes a stray hair behind my ear.

I look away, something mixed between embarrassment and excitement, but his hand finds mine, and he moves it to the space between us. He doesn't squeeze, doesn't push, just holds on like it's the most natural thing in the world.

"Forever's a long time, Zane." I find myself saying, trying my hardest to focus on anything to keep myself from looking at him.

"I know." Zane is quiet but sure."Does that scare you?"

I finally look at him, his eyebrows are pinched together, and his eyes are full of nerves again. It's not often he shows this side of himself, unsure and unguarded. I don't like seeing this version of him. I like the quiet confidence that oozes.

I swallow hard. Like I'm trying to swallow the fear this conversation brings. We're eighteen, forever wasn't in my vocabulary a few months ago.

"I want to travel," I say quietly, like I'm admitting something fragile. "I want to see the house my Nonno built for my Nonna. I want to taste food in different countries, watch sunsets on different sides of the world, do things I've never even let myself picture before."

Zane nudges his knee against mine. "Then do them," he says. "Tell me more."

I exhale, eyes still fixed anywhere but him. "I want… a life that feels big. Full. I want memories I haven't made yet. I want to feel like I chose my own future instead of letting it happen to me."

He's quiet for a moment, and when he speaks again, his voice is soft but steady. "That doesn't scare me," he says. "I want those things too. Maybe not the exact same ones, but… I want a life that feels like it's mine. I want to go places. I want to build something real. Something that means something."

I finally look up at him, surprised. "You do?"

His eyes flick to mine, honest and unguarded in a way that knocks the air out of me. "Yeah. And I want all of it with someone who actually sees me." He shrugs, trying to play it off, but his voice betrays him. "Someone like you."

My chest twists in that terrifying, perfect way that only he can cause.

"Yeah," I whisper. "It scares me."

His eyebrows pinch the way they always do when he's trying not to show how much something matters. "What scares you?"

I look away again, heart pounding. "How much I want it," I say. "How much I want… all of it. With you."

I can see him out of the corner of my eye, studying me. He doesn't respond right away. It isn't until the worry leaves his eyes that he gives me his response.

"Good." He releases my hand and pulls me into his body, his arm draped over my shoulder.

I can feel the beat of his heart steady out on my shoulder blade, and in turn, I melt myself into him.

"We can be scared together, Remilia." He says into my hair as he places a soft kiss onto my head.

I bite my lip and lean into him a little more. "Scared together, huh? I guess that makes us official or something." I let out a nervous, breathy chuckle.

With the swing creaking beneath us and the cicadas singing their endless song, all I can hear is Zane's quiet laugh, mouth still against my hair.

"Yeah," he breathes out. "Yeah, it does."

Sixteen

☾

Remi

It's been four days since Zane, and I made it official. Four days of walking the halls of Copperridge High with my stomach doing flips every time I hear his voice behind me. Four days of me replaying the porch swing moment like it's the only movie I'll ever want to watch.

It's also been four excruciatingly long days of me helping my parents out at Nonna's. I've barely seen him. I've spent the last four days wiping tables, serving bread, and listening to gossip I wish I could unhear. By the time I'm dragging myself out of the shower, my phone buzzes with a text from him, and I'm too tired to do anything other than fall asleep smiling.

So the only time I've seen him is at school. Quick glances in the hallway. Knee brushes at lunch while we were entertaining our friends. It's not enough. Not nearly enough. I miss him.

Which is why, when he shows up on my front porch with his guitar case in his hand and a look in his eyes like he's been waiting for me all week, I know something's different. I sure have missed that smirk, standing on my porch.

"Hey, you," I say, throwing my arms around his neck.

"Mmhmm, I've missed you." He says, wrapping his free arm around my waist. "Come with me." It's a plea, and I'm happy to oblige.

My head rears back to see his face, "Where to?"

"You'll see," he says, setting the guitar case gently on the porch. "Just.. trust me." His smirk deepens.

Trust him? If he told me to jump off the roof, I'd be climbing the vines by the time he got the instructions out. I roll my eyes at the butterflies settling in my stomach, but the smile slowly takes over my face.

"Fine. I'll go." I say, stepping back and crossing my arms. "What do I wear? I've already changed into my lounge clothes." Trying my best to sound a little off-putting.

"What you have on is fine, you may want a jacket though." He says, raising one eyebrow like he doesn't want to tell me anymore.

"Okay, fine, I'll be back." I throw my hands down by my side and walk up the stairs to get a jacket, leaving Zane in the entryway.

Minutes later, I'm trotting down the stairs to see my Mammà hand Zane a bag.

"Uhh, am I missing something?" I make my entrance known.

"Remi, you ready?" Zane asks as my mother scurries away to the other room.

"Uh.." Deciding whether or not to let it go or dive right in. Whatever, I just want a good night. "Sure, yeah, I'm ready."

Zane opens the door and leads me out to the passenger side of the truck. He opens my door and then sets the guitar and the mysterious bag he got from my mammà in the back seat before he climbs in. He doesn't talk much during the drive, the windows are cracked, and the mix of sunshine and the warmth from the last bit of the warmer fall weather floods in. The radio is low, just a faint hum working as background noise.

I'm stealing glances at him throughout town, his profile being softly lit by the sun. He's got that look again, the *im in deep thought,* the one where his jaw is set and his lips are forming a tight line, his eyes stay soft. Why is he being so quiet? We haven't seen each other in nearly a week.

It isn't long before he's pulling off the main road, there are no houses for miles. Surrounded by mountains and fields of nothing but nature. I know exactly where we're going. He slows the truck, then pulls off near the ridge. I love it here, especially at sunset.

"Come on," he says, grabbing the guitar case and the mysterious bag before I can even unbuckle my seatbelt.

Waiting for me at the front of the truck, he grabs me by the hand and says nothing as he leads me that way until we are in the clearing overlooking the ridge. Surrounded by trees, our shoes crunching on the gravel beneath us, and the smell of cedar all around, the view here is the icing on the cake. The sun is melting onto the horizon, streaks of gold, orange, and copper come into view.

He lets go of my hand and pulls out a blanket from the bag along with a thermos, cups, and a few containers. Setting his guitar case down next to the blanket, he kicks off his shoes and steps onto the blanket. I'm so glad I wore matching socks today, I'd have to explain why I hate matching my socks.

"Remi," I look down to where he sits on the blanket, hand held out, stretched towards me. Asking me with words to come join him on the blanket. I grab his hand and kick off my shoes, sitting down next to him on a burn-orange blanket that matches the color of the leaves.

"Zane," I whisper, wanting to know what this is all about.

"Can I play you something?" His eyes avoided mine.

"I'd love that," I sit to face him, hands hugging my knees.

I watch him as he reaches for his guitar case. It's covered in stickers, and I have the urge to ask him about each and every one, just to hear him tell me stories. He flexes his jaw right before he clicks open the case, the slight shake of his hands telling me he's nervous. He takes his time unlatching all of the latches before he finally clicks it open. Running his fingers down the strings, he finally pulls the guitar out of the case. It's much older than I expected. Scuffs and scratches fill up most of the space, it looks like it's been played more than it's been protected.

When he finally settles it into his lap, his shoulders tense like he's about to give a speech. For a split second, I think he might back out, but then his thumb brushes over the strings, and the sound blooms into the quiet air. Low, warm, uncertain until it steadies, like him.

I can't look away.

It doesn't take long before he's lost in it. His fingers dance over the strings, while he closes his eyes and gets lost in the rhythm he's creating. It's beautiful, and the background of the copper ridge is casting a glow onto him, lighting him up from behind, making all of this more magical than it should be.

The nervousness is back in him, his eyes open, and he seems unsure. It lasts only for a second before he's back into his rhythm. It's not until he starts humming that I understand what's happening. His hum is low, barely audible until he finds his footing. I didn't think I could sink any further than I am, but here I am, sinking.

I let go of my knees and sit back on my hands, enjoying whatever song he is playing. His hum lingers, as if he is trying to find the courage to let the words fly out. Even the sunset is holding its breath in anticipation for the next strum, the next note he's going to hit. His humming becomes more uniform, he's more certain in it. That's when I hear it, his voice breaking through with words and not noises.

"You're the light I didn't know I was chasing. The warmth in the cold I was braving."

My breath hitches, and my chest tightens. I don't realize I've stopped breathing until my lungs start to match the burn that's happening behind my eyes. The warmth, is this about me? His strumming slows, and I'm instantly sad. I don't want this moment to end. The last note he plays hangs in the air, suspended through time and space. He opens his eyes, but he's still looking at his guitar. He flexes his hand around it before he looks up to meet my emotion-filled eyes.

I don't clap, I don't breathe, I don't dare do anything that might break the spell. My fingers curl into the blanket, holding on, because if I let go, I'm pretty sure I'd float right off this ridge.

Fourteen-year-old me wrote letters to a boy who sang to me in my dreams, to a boy who felt unreachable, impossible. Now here he is, sitting in front of me, making my heart forget how to beat in rhythm.

"Zane.. I breathe out breathlessly. *Pull it together, Remi.* "Zane, you can't just do that.. I mean.. Now every concert I go to will fail in comparison to this moment."

A crooked smile tugging at his mouth, he shakes his head from side to side, putting the guitar back in its case.

"Good." He looks at me over his shoulder, eyebrows raising. "Then you'll remember this one."

"No one has ever shared something so… intimate with me," I confess.

He leans back onto the blanket, resting his head on the guitar case, which looks pretty uncomfortable if you ask me. Resting one hand on his stomach, he reaches for me, wrapping his hand around my wrist.

"Come closer." Another plea.

I study him a beat longer before I make my way over to his side of the blanket. I lay my head onto his stomach and look up towards the sky. His hand moves to play in my hair, brushing it out with his fingers. I turn my face to look his way. He looks so relaxed, so different from how he looked playing my new favorite song.

"Is there an encore?" I whisper.

He pushes out an airy laugh, "If you want one, there can be."

I give him a cheesy smile, one that makes me turn away from him, focusing on the copper sunset happening just over the ridge.

"I guess that makes me your number one fan," I say, still looking at the sunset.

"That's perfect, I've only ever wanted one fan anyway." He laughs a throaty laugh.

We lay like that for the next ten or so minutes until the sun is no longer visible and the chill in the air sets in. The way he talks without words, he fills the quiet, but not always with noise. Sometimes it's with a simple touch or look that can tilt my world on its axis. This was exactly what I needed after four days of not seeing him. He sits up, and my head drops to his lap. He looks down at me like he is trying to commit this moment to memory, searching my eyes as his hand wraps around my neck while his thumb runs back and forth over my earlobe.

"I brought you something." He says quietly, still studying me.

My smile grows slowly, stretching until my cheeks ache. Something shifts between Zane and me in that moment. I can't explain it, I can only feel it.

"What is it?" I whisper, afraid to disrupt whatever is building between us.

He reaches into the pocket of his hoodie and pulls out something small, so small he rubs it between his fingers. It takes a second but he finally makes it visible to me, it's a guitar pick.

"I've had this since I learned how to play." His voice is low, like he's letting me in on a secret. He hands me the pick, it's black, smooth, and worn like it's been well used, and it has a tiny crescent moon drawn in silver ink. "I figure you should have it for the first time I played for you.. kinda like proof." His voice was low and shaky.

"Oh wow," I say, inspecting it. "Thank you for this." I sit up onto my knees, still inspecting the guitar pick in my hand. "Seriously, Zane, this means so much, and the fact that you've carried it with you as you learned how to play. It has meaning, though. I love it." I throw my arms around him and kiss his cheek as I go, quick but certain.

"That's not all, I had Elena make your favorite coffee." He says she packed way more than that, though. Something about dipping it in the coffee. I'm not sure, actually."

With excitement, I pull out one of the biscotti cookies and dip it into the coffee, holding it up for Zane.

"Here, try this. It will change your life."

Zane looks at the cookie, and then back to me, unease settling on his face.

"Is this the Italian version of cookies and milk?" He says, face scrunching into a soft laugh. Nonetheless, he leans forward, his lips brushing my fingers for a split second before he takes the bite. He chews, moving his head side to side, debating whether he likes it.

"Well?" I tease.

Zane swallows the cookie, smiling like he knows a secret I don't. "It is American milk and cookies, only better." He adds at the end. "Does your family cook anything bad?" He asks with a chuckle.

"If only my Nonna were here to tell you about the first hundred times she tried to teach me to make bread." The confession left my lips, half happy, half sad.

I lean into him, facing the fast-fading sunset. Both of us melt into each other as the sun meets the earth's horizon. The ridge is quiet now, crickets chirp, and windblown leaves fill the space between our breaths.

We don't talk after that. We sit and enjoy the silence, just the two of us, pressed close. We sit there until the day disappears, and we can't see our hands in front of us. This week has been terribly long, but this, this calmness, it's the perfect way to end the week.

Seventeen

☾

Remi

The air in Copperridge smells like autumn and sugar today, more like kettle corn, cotton candy, candied pecans, and something warm I can't name. The square is packed, people buzzing everywhere, the whole town pretending the world is simpler than it really is. It's almost unrecognizable. The square is covered with string lights, waiting for dusk to set in, hay bales everywhere, and pumpkins waiting for their time to shine.

Joss and Maddie are arguing over which booth to hit first when I spot him, Zane. My Zane. The one who sang to me last night on the ridge, snuggled up with a warm cup of coffee and the best view in town. I'm not talking about the sunset either. He stands there in a flannel shirt, sleeves rolled up to show off his sculpted forearms and that half-easy smile that flips my world upside down. He's leaning against the fence next to the ticket stand, unaware of the effect he has on me, even from a distance. He's standing there, arms folded, looking like he belongs on someone's fall Pinterest board.

"If you're going to stare, at least blink." Maddie nudges me out of my trance.

Rolling my eyes in her direction as I reply, "I was going to blink, I just… did it slower than normal, duh."

Joss snorts, "Good one. Should we leave you here to pine, or do you think you can walk without tripping over your own heartbeat?" She raises one eyebrow as she spews her words my way.

I roll my eyes at her, too, and push her toward the ticket booth. "You two are exhausting!"

They are still laughing when he looks up, looking directly at me, it's almost like he knew I was here before he saw me. His grin spreads wide when our eyes meet. That smile gets me every time I see it. Now my smile matches his, and I'm sure my face is bright red by now. He pushes off the fence to meet us halfway, moving so effortlessly through the sea of people that separates us, like he's been walking in my direction all his life. I can smell the cedar coming off his skin as he gets closer.

"Don't say anything embarrassing." Maddie taunts me

"Oh, I'm sure I will." I give her my knowing side-eye.

"Hey," Zane says, stuffing his hands in his pockets, making his shoulders shrug in an unintentional way that makes him look way too good for his own good.

My smile reaches my eyes. "You actually came."

"You thought I wouldn't?" his head tilts to the side, eyebrow arching. "The entire town is shut down, Remi." He pushes out a laugh, which tugs at my heart.

"Didn't know you would trade sunsets on the mountains for carnival rides and junk food." I quip.

His eyes roam mine, instantly going back to last night on the ridge.

"So," Joss voice slices through the moment. "Should we get the popcorn for this show?" Pointing back and forth between us.

I swear my eyes might get stuck from the number of times I've had to roll them at these girls today. Shaking my head, I cut her a look that says I'll be paying you back later. Zane glances between Maddie and Joss, that smirk tugging at his lips.

"I see you brought your bodyguards." With his eyebrow raised in a silent dare.

"They brought themselves." I cough out a laugh and step towards him, wrapping my arms around his waist.

"Don't worry," he announces, louder than the *hey* he just gave me, this one is for the group. "I have some backup coming too."

"Oh god," Joss says, throwing her head back in frustration.

"Please, no, Eli? Again? I cannot deal with the mustard king today?" Maddie says frantically. "Please tell me it's not Elli." She begs.

Before Maddie can even finish her plea, a voice cuts through behind her.

"Did someone say my name?" It's Eli.

He appears from the crowd, carrying two caramel apples: one already half-eaten, the other held out like a peace offering. He's got his backwards ball cap, that ever-present chain, and a grin that says he *thrives* on chaos.

"More like someone spoke of the Devil…" Joss retorts, laced with attitude and something else.

"Relax," Eli says, holding the apple out toward her. "I come bearing sugar and charm." His smile reached both sides of his face.

"You said sarcasm wrong." Her eyes are doing some rolling of their own now.

Putting one caramel apple hand on his chest, "You wound me, Josselyn."

Maddie leans in close to Zane and me. "If they don't make out by Christmas, I'll eat my own pumpkin."

I choke back a laugh, Zane's eyes catch mine, thinking the same thing, it's *only a matter of time.*

"Okay, enough flirting, you two." I step between them, slipping the caramel apple stick from Eli's hand. "Let's get to the pumpkin carving tent before the nightly news consists of your murders, instead of my victory."

"I'll meet up with you guys after, I've got to drop this off to your mom, Remi." Maddie holds up a grocery bag full of coffee. My mom is helping out at the Copper Cup booth this year.

The pumpkin carving tent smells like cinnamon, hay, and the thrill of competition. Strings of orange lights illuminate the canopy, and the sounds of knives scraping pumpkin guts act as the official background noise of the competition. My head snaps to Zane, who is already looking at me, and my eyebrows shoot up to my forehead. I may be a little excited about this.

"Okay, teams of two!" The volunteer speaks into her loudspeaker. Her voice is way too chipper for the mess we are about to create in this tent. "You've got thirty minutes to carve your pumpkins, the best team wins free funnel cakes AND bragging rights for the season."

Eli's eyes light up. "You hear that, Josselyn? It's our destiny calling."

She gives him a sharp look that could possibly cut their pumpkin in half. "You're on your own, mustard king, I'm not messing my manicure up for this mushy mess." She picks her hands up toward her face, inspecting her nails.

"Fine." He says, slamming his tools onto the table, "But when I win, I'm not sharing my funnel cake."

Zane glances at me, a little smile forming. "We're doing this?"

I raise a brow, a challenge on my tongue. "You scared?"

"Terrified," he admits, pulling out a stool for me anyway.

His flannel sleeve brushes my arm when I sit, and that tiny bit of contact sends a warmth through me that no fall candle could ever replicate. I close my eyes and inhale, trying to control my teenage hormones. We start scooping out pumpkin guts, and I'm instantly reminded why I hate this part.

"Ew," I groan, my face contorting up into an evil snarl, flinging a handful of orange slime into the bucket.

Zane laughs quietly. "You're supposed to carve the pumpkin, not fight it."

"I'm… multitasking," I say, chin raised.

A glob lands on his flannel, and my mouth drops open. "Oh my gosh, I didn't—"

He looks down, then at me, a smirk pulling at the corner of his mouth. "Guess I deserved that for teasing you."

"Guess you did," I say, unable to hide my smile.

Across the table, Joss and Eli are already in a full-blown argument about "creative direction." I guess Joss did join in the pumpkin-carving fun.

"It's supposed to be a cat!" Joss insists.

"It *was* a cat," Eli says, "before you decapitated it."

Zane's knife glides through the pumpkin with practiced ease. The design emerges—clean, simple lines, steady hands at work.

I tilt my head. "What are you carving?"

He pauses, just long enough for his eyes to flick up to mine. "A ridge," he says softly. "With a sunset behind it." He peeks up at me behind those thick, full lashes.

For a second, I swear all the noise fades, the chatter, the laughter, even Eli yelling something about "pumpkin rights." It's just the two of us, the smell of spice and rain in the air, and the faint sound of a band starting up somewhere across the square.

"Of course you are," I whisper, smiling so hard it makes me aware of the migraine creeping in.

I'm completely covered in pumpkin insides by the time our thirty-minute timer goes off. Joss and Eli are in the corner, still arguing about whether or not the cat he carved is abstract or animal cruelty. The smell of cinnamon sugar and my personal favorite, kettle corn, lures us back into the heart of the festival. We walk around and play games until the string lights start to flicker on.

"Okay," Eli has his hands on his hips, "Who is brave enough to challenge me in a game of ring toss?" He points to us one by one.

"There's no way I'm paying to play that stupid game." Maddie deadpans.

"One, aren't you like the richest girl in town?" Pointing to Maddie, who answered by rolling her eyes. "And two," he scoots towards Joss, rubbing his shoulder onto hers. "You wanna play?"

"Oh gosh." She huffs, knowing she made a mistake.

"Someone sounds scared." He walks away, matter-of-factly.

The next few minutes are nothing but pure chaos. Maddie is screaming at the top of her lungs, cheering the two of them on. I'm laughing so hard my stomach hurts while Zane steps in to 'help' Joss aim. Which backfires when she begins arguing with him and accidentally flicks the ring back, hitting Eli in the lip and making him bleed.

"Even in failure, you're violent, Josselyn." He tugs at his lip with his thumb.

"Maybe next time, duck, genius." I see the way her lips pull up into a smirk when she turns away from him.

Zane slides up beside me, his scent invading my nose as he does so. "You know, we can skip the games and go straight for the funnel cake."His eyebrows shot up as his soft waves fell into his eyes.

I look up at him, mesmerized. "Are you bribing me with fried dough?" I say, pushing his waves back from his face.

"Would it work?" His smirk slowly made an appearance.

"Probably," I laugh at myself.

Before we can decide something in the sky shifts, a shift that whispers trouble is coming. I look up to the sky, a cold drop hits my cheek, and then another. I should've known.

"Rain!" Maddie squeals, putting her hand out in front of her as if she wants to catch it.

"It'll probably pass," Eli says confidently, seconds before the downpour starts.

Everyone around us screams and bolts under the nearest tent, but we're standing in the middle of the blocked-off road in front of the games, which is all uncovered. Tarps are being thrown out over games, while other booths are pulling things inside. I grab Zane's hand without thinking, fingers slipping together easily, and we take off running through the square. He laughs, loud and real, and I can't stop laughing either, my hair sticking to my forehead, shoes splashing through the puddles.

"Where are we going?" His voice cut through the sound of rain.

"Nonna's!" I yell back at him.

We reach Nonna's, and we're drenched from head to toe. The bell above the door jingles as we stumble inside, both of us shivering and out of breath. The smell of espresso blankets us as we walk to the back, where we keep the cloth napkins, which will double as towels. My parents closed the restaurant for the fair; it's usually a ghost town in the evening when the fair is in town.

"Thank god Nonna's is on the square, huh?" I say, squeezing my hair with the cloth.

Zane nods, running the makeshift towel over his face, before letting out a sigh. When he pulls the cloth down, he's smiling, his honey eyes lighting up as he does so. I pull out my phone, pretending to check the time, and I snap a picture. Knowing I won't be getting any sleep tonight, I'll be staring at this picture until my eyelids betray me.

"You two look like stray cats." My Papà's voice is loud behind me.

"Wet, stray cats, Papà." I reach to hug him, but he takes a step back, putting his hands up.

"You're not going to get me wet teroso." Taking steps backwards.

"Tragic," I give him a grin as I squeeze the water out of my sleeves over the sink. Papà says something under his breath, but I can't quite make it out.

"Did you bring the rain with you, Ragazzo?" My Papà directs his question to Zane.

"Yeah, I guess I did. Sorry about that." He jokes.

Papà waves it off. "No, no. Rain means good luck." He nods toward the espresso machine. "You want coffee?"

"Yeah, that would be nice. Thank you, Sir." He says, taking off his flannel to squeeze it out over the sink.

"How do you like it, the coffee?" Papà asks Zane.

"Nonna's way, please." He replies, his focus still on his flannel.

As soon as the words slip out of Zane's mouth, my eyes meet my dad's over Zane's bent-over shoulder. Papà's eyes are soft and searching, probably trying to figure out when Nonna made her way into Zane's world. Something flickers there, a tight twitch of his lips, and then he turns around to make the coffee. Zane and I finish trying to dry ourselves off and take a seat in front of the espresso machine at the bar.

"Here's your coffee, figlio." Papà sets the cup in front of Zane and turns around to make another coffee.

My body goes stiff and my eyes balloon. No one has ever called him that, at least to my knowledge, and not to the capacity of meaning something to someone other than Aunt Cami or Greyson.

"Thank you, sir," Zane says quickly, wrapping both hands around the cup like it's the only thing keeping him steady. He takes a slow sip, and when he looks back up, his brows are knit together just slightly. "What did he just say?"

I bite my lip, fighting the smile tugging at the corners. "Figlio," I repeat my father's words to him, while he sits behind the warmth of his coffee. "It means son."

He freezes for a split second, his eyes flick toward the counter where Papà's humming to himself, then back to me. "He called me... son? "His body leans forward as the words pull him by a thread, his eyebrows pinch together, and his words come out rushed.

The meaning hits him, and I see it instantly, the faint pink blooming across his cheeks, the glassy sheen in his eyes. It's not just a word to him. It's something more.

"Don't let it go to your head," I tease. "He still thinks no one's good enough for me."

Zane leans back slightly, processing, a soft smile breaking across his face. "Still," he says, voice low. "I'll take it."

The sound of rain against the windows fills the quiet between us. For once, he doesn't rush to speak, and neither do I.

Eighteen

☾

Zane

I can't stop hearing it.

Figlio

It's been on replay ever since it happened last night, a word that doesn't belong to me, but somehow landed. Nico said it so casually, he must not have known the weight it carried for me. I didn't. Like it didn't split something deep inside of me. It wasn't just that he called me *son*. It was how he said it. His tone was warm and certain, as I'd already been claimed by something I never knew I was missing. I've been called a lot of things, most of them forgettable. Not that.

When you grow up without roots, you don't know what you are missing out on. You don't know what it feels like until someone hands it to you in a coffee mug without thinking.

Here's your coffee, son.

Like it's safe, like it can't be taken away. Maybe he didn't actually mean son, I should have brushed it off. Maybe he meant kid or buddy. The weight of the word *son* sits in the middle of my chest. Then there is Remilia Moretti, whose body went completely rigid when he said it. What was that about? Her sarcasm masked the fact that she felt that same weight.

Just when I think I've figured her out, she shows me something new. She's sunshine and sarcasm, chaos and calm. She talks like she's fine, but laughs like she's trying to convince herself of it. When she looks at me, really looks at me, it's like the noise in my head finally falls silent. My calm.

Official. I'm not certain what that means, what "we" means, but if it isn't love, I'd still choose her. I'd still choose it. I've spent most of my life keeping people just outside the boundary line. Where can I be safe and guarded? Somehow, she's inches away, and I don't remember when I let her in. I've spent most of my life assuming nothing good stays. That people leave. That houses are temporary, and so are promises. Official sounds like it should mean forever, but I don't know if I'm allowed to hope for that yet.

The rain from last night has already dried up, leaving behind that clean, cool air. The kind that makes everything smell fresh and new again. I move slowly, letting the morning stretch long. The house is quiet except for the quiet melody, coming from my aunt Cami, singing along to something in the kitchen. She's at the counter when I walk into the kitchen, hair pulled back, coffee in hand. The smell reminds me of Remi.

"Well, well. If it isn't Mr. Sunshine himself." Leaning against the counter, mug in front of her face, grinning over the cup. "You look like you've got something stuck in your head, kid."

I grab an apple from the bowl, though she's not wrong, and I shrug. "Just tired."

"Tired looks a lot like smitten these days." She pins me with her eyes.

Luckily, I took a bite of the apple, so I opted for a slight shake of the head.

"It's okay to like her, you know." Her tone softens.

I swallow the apple "I do" before I can stop myself. "I just don't know what to do with that." Meeting her eyes across the counter.

"Maybe don't do anything about it." She shrugs her shoulders. "Maybe just live in it." She sets her mug down on the counter. "You've spent so long building walls, Zane. You don't have to live behind them forever." Her eyes are full of silent pity.

I nod, staring down at the apple in my hand. "Yeah, maybe."

Her smile breaks the weight in the room. "Now go take a shower, you smell like someone who had a life-changing revelation and forgot deodorant."

"Noted." I huff, not being able to contain the laugh that escapes me.

I'm finished with all of Aunt Cami's to-do list, and double-applied my deodorant. Thanks, Aunt Cami. The sky is a soft gold by the time I leave the house. The in-between light where the world feels half-awake, half-asleep. Like, even the earth is holding its breath.

I drive slowly. The road to the square is familiar, but it feels different tonight. Like I'm seeing them through someone else's eyes. Maybe hers. Remi's stormy eyes. She seems to find beauty in everything. The cracks in the sidewalk, the way the clouds look heavy before a good rain, the song she swears the birds are singing. It's like she's tuned into a world I've not yet visited. The sun is sinking fast when I pull into the parking lot behind the fair. The festival lights give it a nice, illuminating glow at night. Everything washed in warm lighting and laughter. The kind of glow that makes everything seem warmer than it really is.

I step out of the truck and shove my hands into my pockets, taking it in for a second. Music threaded through the noise of people talking and shopping. It's busy. But when my eyes find her in the crowd, the world stops.

She's standing underneath a street light, lighting her up. She looks angelic. Her hair reflects the light, the way her laugh bounces over the top of all the noise like it's her backup singer. It's like the whole town rearranged itself for her. She's wearing an oversized sweater, her sleeves bunched up, her elbows poking out. She's mid-story, hands flying around in the air, making Joss, Maddie, and Eli laugh along with her. She's an anomaly. I pull out my phone and snap a quick photo of her, standing there, taking my breath away under the glow of the lights.

She looks over before I have the chance to call her name. Tucking her hair behind her ear, she gives me a slow smile, her hand coming up to wave in my direction. She hesitates for a fraction of a second, and then her feet are moving in my direction.

I don't move, I just stand there and watch.

When she finally reaches me, she tilts her head, "You look like you've been standing here for a while."

I shrug my shoulders. "You were glowing under the lights. I wanted to commit it to my memory. Forever."

She throws her head back and laughs. It hits me like a warm blanket in the cold night air. She shakes her head, trying to shake off the happiness. It looks good on her, happiness.

"Hi," she says, voice barely above the noise of the crowd.

It should be simple, that one word. But it knocks the air right out of me.

"Hi, angel." I reach for her, bringing her body into mine.

It slips out before I can stop it, quiet but sure. Her lips part, just a little, like she's not sure what to do with it. With me. Then she smiles again, the kind of smile that could make a person believe in things they shouldn't.

For a second, everything else fades, the music, the laughter, even the Ferris wheel spinning behind her. It's just her, looking at me like maybe I said something right for once. She blinks, her eyes full of hope when they open.

Grabbing my hand, "C'mon. Let's go find the others before we have to break up another Joss and Eli fight."

I follow with ease because it's her. I think I'd follow her anywhere if she let me.

The sun has set. Remi indulges in her free funnel cake from winning the pumpkin carving contest. She holds it in one hand, powdered sugar all over her sweater, like she lost a snowball fight. It's cute.

"You're supposed to eat it, not wear it." I tease.

Her nose scrunches up, and her eyes turn playful. "Yeah, well, you try cutting it and eating it. Let's see what you look like after."

I grin. "So you're admitting defeat?"

"Never." She rips off a piece, smirking. "Here. Since you're so perfect."

Before I can protest, she presses it against my mouth. Warm, sweet, messy. I laugh, trying not to choke on the powder.

"That was an ambush." I say around a mouthful.

"Some call it an ambush, some call it strategy." Her tone is sassy but soft.

We wander between booths, bantering and bumping shoulders. We pretend not to notice how often our hands brush. Eli's voice carries from the dart game, Joss yells back, and Maddie's laugh cuts through like a bell. The world is loud and alive, but still feels like ours.

Remi stops in front of a photo booth. "We should take one."

"I don't take pictures," I start to say, but she's already tugging me inside.

Flash.

She sticks her tongue out in the first one.

Flash.

I'm caught smiling in the second.

Flash.

She's laughing in the third, her head on my shoulder.

The strip slides out, still warm. She waves it dry and tucks it into her pocket like a secret.

"Insurance," she says. "In case you ever pretend this didn't happen."

"Guess I'm caught, then."

She smiles, stepping closer, the lights outside spilling gold across her face. "Good."

Somewhere in the distance, the Ferris wheel creaks to a stop, the lights blinking in invitation. It's my turn to drag her somewhere.

"Let's go," I say, grabbing her hand and pulling her behind me.

The Ferris wheel groans as we climb in. The world below glows like a lantern-lit dream. Remi slides beside me, knees bumping. The air carries a mix of vanilla, coffee, and just… her. She tucks her hair behind her ear, but the wind messes it up again.

"You're smiling," she says, like she's caught me doing something rare.

"Am I not allowed?" trying to contain the smile.

She shrugs. "You just don't give it away often."

The cart lifts higher, the crowd shrinking into dots of color. From up here, Copperridge looks small, almost peaceful. For a second, I forget the noise, the people, the way the lights flash and fade. It's just her and me. The cool night air slips between us, and she instinctively moves closer.

"You're right," I say finally. "I don't give it away easily." I look over, and she's watching me, eyes softer than I've ever seen them. "But you make it easy."

Her lips part slightly, and she laughs under her breath, trying to look anywhere but me. "You always do that."

"Do what?" My smile stays in place.

"Say something that makes my chest feel too small." It comes out as a whisper.

I grin, leaning back, letting my arm rest across the back of the seat. "Maybe your heart's just growing."

She looks at me, really looks. "You ever think about how weird it is that a town this small can hold this much magic?"

I glance down at the square, lights flickering like fireflies, and then back at her. "I don't think it's the town," I say quietly. "I think it's you." My chin lifted to point at her.

She doesn't reply right away, just lets her head fall against my shoulder. My arm wraps around her automatically, the movement instinct more than thought. She fits there so easily, it almost knocks something loose in me, like my body was made for hers. Her weight settles against my chest, warm and soft, and I swear I can feel her breath syncing with mine. There's this pull in my ribs, something quiet but certain, like holding her is the most natural thing I've ever done. Her hair brushes my jaw, soft and unintentional, and it does something to me I'm not ready to name out loud.

The wheel stops at the top. The air is colder here, thinner. Below us the fair goes on, laughter, music, motion. But up here, it's still.

She tilts her head up, and for the first time, I let myself meet her halfway.

The kiss is quiet. Not a rush, not a promise. Just a moment suspended between heartbeats and starlight. If I believed in fate, I'd say my whole life has been crawling toward this second. The boy who learned to live in the cold finally found a place that feels warm enough to stay.

When we pull apart, she smiles against my shoulder. "You always know when to say nothing."

I rest my chin on the top of her head. "That's because sometimes words ruin it."

Remi's fingers trace idle circles on my palm, small, absent-minded, like she doesn't realize what she's doing. I do. Every touch feels like something permanent. When our feet touch the ground again, she looks at me like she's trying to memorize my face. Like maybe she's scared this will fade.

"It's weird," she says softly. "How something can feel like a beginning and an ending all at once."

"Maybe it's both," I tell her.

She smiles that soft, crooked one that makes me forget how to breathe. She threads her fingers through mine as we walk away from the wheel. The music fades behind us, replaced by the rustle of leaves and her laughter echoing off the square. If I could keep one moment, one version of the world forever, it would be this. Her hand in mine. The air is heavy with autumn and sugar. The sound of her voice saying nothing at all, but meaning everything.

Nineteen

☾

Remi

The world feels softer this morning, which is annoying because it's definitely Zane's fault. Everything reminds me of him, the quiet birds, how the air feels easier to breathe, with him, everything is so effortless and easy. He makes the world brighter, which is strange, because he only wears black or grey. Even the flannel he had on the other night was black and grey with pops of blue lines intertwined.

I'm playing it cool, though, pretending that I'm not the girl who spent an hour staring at her ceiling this morning, reliving every detail of the Ferris Wheel last night. I refuse to be the Remi who is stuck in her head and stuck in the past today. I'm choosing to live in the now, even if it feels like I'm the leading character in my new favorite romance movie.

We were all invited over to Zane's house for dinner, Aunt Cami's way of getting to know his friends. Maddie and Joss show up ten minutes late to my house, good thing I already anticipated this and told them to show up fifteen minutes before the time Aunt Cami gave me. Maddie came equipped with a box of cookies from the Copper Cup Cafe, saying she supervised their cooking, so they're 'homemade'. While Joss just nurses her pumpkin cream cold brew, seemingly hiding something, she's always quiet when she has a secret she's not ready to tell.

"Are you nervous?" Maddie asks as we take our short walk over to Zanes.

"Why would I be nervous?" I snap my head her way.

"Meeting the aunt, big family dinner energy. I can already smell the awkwardness." Joss says over her coffee.

"It's not like that." I quickly say. "Cami is super sweet, and we've met before."

Joss smirks, "So, it *is* like that."

"You're the one who should be nervous, *Josselyn.*" Using her full first name, just like Eli does. " I was told when Eli heard you were coming, he planned to stay another day just to be at this… How'd you put it, 'big family dinner'? " I point my glare in her direction.

We arrive as soon as I finish my jab at Joss, and I can already hear the laughter spilling from the open windows. His house feels so welcoming, it's the kind of house with too many pictures on the wall and furniture that doesn't match, but it gives off only one vibe: *home.* The scent of sweetness hits me, freshly baked chocolate chip cookies. Zane told me they're his favorite, and Aunt Cami will do anything to see a smile on his face.

Cami meets us at the door wearing an apron covered in powder and a smile that feels an awful lot like a warm hug. I swallow down fear as soon as she opens the door. I guess I am kind of nervous.

"Hi Aunt Cami." I go in for a hug anyway. "This is Maddie, and Josselyn." I point to the two girls behind me.

"I've heard enough about you two, I feel like I know you girls already," Cami says, hugging Maddie and Joss. "Come on in, Zane is in the kitchen pretending to help."

Pretending was right, when the kitchen comes into view, I see Zane leaning against the counter, sleeves pushed up around his forearms, trying to look casual but failing miserably. His smile meets me before his arms do, small, knowing, like he has been waiting all day for this moment. He pushes off the counter to meet me in the middle, arms wrapping around my waist and picking me up, spinning me in a circle.

"Hmm, I missed you." He whispers into my neck.

"You just saw me last night, Zane." I giggle

"Um, hello, we're here too." Joss interrupts our moment.

"Yeah, hi to you, too, lover boy." Maddie chimes in.

Zane laughs, actually laughs. It's so rare, I want to bottle it up and keep it all to myself. He is still spinning me around the kitchen when Cami's voice breaks his spell.

"Lennox Zane. You put that girl down and greet the rest of the guests. Don't be rude." She was waving her wooden spoon around in the air.

The whole room freezes, or at least to me it does. He suddenly drops me on my feet and says hello to the girls while I'm still stunned in the place he dropped me.

"What did she call you?" I whisper to myself, or so I thought.

"Just his full name, sweetheart. I only have to use it when he has lost his manners." Cami says over her shoulder, stirring something on the stove.

Zane is trying his hardest to make conversation with Maddie and Joss, asking how their time was at the fair and blah blah blah, doing everything in his power not to turn and look at me. His body is tense and rigid, like he doesn't want to face it, to face me. His silence slices through me like a perfectly ripe tomato.

"Full name?" Joss repeats Cami. "As in, you didn't know you were out here dating a Lennox and not a Zane." She accuses.

"Like the name of a luxury air conditioner," Maddie deadpans

"Or a toothpaste brand." Eli makes his grand entrance from down the hall. Joss rolls her eyes immediately.

"Or a villain from a Netflix drama." Maddie erupts in laughter, and Joss joins in right behind her.

I shoot them both a look that says I will murder you as soon as we leave this house. Meanwhile, Zane is still doing his best not to look my way. His face is low, like he's embarrassed or ashamed.

"It's a good name." Cami throws over her shoulder.

"It's a name." Zane spits out.

The silence that follows flattens out the emotion in the room. Cami clears her throat and says something about salad dressing before she conveniently slips into the dining room. Maddie and Joss give each other a look before they announce they are going to help set the table. Seconds pass before Joss appears again, pulling Eli's shirt until he gives in and follows her into the dining room.

"Lennox." I test out the name for myself. It feels so familiar, but I can't place where. "That's your first name?"

"Yeah." He whispers, his head staying low.

"I know we've only been official for like four minutes, but I was sure I knew your name." I take a step closer to him, testing the air between us. What else don't I know? My heart sinks a little.

"It's not exactly my favorite subject, Remi." His tone is sharp, but not mean. "My parents named me after a casino." He says, shaking his head like he's trying to shake off the memory.

"A casino?" My eyes are bulging. "Like bad decisions and slot machines?"

"Exactly." His laugh clipped, humorless, sarcastic even. "The Lennox Grand in Tulsa, Oklahoma, of all places. It's where they met, where they had lost everything. They thought it would be poetic. Turns out, it's just pathetic."

He delivers that line like it's a joke, but it doesn't land right. It feels more like a bruise.

"Hey," I say softly, stepping into his space. "You want to know what I think?"

"Always." He says, turning at the pace of a snail to face me.

"I think it's a good name, it's just used wrong." Grabbing his hands.

Zane tilts his head to the side, asking a question without words.

"Maybe Lennox started as something broken," I say softly, squeezing his hands. "But names get rewritten. People do too. It doesn't have to mean what they meant. It can just mean... you."

His eyes soften, and I can see the tension rolling off his shoulders. He lets out a quiet laugh, one that sounds more like relief. It's ironic how the things meant to hurt us sometimes turn into the things that remake us.

"How do you make everything sound easier than it is?" The sadness in his eyes softens a bit.

"It's the Italian accent that I *don't* have, I can just make it sound... better." I smile to myself, hoping that didn't come off as cheesy as it sounded coming out of my mouth.

"Let's hear it." Zane takes a step forward, invading my space now. "Say it again."

"Say what?" I look up at him

"My name Remilia, say my name." He breathes out. "And don't you dare leave out the nonexistent accent."

I take my time, trying to figure out how I can make Lennox sound Italian. My mind comes up empty, and I settle on normal.

"Lennox," I say with a smile.

He closes his eyes and exhales. "You're right, it's the Italian accent you totally don't have." He opens his eyes to meet mine. "You make everything better."

"Remilia and Lennox." Floating off my tongue like I'm walking on clouds.

He laughs under his breath, "Remilia and Lennox." He repeats. "It sounds like a bad band name."

"Sign me up, I guess." I let out a laugh.

Zane's eyes on me in this moment are a lot to handle, that's why I'm almost thankful when Joss busts open the dining room door.

"I mixed this." Holding up a bowl full of salad. "With my hands, it's art." Her smile reached her eyes, and she was proud of herself.

"Now come eat," Eli yells from the other room.

"That's horrifying," Zane responds to Joss' art. He pauses as he looks back at me, he gives me that smirk I'm obsessed with, and he nods towards the dining room before grabbing my hand and pulling me behind him.

Zane pulls my chair out before sitting next to me, his hand brushing all the way across the top of my shoulders as he goes. It probably looked like nothing, but to me it was everything. I turn my head to look at him, and he is already looking my way, with a small grin and soft smile.

Remilia and Lennox.

Laughter and chaos filled the air. Surprisingly, Joss and Eli haven't argued yet, which should one hundred percent raise some red flags. The chocolate chip cookies quickly became everyone's favorite. Eli has gone back at least four times already. Cami has called everyone sweetheart, the girls definitely felt at home here. Zane looks content. I don't think I've ever seen him so relaxed, shoulders slumped, an easy smile that never left, color back in his cheeks, and even a full belly laugh.

"Thank you for inviting us over for dinner, Aunt Cami." I lean in, giving her a goodbye hug. "Im not sure what was better, the food, or seeing Joss and Eli get along for once."

She laughs and leans closer into me, whispering in my ear for only me to hear. "I was there when Eli was born. I've seen him grow at every stage in his life. He has never, and I mean never, looked at someone the way he looks at her."

I pull back, eyes wide. "You think?"

"Oh, sweetheart, I know." She says with a wink, moving on to hug Maddie.

There's nothing better than the Tennessee air in the fall, it's cool, crisp, and refreshing. Zane stands on the porch, hands shoved into the pocket of his black hoodie, laughing at something Eli is saying. While Eli stands there holding the jar of cookies like a newborn baby, shoveling another cookie into his mouth. Joss is standing between the two of them, her eyes lit up, watching Eli with that *'give me your attention'* face.

Maddie loops her arm through mine. "That was actually fun." Nudging me, " I don't know what was better, the food, or watching Joss blush."

"I don't blush," Joss spits out.

"That sounds like someone who was blushing would say." Maddie spits back at her.

Zane falls into step beside me as our friends argue ahead of us. Eli looks like a human tennis ball trying to keep up with their conversation while the girls go back and forth on either side of him.

"Your friends are something else." His eyebrow reached for his hair.

"Are you surprised by that?" My head is tilting to one side.

"No." He shakes his head. "Just an observation." He says, "They care about you."

I study him for a second, not sure where he's going. Those two have been in my life since kindergarten. One has practically lived with me, and the other, well, Maddie and I have a strange dynamic.

"And you don't?" Accusations rolling off my tongue.

"Didn't say that." His smile softens. " I just like seeing you laugh, and those two." Pointing ahead of us at Joss and Maddie. "They make you laugh."

We walk hand in hand for the rest of the way, his warm body pressed against mine, thumb rubbing back and forth against my hand. This is nice, so nice I want to say it aloud, but I don't want the closeness to stop. So I don't, I just hold his hand and let the closeness do the talking.

"Hi, Elena. I'm loving that sweater on you. Can I borrow it?" Joss asks as we walk up the stairs to the porch.

My papà shakes his head, "Sempre questa ragazza..." his hand in the air.

"What did he say, Remi?" Joss tosses over her shoulder to me.

"Again with this girl," I whisper so only Zane can hear.

He chokes out a laugh while my friends introduce Eli to my parents. My mother looks at me from over the top of them all, she winks, and I know exactly what she's trying to say without saying it. *Happiness looks good on you.* It's something my Nonna used to tell me when I was growing up. The smile I give her back says it all.

"Ah man, I hate to miss it, but I promise to come back for the next one." Eli delivers a promise to my parents.

"What are you missing?" I ask

Maddie turns around, excitement etched all over her face. "Tomorrow is homemade pizza night at the Moretti house, and I personally cannot wait."

"You too, figilo." My Papà announces to Zane.

"Wouldn't miss it," Zane says, smiling down at me. I don't miss the way his chest swells at the word figilo.

Twenty

☾

Remi

Pizza night at the Moretti house always feels like a full-contact sport under stadium lights. The atmosphere is loud and charged with competition, today is no exception. Floors and counters are covered in flour, and sauce is caked onto every inch of the kitchen island and the stove. Papà yelling demands from every corner of the kitchen, 'too much basil, not enough passion'. Mammà is blaring an Italian pop song while Joss fails at singing along, knowing only one word: *amore*. Maddie is on the kitchen island, trying to make her dough Instagram-worthy, which only means there's more mess than there should be.

Then there is Zane.

He's standing next to Papà, sleeves rolled up, hands dusted with flour, trying to spin a ball of dough in the air like it's easy. Take my word for it, it is most definitely not easy. The moment he tosses the dough in the air, it folds in on itself and smacks him loudly in the shoulder. Joss and my Mammà try hard to conceal their laughter, but it doesn't work.

"You were supposed to catch it, Carter," Maddie shouts. She's probably living on Instagram right now, and he will kill her for that later.

"Dio Mio! You look like you're fighting the dough." Papà huffs out, his hands flying in the air like a true Italian.

"I am fighting it!" Zane laughs out. "It started…" he looks around the room."It started…it."

The entire kitchen breaks out in laughter, even Papà. I can't help but look around the kitchen, full of things I love and smile at. It's loud in here, which isn't unusual; it's alive, and it's definitely messy. Zane glances my way across the kitchen, and I swear he looks like he has been here for as long as Maddie and Joss. He looks comfortable here, like this isn't his first time at homemade pizza night. The smile creeps across my face when I realize I want him here for at least a hundred more.

And wow, I love this. Wait. Did I just think about love? As in a room full of things I love. Nope. Absolutely not. Delete. Backspace. Rewind. Cancel subscription. I definitely didn't sign up for that. The smile that creeps up anyway when I realize I want him here for at least a hundred more nights.

Papà's playlist switches mid-song, and suddenly the room is filled with an old Italian ballad, one I haven't heard in forever. I'm looking down at the dough in my hand, I'm frozen, it's one of Nonna's favorites. One note is all it takes to rip open a memory, sweet enough to ache, sharp enough to hurt. With pools forming behind my closed eyelids, I feel mammà's eyes on me. When I get the courage to open my eyes, her head tilts to the side ever so slightly with a look that says *Come on, piccolina, you know what to do.*

Before I can even gather my thoughts together, she's invading my space. She reaches for me, grabbing my flour-covered hands, and pulls me to the middle of the kitchen.

"Mammà, no" I plea. Unsure if it's another headache making the room spin or the bittersweet memories of my Nonna.

"Sì sì," she insists, already spinning me under her arm.

Papà starts snapping his fingers, making his way to us, like the center of the kitchen is our own personal dance floor. I trip under my own two feet, which gains me a round of applause, like I'm performing surgery, and they're watching from the gallery. What surprises me most is when Zane makes his way to us, swaying to the beat, leaving his oven mitt on the counter, next to his mangled dough. He steps forward, looking uncertain but willing, like he's choosing this chaos, choosing us with every sway.

"You dance?" My breath is short and choppy, snapping and swaying to the beat.

"Nope." He grabs my hand anyway, spinning me under his arm.

He is careful and sure at the same time, enjoyment written all over his face. He moves his body, but his feet stay planted. It's almost like he doesn't really dance, just living in the moment, here with me. He smiles and spins me the wrong way, right into my Mammà.

"Careful, figlio. We replaced the drywall last year. I don't want to have to do that again." My Papà warns, a grin on his face.

The music drifts through the kitchen, soft and familiar, like it's been waiting for the right moment to show up. For a second, I can swear I see Nonna standing in the corner, clapping to the beat, flour covering her apron.

"She used to dance with me, right here." My voice is low, and I direct my words to Mammà.

"That means you're in the right spot, Ragazza Mia." Her tear-filled eyes squeeze my hand.

Zane sneaks next to me, wrapping his arm around my shoulders, smiling down at me, like he's been let in on a secret. The next song drifts in, flour now covering the floor, but I couldn't be happier.

After the dancing dies down and the kitchen looks like a bakery exploded, quite literally, there is flour in the silverware drawer and in Maddie's hair. Papà claims it's part of the creative process of cooking, while mammà stares at him wildly from across the kitchen, where she is setting the table. Oddly enough, it feels like any other Friday would.

Joss and Maddie start pizza night off the way they do every time, re-telling stories from all the pizza nights that came before this one. Each one was filled with nothing but laughter, dancing, and a huge mess to clean up at the end of the night. Let's just say, Zane isn't the first person to burn the crust during one of these special nights.

It feels like everything is moving more slowly now. The way Maddie throws her head back when she laughs, Joss's gestures so big she almost knocks over her drink, my Papà pretending to clutch his pearls, while Mammà's face lights up when Joss finally gets to the point. I don't even think Mammà knows she has a dusting of flour on her cheek. Even Zane, his eyes growing as he watches all of the chaos unfold. The sleeves of his shirt were stained with pizza sauce splatters, his laugh blending in with everyone else's. It's like he stepped into my movie, but now he feels like he belongs.

I just sit back and watch, taking everything in. After Nonna died, I always felt like a piece of me was missing. No one can ever take her place, that's a no-brainer. Here in this moment, sitting around the table with all the people who make my heart swell, I don't feel that empty piece anymore.

Papà is laughing at something Joss says when the sound in the room dips; it's like someone turned the volume knob all the way down. My first thought is: one song switching to the next. No one else is phased by it. They continue as if the volume is the same. My head begins to move frantically between Papà and Joss, trying to hear their banter when the lights dim, I can barely see anything.

My head goes light, almost hollow, the air thick and slow entering my lungs. I'm gasping for more air, but I feel like I'm breathing through a straw, a coffee stirrer, actually. My hearing tunnels before my sight does, voices thinning like they're slipping underwater. I blink hard, but that doesn't help. The edges are closing in on the charcoal blur in between them. Even the flicker of the candlelight goes grey as my chest struggles to rise and fall.

I grip the edge of the table, trying to steady the room, my head bowed low. My fingers lose, chest still straining under the breaths I'm trying to take, the sound of the radio statics in and out. Zane is up before I realize I'm falling, the bowl of olives sent flying in the air as I try my best to get a grip. Something clatters to the ground, I can't tell if it's my plate or the olive bowl. I feel hands under my arms, the back of my neck slick with moisture.

"Hey," Zane says, holding onto my limp body.

"Remi, look at me." Panic laced his voice.

The room narrows to his voice, and I squint my eyes trying to see his face. The smell of pizza sauce and flour. The warmth of his hands around my waist, trying to hold me up.

Then it all folds in on itself.

Twenty one

☾

Remi

Voices flow in and out, blending in with the chairs scraping across the floor. Panic mixed into voices all flooding in at once. The smell of burnt pizza crust still wafted in the air, turning my stomach upside down before I even opened my eyes completely. Cool, wet fabric on my forehead, a fringe blanket draped over my body, the kind she claims are only for decorations. I'm on the couch. I can feel Mammà's slender fingers running through my hair the way she used to when I was little and had a fever.

Somewhere nearby, I hear Papà. His voice is low, panic lacing his words. He is hiding it the best way he knows how, in Italian.

"Non l'hai vista, Elena," he says, his voice trembling. "È rimasta immobile, completamente immobile. L'ho chiamata tre volte prima che si muovesse. *Tre volte!*"

You didn't see her, Elena. She went still, completely still. I called her three times before she moved. Three times! His voice trembling, it's been a long time since I've heard the unsteady version of Nico Moretti.

I almost didn't want to open my eyes, my Papà never panics. There's something about hearing your parents freak out, it makes you feel smaller than you already are. I can't listen to him like that any longer, he's the man who isn't afraid of anything. He is the biggest, strongest person I know.

I clear my throat to make sure it's working and say, "In case anyone was wondering, I'm alive," forcing my voice to sound lighter than I feel.

The entire room goes quiet.

"Uffa, Remilia Giuseppina." Papà's words come out rushed. "Don't do that again!" He demands.

"Do what, Papà? Wake up?" I mumble, rubbing my eyes, willing them to open.

"You scared ten years off of my life, Remilia." He lets out a half-laugh, half-groan.

I finally open my eyes, but it's a strain. The sunlight is fleeting, but the rays are still visible and painfully shining through the windows. When I'm finally able to focus, I meet Mammà's eyes, worried, saying more with her eyes than she ever could with her words.

"Im Okay." I lie. Leaning into her cool hand on my cheek. My head feels like it's spinning on a hamster wheel. I reach for the first explanation I can give them to excuse my fainting.

"The smell, the pizza that Papà let Zane burn." It's the only thing I can think of. "That's what did me in, the smell," I repeat, trying to believe myself. "It was so bad." I look up to Mammà, trying to decipher the look on her face.

Papà lifts a hand to his chest, scandalized. "*Assassinate?* My bread?"

"Papà, that smell could knock someone unconscious," I banter, doing my best to sound playful.

Mammà stifles a laugh, her shoulders shaking as she passes me a glass of water. "She has a point, amore," she teases.

"Maddie and I will open the windows and then give you guys some space," Joss announces to my parents as she walks my way. "Feel better, Rem." She bends down and kisses my cheek. "Let me know if you want to cancel tomorrow's study session."

I give her a tight smile and a nose scrunch, that's all I can muster up at the present moment. Maddie nods my way and begins to open the windows around us. They make their way to the kitchen windows, and then they quietly dip out of the back door. When I look back at the living room, I see Zane sitting in a chair in the corner. His elbows were on his knees, and his head hung low.

The air rushes in, cool and fresh from the windows the girls opened, surrounding my body and enveloping me in. I close my eyes and breathe it in, making a show out of it to keep the lie alive.

"See, breathing better already," I say in Zane's direction. He doesn't budge.

Mammà pins me with a *I know better* stare. "Im going to go turn the fans on." She looks to Papà, "Nico, come with me in case I pass out too." She giggles. "Wouldn't want you to lose ten more years now, would we?"

Papà shakes his head and follows Mammà's lead towards the kitchen. I watch them leave. Papà twirls her around, saying, "Let's *turn the music back on* in Italian.

"Hey," my voice is soft, turning back to Zane, whose head is still low.

His hands stop moving, but he doesn't look up at me just yet.

"You can breathe now, I'm okay." I try, but there is still no movement from him. "Come sit with me." I pause, "Please." My plea is coming out softer than before.

He finally lifts his head, his eyes searching mine, looking for some ounce of reassurance. His movement is slow, the way his thumbs twirl over each other, even the way he swallows, the bob of his throat, like he is swallowing a truth he isn't really sure of. On exhale, he stands, eyes still locked on mine.

When he finally crosses the room, the sound of his boots on the hardwood floor feels louder than it should. He sinks down on the couch next to me, and his body goes into the same position he was in across the room in the chair. His elbows are on his knees again, his head hung low, and his hands are still clasped in front of him.

"I didn't know what to do." His voice breaks. "You just… You scared me." He lifts his head a little, eyes still on the floor in front of him.

I reach for him, rubbing circles on his back, comforting him. "Seems to be my specialty tonight." I crack a smile, hoping he will follow me into lighter territory.

He huffs out a laugh that sounds more like a pained sigh. Sitting criss-crossed under the decorative blanket, I scoot closer to him until my knees are touching his leg. I move my hand to go over his clenched hands, his skin hot to the touch, and I give him a squeeze.

"Hey, I'm okay. Look at me. I'm okay, Zane." Basically begging him to believe me.

"You don't look okay." He reaches for my face, and on instinct, I lean into that touch. "You're pale, lifeless, Remi." He says softly.

I close my eyes, there's nothing I can say to make this better for him. I almost tell him the truth. That I'm scared too. That the darkness took longer to let go this time. But if I say it out loud, it becomes real, and I'm not ready for real yet. For a moment, neither of us moves. My face lay in his hands, the music humming softly from the kitchen, the cool breeze wrapping us in the fresh air.

"You stayed," I manage, pushing the words out.

"Where else would I go, Polaris?" His voice is cracking.

I open my eyes to meet his, glassy with fear.

"I'm sorry, Zane, but in order not go through this again, you won't be allowed to make the pizza dough anymore." I smile big, hoping he will match mine.

He searches my face once more, "Okay, Remi," he brushes his thumb across my cheek. "Okay, Angel," he whispers.

He stays that way, running his thumb back and forth on my cheek until the tension rolls out of us both. The music shifts to another song, and I can hear my parents murmuring quietly over the running water. They'll be in there a while, cleaning up what was left behind from our tragic attempt at pizza night.

"You should get some rest," Zane announces softly, pulling my attention back to him.

He is right, I'm so tired, too tired to even go to my bed. I snuggle into the couch and watch as Zane pulls the blanket over my shoulders. His eyes are soft again, not so tormented by my fainting spell in the kitchen earlier.

"Will you stay until I fall asleep?" I ask mid-yawn.

"Of course. I'll always stay, settling himself into the other side of the couch.

The room is stable, no more spinning, the faintest smell of burnt pizza coming from somewhere in the distance, and the hum of music threatens to pull me into slumber quickly. I can feel Zane's warmth at the end of the couch, and I wish I had the energy to scoot closer to him. Before I can even finish that thought, I'm pulled under.

The next morning

The light creeping in from the curtains is much softer today, or the pain behind my eyes is weaker. I blink a few times, trying to place where I am, trying to understand what happened last night. It takes me a beat, but I remember. The fainting, the pizza smell, the worry etched on everyone's faces. I'm still on the couch, wrapped in the blanket that's only for decoration, only someone layered it with something heavier.

I push myself up slowly, not wanting the room to spin like it did last night. My throat is dry, but at least my head is still. There's a pen and a napkin on the coffee table in front of me.

"Didn't want to wake you. Text me when you feel up to it. -Z"

Seeing his initials on that napkin sends an annoying pang in my chest and a flutter in my stomach. I run my fingers over the ink, feeling the indentations on the other side. I close my eyes and inhale, wishing he were still at the other end of my couch. Luckily, my phone is right next to the napkin. It's like he was willing me into feeling up to it as soon as I woke up. I smile to myself because only he would.

The smell of freshly brewed coffee gets me off the couch. I can hear Mammà stacking the dishes into the cabinets.

"Good morning, bambina." She calls out over the noise when she notices me in the doorway.

"Good morning Mammà. "Yes, before you ask. I feel much better now that the smell is out of the house," I say as I walk toward her and wrap my arms around her.

Papà pops his head up from his newspaper when he hears me. He points to the glass of orange juice and the plate of toast in front of him. "Eat. Doctor's orders."

I greet him with a smile. "You're no doctor, Papà."

"I was last night." His tone is stern, but his face is haunted. Flashes of the fainting episode are still on his mind.

"You should take the day and rest," Mammà suggests, sitting next to me at the table.

"Mammà, I'm okay, it's just studying, not skydiving. I'll be okay." Pleading my case.

Papà mutters, " *Stubborn just like your mother* under his breath in Italian. Mammà and I pin him with the same look, which makes him laugh. The tension leaves his body as he shakes his head. Okay, maybe we are the same.

"Im going to get a shower in, I promise not to faint in there." I tease.

"Don't joke about that, Remilia." My dad spits out.

"Nico, she's kidding." Mammà swats his arm and shooes me away.

I escape down the hall before either of them can change their minds. The hot water hits my shoulders, and for the first time since last night, I can finally exhale. The steam wraps around me, washing away the scent of smoke and panic.

My phone buzzes from the counter. It's Zane.

Zane: You Alive?

Remi: Yes, barely. My Dad is hovering like I'm about to fall over at any moment.

Zane: Reasonable Concern. He probably thinks you're turning into a fainting goat.

Remi: Wow, thanks for the visual.

Zane: I've seen sturdier flowers.

Remi: Keep talking, and I'll tell him not to let you come over for pizza nights anymore.

Remi: And he will because I'm his favorite.

Zane: You're my favorite, too.

I stare at the screen for a minute, too smitten to do anything except stand here with this stupid grin on my face.

Remi: Nice save.

Zane: Lol. Are you really okay? I'm worried about you.

Remi: Yeah, just a headache hangover now.

Zane: Next time, I'm wrapping you in bubble wrap.

Remi: If that's what you're into.. hot, I guess?

His reply comes slower this time.

Zane: You scare me, Remi.

My thumb hovers over the screen. I want to make a joke, to send a meme, anything to dodge the heaviness of this conversation.

Remi: I scare myself.

Zane: I'll see you later.

Remi: Yeah, I'll let you know when I'm done with the girls.

I throw on jeans and my softest sweater, pull my hair into a slick back, and before my parents can protest, I slip out of the front door. The morning air smells like rain and cinnamon, Copperridge's signature scent. Fresh air, that's exactly what I need.

The Copper Cup Cafè is already booming with people when I walk in. The ring of the coffee bell, the plates clanking together, and the sound of the cash register opening and closing. This is exactly what I need to feel normal again. Maddie and Joss are already here, they have claimed our usual table near the window and are armed with caffeine and zero productivity.

"Look who survived pizza night," Maddie calls as I slide into my seat.

"Barely," I say, pulling at the sleeves of my sweater.

Joss grins, stirring her latte. "Your dad texted the group chat and said you blamed him and Zane for burning the dough and fainting."

I groan, "Of course he did."

Maddie leans in, eyebrows raised. "So.. Zane stayed all night?" She nudges me with her shoulder.

"He might've," I say, still picking at my sweater.

"Remi, you passed out, and he turned into McDreamy." Joss retorts.

I roll my eyes at them. "You two are annoying this morning."

"True," Maddie says. "Drink your coffee before you faint again, these arms can't catch you, they're decorative."

Maddie's laptop is open, but she hasn't looked at it once. She is too busy with her phone, it keeps vibrating, she keeps sighing, and then pretending that she's not sighing. She looks annoyed, and then she brushes it off as soon as it comes.

Joss leans over towards Maddie. "Okay, hun, what's going on? You look like you're planning your own funeral." Her eyes were bulging.

Maddie flips her phone upside down on the table and stops breathing. "It's just my mom, she wants me to come into the office next week." She says, rolling her eyes.

"The office." I pause. "You mean the empire?" I say matter-of-factly.

"Please don't call it that." She brings her hands to her eyes, rubbing hard.

"You're literally a Whitmore." Joss quips. "As in Whitmore Holdings," She adds matter-of-factly.

"You make it sound like a cult." Maddie throws her hand in the air.

"Isn't it tough?" Joss rebuttals. "Matching sports coats, yearly vacations in Aspen. Did I mention the money?" Joss taps her chin.

Maddie picks up a sugar packet and throws it at Joss. "It's not like that. I just… I don't want to spend my life making PowerPoints about stocks I don't care about. My mom's already lined up someone to 'shadow' me while I learn the ropes."

"Shadow?" I raise an eyebrow. "What, like a corporate babysitter?"

She shrugs. "Security, technically." She fidgets with another sugar packet. "Which is ridiculous because the college they'll choose for me has more cameras than the Pentagon."

Joss grins. "So he's probably old and boring and wears too much cologne."

"Oh, Maddie," I say slowly, trying not to smile.

Her glare could burn through steel. "Can't I just hide in your luggage when you go to Spain this summer?"

My smile widens. "I don't personally own any luggage that big, unless you're willing to let me borrow that Louis Vuitton."

Maddie groans and hides her face behind her cup. "Can we please talk about anything else before I develop a trust fund rash?"

The laughter that bursts out of Joss and me is way too loud for a place with exposed brick and acoustic music. Half the café, including Georgia behind the counter, turns to stare at us like we've escaped from the zoo.

"Okay, okay. We will behave." I say, wiping a tear from my eye.

Hours slip by us between the caffeine and the town gossip. The buzz of the cafe drops to a lull. It's only when my stomach growls so loud that Maddie jumps that I realize how long we have been here.

"Nonna's anyone?" Packing up my books into my bag.

The walk to Nonna's is barely two doors down, but we stretch it out anyway. The evening light has turned Copperridge gold, the kind of glow that makes everything look softer, the bakery sign flickering, the breeze carrying the smell of sugar and roasted coffee beans.

Joss loops her arm through mine, still talking about something ridiculous from class. Maddie trails behind us, phone in hand, pretending she's not checking for another text from her mom.

When we reach the corner, the air changes, it's warmer, richer, and the unmistakable scent of garlic and fresh bread wraps around us like a welcome home. My smile comes as quickly as the air changes, and I inhale the smell of fresh, non-burnt bread.

"Okay, whoever's cooking tonight deserves a medal," Joss says, closing her eyes and inhaling dramatically.

"Both of my parents are working tonight," I mention.

We round the corner to Nonna's, and that's when I see them. Zane is standing with my parents outside the restaurant.

My Papà's laughing, full-body, hand-on-the-shoulder laughing, while Mammà's smiling in that way that makes people feel instantly forgiven for whatever they've done. Zane's got one hand in his pocket, the other holding what looks like a to-go cup, shoulders relaxed like he's known them forever.

Maddie whistles low. "He's either getting recruited or interrogated."

"Or adopted," Joss adds.

"Or worse," I mutter. "He's charming them."

Joss bumps my shoulder. "You say that like it's a bad thing."

The smell of roasted garlic hits us full force as we step closer: basil, tomatoes, and toasted bread. Nonna's smells like comfort, like home, like every childhood memory that still lingers in the corners of this town and the corners of my mind.

My mother spots us first, waving her hand high like she's flagging us in for landing. "Girls! Perfect timing! We were just talking about dinner."

My Papà claps Zane on the back. "We've invited him to stay. He's already family now."

"Family?" I repeat, pretending to be horrified. "You've known him for five minutes."

"That's four minutes longer than it took me to decide I liked your mother," Papà says, holding the door open with a grin.

I jerk my neck back, "Oh." That's all I can say.

Maddie smirks. "And this is why Remi's doomed. Charm clearly runs in the family."

Inside, Nonna's glows warm and golden, the sound of clinking glasses and laughter spilling from every table. The girls rush to our usual booth by the window while Zane hovers beside me, waiting, that cautious look in his eyes like he's wondering if he's really invited.

"Come on," I tell him. "You've already survived my dad once today."

He gives a quiet laugh, following me in. "Barely."

Papà slides behind the counter, gesturing toward the ovens. "You girls eat. I'll bring something out. No arguing."

Mammà adds, "And no passing out."

"Mammà," I groan, burying my face in my hands.

"Just saying," she teases, kissing the top of my head before disappearing into the kitchen.

Zane leans closer, voice low. "She's turning that into a joke?"

"Seems so," I sigh. "She's Italian, we cover everything in marinara." I shrug.

"I guess we will have to make the next pizza night memorable for another reason," I say it light, easy, like we're just talking about burnt crust and not the way the world went black around the edges.

Twenty two

☾

Zane

The sound of laughter still hums in the background. Plates are being scraped clean. Voices soft now, stretched with comfort. That's what Nonna's Restaurant feels like, a home away from home. The lights are dim, the air is warm. It's like the walls are reflecting what they see, remembering who built them.

She's at the center of it all. My Polaris, Remi. Head tilted back, laughing like it costs nothing. But I can see the tremor in her hand as she reaches for her glass. The way her eyes dull when she thinks no one is watching. The way she keeps bringing her hands up to her eyes to give them a good rub. She's got a headache.

She says she's fine. She *always* says she's fine. Everyone around her is falling for it. The lie she's trying to tell. Who is she really lying to, all of us? Or herself? Does she even believe her lie?

Joss mentions something about Maddie and her family's money. The whole table erupts in laughter again. I laugh when

I'm supposed to, but my chest stays tight. Noise is easy to fake. Breathing isn't.

When the conversation turns into something light, I take my chance. I stand and say something about getting air. No one notices except her. She always notices. Remi's eyes find mine, curious, soft, the kind that follows you even when you look away.

I walk towards the back, finding the quiet pulse of the kitchen. The air changes here, quieter, heavy with garlic and steam. Her parents are cleaning up, a dance they've done over and over again. That's apparent by the way they work around each other, like they've done it forever.

I wait in the doorway, unsure how to start. Or if I even should. Her mother, Elena, is the first to see me. Too late.

"Come in, Zane. You don't have to hover." She shouts.

So I do. I enter the threshold, and somehow it feels like I've been invited into something sacred.

"I uh.." Searching for the right words. "I just want to thank you," I manage. "For dinner. For letting me..."

"For letting you be here?" Nico waves me off. " Nonsense. You belong, *figlio mio*. Stop thanking us." He continues to wave his hands in the air, like he's not too pleased.

That word again, *Figlio*. It lands somewhere deep. Somewhere unguarded. I finally pushed out the breath I was holding onto.

"Can I ask you guys a question?" I swallow hard.

Both of them stop what they're doing. The room goes silent. Elena dries her hands on a towel, and Nico puts the broom to the side and leans against the counter. Giving me their full attention.

"When she uh.." I can't even say it. "Remi, when Remi fainted." I swallow the lump that's in my throat. The image won't leave my head. "It's like she wasn't even there. She —"

"We know," Nico says, his head hung low.

"She's had migraines since she was little, but this one." Elena stumbles over her words, worry etched all over her face. "This one was different."

Nico reaches for Elena, rubbing her back. Like Remi has done for me many times. Comfort.

"The doctors, they say it's stress or hormones. They don't really know, they're never sure." He pushes out softly.

The weight of the silence that comes while Elena and Nico have a silent conversation with their eyes is almost deafening.

"She will kill me for saying this, but you should keep an eye on her." She lifts her head to look my way. "She will be okay, but we all need to keep a close eye on her."

I don't know what to do with that. I look down at my feet. I'm still trying to figure out how to breathe when she smiles. Nico's hand lands on my shoulder, he turns me around, and gives me a little nudge back out towards the tables.

"Go, have fun. Leave the heaviness for us, ya?" He nods, answering the question for me.

"Yeah," I say somberly.

My chest feels lighter, and my breathing is a little more fluid. At least I'm not the only one worried. Stepping out of the kitchen, I'm instantly aware of where she is. Her hand is propping her head up. She's listening to Joss and Maddie argue over something. Her eyes are half-lidded, relaxed. She must feel my eyes on her, because she looks over at me. Watching me watch her. Her mouth forms a smile, lazy, but real. That's all it takes for me to be undone. I make my way over to where she is.

I slide into the booth next to her, letting my knee bump into hers. "Hey," I say, my mouth forming a smile on instinct. Breathing her in, coffee and basil. Always.

"Hey, yourself." She bats her eyelashes.

"You okay?" I study her.

"Im more than okay." She smiles up at me.

"Let's get out of here. Fresh air, no pizza fumes, no Maddie and Joss arguments. Just us." I run my hands up and down my thighs. Anxiously awaiting her answer.

"I'd love that actually." Adoration filled her eyes.

We drove around the town for a few minutes and eventually landed back at her house. Parked in her driveway with the headlights cutting through the thin layer of fog. Both of us just sit there in the silence. Her hand was over mine in the center seat. Neither of us is moving. Neither of us wants to break the silence. Silence never scared me. It used to, when I was younger, it felt like proof that no one was listening. Somewhere along the road, it changed. I realized the silence wasn't empty. It was honest. You can't lie in it. You can't hide behind it. It's where the truth sits quietly and waits for you to notice.

That's why I like it with her. Remi doesn't fill the quiet just to hear her own voice. She lets it stretch between us, soft and alive, like it means something. With her, silence isn't distance, it's understanding. It's being seen without having to explain yourself.

Copperridge is quiet, especially at night. The kind of quiet that forces you to listen to the leaves rolling, the bird chirping, or the gravel beneath you crunching. Porch lights begin to flick off one by one. Somewhere in the distance, a dog barks and then stops. It's like the entire town shuts down.

"I don't want to go inside yet." It's almost a whisper.

"Then don't."

She turns towards me, a smile tugging at her mouth. "That easy, huh?"

"Some things are." I raise an eyebrow.

I love the way it feels under the weight of her gaze. I love the way her cheeks sit nice and round at the front of her face, how the freckles dance across her nose. The way her hair always falls perfectly around her face, like it knows she's the star of the show. I wonder if she knows how beautiful she is. We sit staring into each other's eyes, waiting for someone to finally make a move. Just being next to her fills the silence, even when she isn't saying anything at all.

"What's your favorite flavor of ice cream?" She asks, a mischievous smile on her face.

"Im simple," I say, throwing my shoulder up towards my ear.

"Let me guess..." She crosses one arm over her ribs and taps her lips with the other hand. "Vanilla," she says.

I lift my cheek, giving her the smirk she loves so much.

"Predictable." She rolls her eyes and reaches for the door. "I'll be back, hopefully with something that has a little more flavor than vanilla."

She disappears inside before I can even think of a good comeback. The light inside spills onto the porch and bathes everything in a golden glow. The door shuts, and I'm staring at a faint silhouette of her in the house.

I lean back in the seat, tapping my fingers against the steering wheel. Vanilla. Predictable. Maybe she's right. But predictability sounds a lot like peace, and peace is comforting. Through the window, I see her moving around the kitchen, hair loose, sweatshirt hanging off one shoulder, opening the freezer, talking to herself like the world's safest kind of chaos.

A few minutes later, she's back outside, two spoons and two bowls. She plops down in the seat and hands me a bowl.

"See?" she says, showing me her bowl. "I bring the flavor."

I take the spoon she hands me and shake my head. "You bring the entertainment."

She laughs and digs in first. "That too."

We eat in silence for a while, the fog thickening around the headlights, everything else fading out.

"Try this," she says, shoving her bowl in my direction.

"It's green." I say disgusted

She rolls her eyes. "It's pistachio, not nuclear waste, Zane. Just try it."

"I don't eat things that look like lawn clippings." I deadpan.

"You don't eat anything that isn't beige or red," She's quick to fire back.

I tilt my head, pretending to think about it. "Accurate."

She scoffs and holds the bowl closer. "Come on, Zane, live a little."

There's no winning when she says my name like that, sharp around the edges but dipped in honey. So I take the spoon, brace myself, and try a bite. It's... not terrible. Sweet, creamy, a little nutty. Definitely not my usual.

"Well?" she presses, her stormy grey eyes wide with excitement.

I shrug, swallowing more slowly just to watch her squirm. "It's edible." I finally gave up.

She shakes her head as her mouth falls open, offended. "Edible?" Her face scrunches in disgust. "You're impossible."

"Hey, I like what I like." I shrug.

She laughs, loud and unguarded, the sound echoing softly inside the cab. The fog outside wraps tighter around the truck, muting the world until it feels like we're the only two people left in it. I don't know what time it is or how long we sit there, just that she's still stealing spoonfuls from my bowl and I don't bother to stop her.

When she finally sets the bowl down, she turns toward me, eyes soft now. "You know, you could've just admitted you liked it."

I smile, leaning back against the seat, my eyes meeting hers again. "Maybe I like the person feeding it to me more."

Her breath catches, and for a second, neither of us says anything. The radio hums low, an old song threading through the quiet. Her eyes can't decide if they want to look at my mouth or my eyes. Eventually, whatever is happening in her mind shows itself. She smiles, breaking the spell. Gosh, that smile.

"Careful, Zane Carter. That sounded dangerously close to Italian ice cream, which is my favorite flavor," she quips.

I drop my chin to my chest and shake it back and forth. She's insufferable. "You're impossible, Remilia Moretti."

That earns me a smile. Remilia. The name itself sounds like a love letter. It dawns on me that I don't know her middle name.

"Remilia?" This time it's a question.

"That's me." She says, her words dripping with sarcasm.

"What's your middle name?" My voice is soft.

The look of disgust that comes over her is both cute and intriguing. She throws her head back until it meets the headrest, and she stares at the headliner of the truck. Pure annoyance.

"That's classified information." She blows out.

"Classified information?" I shoot back at her, one eyebrow raising in confusion. "C'mon," I nudge her knee.

She jolts her head up, giving me a look that screams, " What? " She rolls her eyes, shakes her head, and throws it back to the headrest. The drama that is oozing out of her right now is absolutely adorable. Now I *NEED* to know what it is.

"I told you mine." The words roll off a little more playfully than I intended.

"Seriously?" She flings her head back upright, looking at me like she's about to pounce. "You introduced yourself to me as Zane, which is your middle name, by the way." Her hands are flying wildly around in the air. "And you," pointing her finger in my direction, "didn't tell me the name you hate, I overheard your Aunt Cami calling you that name." Her neck looks only similar to a snake right about now. "Lennox." She finally spits out.

"So you hate it?" I ask hesitantly.

That earns me another eye roll. Cutest attitude ever. "Lennox sounds like a bad spy name from a low-budget film anyway."

"Better than Remilia -Mystery Name - Moretti," I whisper.

She lets her guard down, and a grin begins to present itself. That is, until the nerves set in. She tucks her hair behind her ear and chews on her lip. She finally gives in, I can tell by the eye roll.

"Giuseppina," She announces as she stares out of the fog-covered window.

"That's.." I pause. " A lot of syllables." I blink.

Her laugh finally escapes, it's soft and unguarded. "Tell me about it. It was my Nonno's name." She reaches up to play with her gold crescent moon necklace, which I've never seen her without.

"Giuseppe. My mom swears it was sentimental. I think she just wanted to make sure no one forgot him." She flings her hands in the air again.

"I didn't though, not once. Even though I've never met him." She looks down at her hands lying in her lap. "How could I? He's laced into everything my Nonna did, everything she said, her favorite colors were his, her recipes." She finally looks up at me. "They're all his." She looks back down to her lap, making sure her hair is still tucked behind her ear.

"I like it," I say softly, reaching over to grab her hand and break her free from the sadness that's consuming her. "Can you text it to me, though? There's no way I'll try to spell that alone." I say playfully.

She glances over. "You like everything."

"Not true," I counter. "I don't like pistachio ice cream." Pointing to her now empty bowl.

That earns me another laugh, smaller this time, like it's just for me. Her eyes linger on mine. If I had it my way, she would never stop looking at me like that. Like she has stars in her eyes, and they're all for me.

"You're not supposed to make me like my name," she says softly.

I tilt my head. "Maybe it's not your name I like."

She exhales, half a laugh, half something else. The air between us thickens, not with tension exactly, but something gentler, something real. The space between us is alive and full of all the things we haven't said yet. Her fingers are still under mine, warm, steady, and trembling just enough to give her away. I lift my hand, brushing a loose strand of hair from her cheek. She doesn't look away this time. There's a silent plea in her eyes. Those stormy eyes. My eyes drop to her mouth. Her lips are full, and if my memory serves me correctly, they feel just as soft as they look. Pillows. I lean in, kissing her softly at first. Making sure to savor every moment of this. The taste of pistachio ice cream on her lips.

My new favorite flavor.

Grabbing her by both sides of her cheeks, I deepen the kiss. Craving just a little more of her. Her hands grip my t-shirt. pulling me closer. Her plea isn't so silent now. Pulling her lips back to mine and gently sucking her bottom lip as I let go. Definitely my new favorite flavor.

When I finally pull back, she's still close enough that I can feel her smile against my skin. Her breath ghosts across my lips, warm and unsteady, and I swear it's the only thing keeping me grounded. Her eyes flutter open, pupils wide, lashes still trembling from whatever that was, whatever *we* just were.

"Zane," she whispers, my name caught somewhere between a laugh and a sigh.

I rest my forehead against hers, thumb still tracing the edge of her jaw. "Yeah?"

She doesn't answer. She just breathes, like she's trying to memorize the air between us. The silence that follows is full but not heavy. It hums. Her head tilts, and that shy, half-smile I love pulls at her lips again.

"That was…" she starts, voice quiet, almost shy.

She looks down, brushing her thumb over my sleeve like she's erasing evidence. "Goodnight, Zane."

I let her go, my fingers catching hers for a second longer than they should. "Goodnight, Remilia Giuseppina."

She smiles, and for a second, all is well in the world. The door clicks shut behind her, leaving me alone in the truck with the faint hum of the crickets. I drive slowly. The streets of Copperridge are empty, washed in that hazy glow that only shows up this late, all soft edges and half-light. My hands still smell faintly like her vanilla lotion, and my hoodie carries her shampoo. It's not much, but it feels like proof that tonight actually happened.

The porch light is still on when I pull into the driveway. I see Aunt Cami in her chair, cardigan pulled tight, a half-empty mug beside her, and her face buried in her book of the week.

"You're late," she says as I walk up the steps. "That's new."

"Lost track of time," I admit, running a hand through my hair.

She hums, studying me with that look that sees too much. "You look different."

"Do I?"

"Yeah," she says softly. "Lighter."

I sink into the chair beside hers, letting the wood creak beneath my weight. "Maybe it's just the fog."

"Or maybe," she says, standing to head inside, "it's the girl."

Her words linger in the air long after she's gone.

I stay there a while, watching the fog roll through the yard, the sky opening just enough to show a few stubborn stars. The night's still buzzing with her laugh, the taste of pistachio, and the sound of her name still warm on my tongue.

Home doesn't feel so far away anymore.

Twenty three

(

Remi

This day started like every other day, way too soon. The smell of espresso and fresh biscotti alone is enough to get me out of bed, though. I can hear Mammà's faint singing from upstairs, she swears she doesn't like those new Italian Pop songs, yet she's humming them every chance she gets. I walk into the kitchen, still rubbing the sleep out of my eyes, just in time to see her swaying her hips as she pours the coffee into her mug.

"It's a little early to start our day off with Roma-Bangkok by Baby K Mammà," I announce.

Mammà jumps, almost spilling her espresso on the counter. She grabs her chest dramatically, like she's clutching her pearls. "*Madonna mia,* Remilia! You scared me half to death!"

"Mi dispiace," I say through a grin. Reaching over, grabbing a warm biscotti off the tray, "Next time I'll be sure to cough first."

"You should be more careful sneaking up on a woman before she has had her morning caffeine." Mammà pins me with a glare. "It's dangerous!"

"I live for danger," I say, dunking the biscotti into her mug before she can stop me.

"Hey!" she laughs, snatching it back. "That was my first sip of peace for the day."

"Then it's blessed now," I quip, stealing a second biscotti just in case.

Mammà shakes her head, still smiling. "You're impossible, *ragazza mia.*"

"Heard that before," I shoot back, pinning her with the same look she gave me.

She leans against the counter, that soft smile fading into something gentler. "You're working again today?"

"Morning shift," I say, sliding onto the barstool. "Joss and Maddie promised to come by for moral support… or free pasta. Probably both."

Her expression softens, but she watches me a moment too long—the look only mothers have that says, I'm worried *but I'll let you pretend you're fine.* The moment quickly passes.

"Eat something before you go," she says, pushing a plate in front of me. "You can't keep living on coffee and sarcasm."

"I've gotten this far," I say with a mouthful of toast.

She laughs and turns back to the stove, humming again.

"Save me some of that espresso, Mammà." I stuff another biscotti in my mouth and head up the stairs to get ready for the day.

"I make no promises!" She shouts.

I quickly take a shower, grab another Essence Super Peptide Gloss, stuff it in my bag, and head out the front door. The cool air chills my skin as I step outside. Copperridge is beautiful in the fall. Piles of orange, red, and gold leaves scatter across the sidewalk like confetti. The whole town still smells like fall, cinnamon, and cedar wood. The drive to Nonna's isn't long, but it's enough to wake me up. I sip on the to-go cup of espresso I swiped from Mammà on my way out as I watch the sun fight through fog.

When I reach the square, Nonna's sign is already shining bright, inviting the world in, the chipped gold paint on the window glistening against the morning sun. The bell above the door rings as I walk in, and the familiar scent of espresso hits my nose first. Followed by the pungent smell of burnt bread, ugh, not again.

"Uffa, Papà," I call out, waving my hands in front of my face. "We need to leave the door open for a little while," I call out, propping the door open and fanning the air in front of me.

"That's my fault, Rem. I'm sorry." Rachel calls from behind the counter.

I instantly flinch. I hope I didn't hurt her feelings. She's my parents' favorite manager, they've been trying to teach her every aspect of the business so they can go with me to Italy this summer.

"It's okay, Rae. I'm going to keep the door open until we get customers in here." I give her a tight smile, trying to conceal my concerns.

Papà rounds the corner, wiping his hands on a towel. "Don't be dramatic, Remilia." He says, plastering a smile on his face.

I hate how he insists on using my full name while we're at the restaurant. I mean, anyone can take one look at my pale skin, big eyebrows, and dark hair and know that I'm Italian.

I roll my eyes and grab a tray from the counter. "You know, Papà, one of these days I'm just going to start answering to Rachel, see how you like it."

He smirks. "Then I'll have two Rachels who don't listen."

Rachel snorts from behind the espresso machine. "Hey, I heard that."

"*Appunto,*" he says, grinning as he disappears into the kitchen.

"What does *appunto* mean?" Rachel whispers over the counter.

"It roughly translates to *that's the point.*" I roll my eyes. "He is dramatic today." I scrunch up my nose.

For a few minutes, everything feels normal. Laughter, clinking pans, and the smell of tomatoes simmering in the back. The kind of chaos that feels like home, but as the scent of burnt bread starts to drift from the oven again, that same dull throb crawls up the back of my skull. I blink hard and shake it off. Not now. Not here. I don't have time for another migraine, especially one brought on by overcooked bread.

I force myself not think about it, not feel the pulse behind my eyes. Grabbing a rag from the counter, I pretend to make myself busy by wiping tables. The same dull throb is crawling up the back of my skull. Im trying my best to shield Rachel and my Papà from seeing my face wince in pain. I've got to get some medicine out of the office without him seeing it and making it a thing. The front door jingles. Joss pushes her way inside, her curls wild from the wind. Maddie follows behind her, already on her phone.

"Wow, look at you, Remi, working before noon." Joss sarcastically spits out, pushing her sunglasses onto the top of her head.

I cock my head to the side. "I could say the same thing." She pointed to the coffee cup in her hand. "Buying your own, instead of mooching off mine."

"Baby step." She smirks. "Did Maddie beat me here? We came to torture you for lunch."

"No, not yet." I shook my head and twirled around in a circle to show her that the place is still pretty empty. It was a bad choice on my part, I'm ten times dizzier now.

"Is your dad training someone new? It reeks of charred something in here." Her face turned up in disgust.

"Unfortunately, not." My eyes are going wide, and my eyebrows are lifting.

"Watch it teroso, or you'll be the one making the bread today." Papà pops his head out of the kitchen.

"Don't tempt me with that kind of power." I mumble, barely able to focus on him. *What's wrong with me today?*

"Anyway," I turn back to my best friend, "You can sit anywhere, and I'll see if there's any non-burnt bread in the kitchen." Speaking loud enough that Papà shouts something inaudible from the kitchen.

As Joss takes a seat at our favorite booth right next to the window, customers start piling in, and the smell has almost dissipated. Maddie comes in and gives me a big wave before making her way over to where Joss is sitting. Part of me wants to think they show up to keep me company, the other part, the logical part, knows they'll show up for the free food.

"Hey Madds," I lean into her booth and kiss her on the cheek.

"Hey, Rem, you doing okay? You're pale." Her face is lax, and she's showing real concern.

"Oh," I touch my face. "Uh, yeah," shaking off the oh crap I must look the way I feel, feeling. "Um, I just forgot to put on bronzer today, and with it being fall and all, I've lost my tan." I quickly recover. "But thanks for pointing out that I look like a bad batch of pesto pasta, Madds, way to make a girl feel good about herself." I give her a side eye.

"I'm sorry, Remi, I just notice things." Maddie shrugs her shoulders.

"I know, hun." I give her a soft smile. "What do you girls want to eat?"

"Well," Joss raises her eyebrows. "I wanted the pesto pasta, but now…not so much."

All three of us fall into a fit of laughter, the doorbell jingles, and instantly, I feel like I'm being pulled in the direction of the door. I knew it was Zane before I saw him. A smile tugs at my lips before I can even realize it.

"There's lover boy." Joss lifts her chin towards the door.

"Yeah, there he is," I say, dazed as 'the most beautiful human' walks in.

"So, I guess we will have the vodka rigatoni," Maddie calls out.

"Yeah, of course. Good choice. I'll be back with some bread." Giving them a tight smile, I hurry over to where Zane and his Aunt Cami have been seated.

"Hi Aunt Cami, it's nice to see you again." I lean down to place a kiss on her cheek.

This way of greeting people isn't very American of me, but I was raised by two deeply rooted Italians. Zane watches me with a smirk on his face and a twinkle in his eye. I've never seen that look in his eyes before. What is that? When I give him my full attention, I'm rewarded with a full smile. He pulls his hands out of his hoodie and stands. I can't help but look at him like he's the creator of happiness, because for me, he is just that. He closes the distance between us. Enveloping me in his warmth.

Zane nuzzles his face into my neck and whispers, "Hi, Angel."

I don't know what to do with my hands, so I hold on to his hoodie and let myself breathe him in, cedar and something sweet, familiar in a way that makes my heart ache. *What is that smell? I still haven't figured it out.*

"Flirting with me won't get you free food," I whisper back.

He chuckles softly, the sound rumbling against my skin. "Not doing it for free food, Remi."

Cami clears her throat, teasing. "I can come back later if you two need a minute."

I pull away, my cheeks on fire. "I'm so sorry."

Grinning as she unfolds her napkin. "It's okay, I was young and in love once, too. Now, what's good here, sweetheart?"

My body goes rigid, *in love?* My entire bloodstream becomes jello. No one has ever said 'in love' and 'Remi' in the same beat. I feel Zane sit back down in the booth, but I can't make myself turn to look at him just yet. *In love,* did I hear that right? Snap out of it, Remi.

"Uh, everything," I say automatically. "My personal favorite is the vodka rigatoni. I've basically forced all my friends to love it, too. You should try it." Im word vomiting all over her right now

Cami laughs. "Good to know."

I finally work up enough strength to look over at Zane, and he's not panicking, completely at ease. Resting his arm along the back of the booth, I give him a nervous smile, you know the one where my eyebrows are still shooting towards my hairline. I couldn't have heard her right.

"You good? You look…" he pauses, eyes softening. "Tired."

This again, "Wow, between you and Maddie, I'm really out here winning today," I say, trying to laugh it off.

But his gaze doesn't waver. "Remi."

I exhale and give him a half-smile. "I'm fine. Just a small headache, promise."

He studies me for another second, like he doesn't believe me, but finally nods. "Okay. But you're taking a break later. Doctor's orders."

"Oh, so now you and Papà are doctors?"

"Only when you're being stubborn."

"Which is never," I shoot back.

That earns me the smile I was aiming for. I turn toward the counter to grab their menus, but when I straighten, the lights overhead flicker, or maybe it's my eyes. A quick wave of dizziness rolls through me, gentle at first, then stronger.

I blink it off and paste on another smile. "Um, someone will be back to take your drink order," I say, steadying myself against the counter as I walk away as quickly as I can.

The next wave of noise in the dining room feels too loud. Silverware clinking, laughter bouncing off the walls, the espresso machine hissing like it's angry at me. My pulse thuds behind my right eye, sharp and steady, like a second heartbeat I didn't ask for.

"Hey, Rem, you good?" Rachel asks, balancing two plates on one arm.

"Yeah." My smile's too quick, too practiced. "Just need some air."

I duck through the swinging door before she can say anything else. The kitchen's hotter than the dining room, the smell of garlic and tomato sauce thick in the air, and for a second I think it's helping, until it isn't. The hallway to the back door is blessedly quiet. I shove the handle open and step outside into a breath of cool October air. The door swings shut behind me, muffling everything. For the first time all morning, it's just me, the wind, and the hum of the town. The chill hits my skin instantly, goosebumps crawling up my arms. I lean against the brick wall, close my eyes, and let the air sting my lungs.

Okay. You're fine. You've had worse. Just breathe.

The smell of the kitchen clings to me: tomatoes, basil, something burnt that won't let go. It twists with the crisp air until I can't tell where one ends and the other begins. A pulse flares again behind my right eye, hard enough that I flinch. The world flickers.

"Ugh." I press my fingers against my temple. "Not now."

The pavement shifts beneath my feet, or maybe it's just me. I blink hard, willing the edges of everything to hold still. The world blurs, smearing like wet paint. My knees stop listening to me.

Breathe, ragazza mia. Life slows down when you do.

Nonna's voice floats up from somewhere deep inside my head. She used to say it when I'd rush through everything, homework, cooking, growing up. I almost laugh at the thought of her scolding me now.

"I'm trying, Nonna," I whisper, swallowing hard.

The back door creaks open behind me.

"Remi?" It's Joss. "Hey, what are you doing out here?"

"Just needed a minute," I say, turning toward her. But my voice sounds wrong, slurred at the edges, fuzzy.

Her brow knits. "You don't sound okay?"

"Yeah, I just—"

The air hums. The light shifts. The smell of burnt bread hits again, sharp and sudden, like the air itself is cooking.

"Remi?" Panic floods her voice.

I open my mouth to answer, but everything tilts. The walls, the sky, Joss's face.

And then,

Nothing

Twenty four

((

Zane

Joss screams from the back of the restaurant. My stomach drops before my brain catches up. Remi. Something's wrong. I can't move, my feet are glued to the floor below me. The air in the restaurant feels all wrong, and the whole place is spinning just slightly off balance. Rachel's at the counter, frozen, eyes wide. Joss is kneeling near the back hallway, her mouth is moving, but I can't hear any words.

By the time I reach her, everything slows.

She's on the ground.

Remi.

Her body's still, her hair fanned out against the pavement. There's a smear of flour on her cheek, absurdly normal, like the universe couldn't decide whether to make this moment horrifying or just cruel.

"Hey. Hey, Remi." Skinning my knees as I drop down beside her. My voice sounds too calm, like it's someone else's. "Come on, open your eyes."

Nothing.

"Remilia," I try, because she always pretends to hate it when I use her full name. My thumb brushes her temple. Her skin's clammy. "Please."

Someone's shouting for help. Rachel? Joss? My ears are ringing too loud to tell. Her chest rises, shallow but steady. She's breathing. Thank God, she's breathing.

"Remilia." Nico rounds the corner just as she's waking up. "Zane. What happened to her?"

"I don't know," I say, which feels like a lie even though it isn't.

"Call an ambulance. Now." Nico shouts to anyone who will listen.

Joss runs for the phone. Nico cradles Remi's head in his hands, brushing her hair from her face. I stay on the floor. I can't touch her, can't make sure she's still here. My hand shakes against her wrist, counting heartbeats I can't keep up with.

"Come on, Angel. You're okay. You said you were okay." i plea.

The door opens again. Nico is spewing words I can't understand. Cami's voice cuts through the noise.

"Zane," She looks down at me in pure horror.

"She just" I struggle to get my words out. "Joss said she just dropped," I say between breaths "One second she was fine, and then…"

Cami's already kneeling beside me. She presses two fingers to Remi's neck, nods once. "Her pulse is there. Keep her on her side." She directs her orders to Nico.

Sirens start in the distance, faint, then grow louder. Every second stretches too long. My chest feels tight, like I've forgotten how to breathe right along with her. I brush her hair off her face.

"You don't get to do this. You don't get to leave me." I choke out, fighting back tears.

The sirens are right outside now. Paramedics flood in, voices taking over, questions I can't process. I just stay there until someone's hand lands on my shoulder, gentle, firm.

"It's okay, Zane, they'll take good care of her."

Joss.

The words should mean something. They don't. All I can think of is how she looked at me just a few minutes ago, laughing, rolling her eyes at something dumb I said. How the smell of burnt bread had followed her around all morning.

How I didn't see it coming.

~~~~
~~~~

Hospitals smell like bleach. I've only ever been in a hospital twice, visiting Aunt Cami last year after surgery and a broken femur when I was nine. Never like this, though. I've never been in a hospital with the fear of someone I love not being able to walk back out with me.

I can still smell her vanilla lotion on my shirt; there's flour on the edge of my sleeve. She's still with me. Every time I inhale, she is there. The waiting room is full of vinyl chairs, vending machines, and anxiousness. I can't sit here. Every time I do, my knee starts bouncing uncontrollably, and my hands start to shake. Standing up, shaking my nerves out of my arms, I begin to pace. The paramedics said she was breathing on her own. They said she had a pulse. I hold onto those words like a rope.

Joss and Maddie are here, whispering across from me, their faces pale. Rachel stayed behind to run the restaurant after giving her statement to the EMTs, her eyes glassy with worry. The whole restaurant must've emptied after the ambulance pulled away. Copperridge doesn't do quiet, not until today.

Aunt Cami is sitting beside me, both hands wrapped around a paper cup of coffee she isn't drinking. She's the only one who's calm, at least on the outside.

"She's young," she says softly, like she's reading my thoughts. "Young people bounce back."

All I can manage is a nod, letting her know I heard her. Words can't even form in my throat. The door at the end of the hall opens, and I don't need to look to know who it is. I'd know that voice anywhere. Nico Moretti doesn't just enter a room, he fills it. He stepped out of the room a few minutes after getting a phone call from Elena.

"Have they come out yet?" he asks the room, accent thick with fear. Elena's right behind him, her hand gripping his arm.

Nico doesn't wait for an answer, he moves toward the nurse's station like he's still running the kitchen, all command and fire, until the tremor in his hands betrays him.

"I'm her father. Someone tell me something," his voice breaking.

The nurse looks up, patient but practiced. "The doctor's still with her, sir. They'll come update you soon."

Elena squeezes his arm again, her voice low but steady. "Nico, *basta.*" Enough.

He exhales, folding in on himself, sitting two chairs away from me. His elbows rest on his knees, head in his hands. He looks smaller than I've ever seen him. No one speaks for a long time, just beeping from a nearby monitor, the distant echo of announcements over the intercom, the soft hiss of a coffee machine down the hall.

Maddie finally breaks the silence. "She's strong," she says, her voice barely above a whisper. "That girl's got fight in her."

Elena's head lifts at that, a tiny smile cracking through the worry. "Yeah, she does."

Nico looks over at me then, and for a second, the weight of everything in his eyes hits me like gravity. "Thank you," he says simply. His voice was barely audible. "For staying with her."

I want to tell him I didn't have a choice, that leaving her wasn't an option, but the words stick in my throat. All I can manage is another nod. The door down the hall opens again. Everyone stands at once. The tension in the room is so palpable you could probably cut it with a butter knife. The doctor steps out, clipboard in hand, tired eyes scanning for a place to land.

"She's stable," he says. "Still unconscious, but her vitals are strong. We're keeping her for observation. We're running some scans now to rule out any neurological causes for the fainting."

"Neurological?" Nico repeats. The word catches like a thorn. I close my eyes and try to keep breathing.

The doctor softens his tone. "It could be dehydration, low blood pressure, or something simple. We just want to be sure."

"Can we see her?" Elena asks quickly.

The doctor nods. "Yes, but only immediate family for now."

Nico doesn't wait for permission. He's already halfway down the hall, his wife right behind him. The door swings open, the sound of his voice spilling out before it shuts again, low, cracking under words I can't make out.

The rest of us stay behind in the waiting room, still caught between hope and fear. Joss leans into Maddie's shoulder, her mascara smudged from crying. Aunt Cami's sitting close to me, her fingers tracing the rim of her untouched coffee cup. I can't sit. I keep pacing. One, two, three turns across the same strip of tile. I can feel the weight of every heartbeat in my chest, but none of them feel like they're mine.

Cami finally speaks, her voice quiet but solid. "You can't fix this part, Zane."

"I know," I say, even though I don't. My throat feels like sandpaper.

Minutes pass, or maybe hours. Time doesn't behave right in hospitals. When the door finally opens again, Nico steps out first. His face is drawn, eyes rimmed red, but there's a steadiness there now, something that looks like purpose. Elena's behind him, her hand pressed to her chest, trying to hold herself together.

"She's sleeping." he says, voice rough but clear.

The relief that floods the room feels like air after drowning.

"The doctor says they're keeping her overnight. They found…" His face changes. "Something on the scans." His voice breaks just slightly on that word, *something.*

I freeze. "Something?"

His head hanging low, looking at the same tile I've been pacing back and forth on. He hesitates.

"They don't know what yet. A shadow, he said. Behind her temple." Nico shakes his head, as if he can shake the image away. "They'll run more tests tomorrow."

Elena sinks into the chair nearest the wall, pressing the heels of her hands to her eyes. Nico stays standing, motionless. No one speaks. The only sound is the humming in the corner and the faint monitor beep echoing from somewhere down the hall.

"Go," Nico says finally, looking at me. "She'll want to know you're here when she wakes up."

I nod, but it doesn't feel like enough. When I reach her room, the door's halfway open. The steady rhythm of the monitors draws me in. She's pale against the white sheets, her hair fanned across the pillow, IV lines tracing down her arm like fragile threads. I sit beside her and take her hand, rubbing my thumb over the inside of her wrist, the same spot I used to trace when she was nervous.

"Hey, Angel," I whisper. "You've got the whole town pacing out there. You'd better wake up soon before your Papà works himself into a hospital bed next to you." The words break halfway out of me, but I keep going. "You're okay. You have to be okay." I'm fighting back tears. "You said you were okay."

I lower my head, resting it beside her hand. Trying to hide the fact that I'm wiping the moisture from my eyes, even though she's not awake to see it. Monitors beeping in the background become my focal point, keeping me from breaking down.

Hours pass by, and the doctors come in to move her to a regular room. We're all here, waiting for her to wake up. Well, most of us. Elena and Nico are in the hall, arguing about which one of them would go back to run the restaurant before the dinner rush comes. Joss and I make eye contact before I look back at the door. She's doing her best to be brave, but her lip keeps trembling, letting her fear show itself.

"Maddie can't, but I'm going to the restaurant. To uh… help. Maybe let them stay here with her a little longer before.. " Her voice trails off, her eyes fixed on the floor.

"Yeah." Still rubbing circles on Remi's hand. "They should be here when she wakes up. I'll come with you."

Remi's hand feels too cool on my palm. Her pulse is nice and strong, though. The beeping on the monitor is the only thing keeping me from crawling out of my own skin.

"I'll drive," I say, looking up at Joss. "Just give me another minute." I turn back to Remi, moving her hair behind her ear. Taking my time stroking her hair, wishing she were awake so I could tell her how important she is to me. To tell her I love her.

I've always been quiet, never regretted that in my life. Now. Now I do. Now I wish I had told her on the Ferris wheel how I felt about her. Those three little words that scare us all so much. Love is such a strange thing. They say love is supposed to make you whole, but maybe it's there to show you the missing pieces. Before her, I didn't know something could feel this necessary. Now it's like my life only makes sense if she's breathing in it.

I lean down to place a kiss on her cheek. "I'll be back for you, Angel. I love you. Please be okay."

I look at her hand, pale against the white sheet, and I realize love is this. It's waiting beside someone who can't answer you. Loving them anyway.

"Okay," I whisper, brushing my thumb across her knuckles. "You win. I'll go."

The words barely make it out. My throat feels like glass. I stand, but it takes everything in me to let go of her hand. It's like peeling my heart off my sleeve, finger by finger. Cami watches from the doorway, her expression soft, knowing. She doesn't say anything, just gives a small nod, the kind that means *I understand.*

When I pull away, her lashes flicker, just barely. A tiny movement, maybe nothing at all, I will take it. I let it carry me out of that room before I shatter. The hallway feels colder now, louder. Joss is waiting by the elevators, twisting her hands together. She doesn't say anything when I walk up, she just nods.

"Ready?" she asks.

"No," my words come out more clipped than I intended.

"I told Nico and Elena what we were doing. Nico says, " *Make sure you stay away from the pizza figilo,*" trying her best to sound amused.

A smile threatens to break its way past my lips. Threatens.

We head toward the exit, side by side. My stride is more sluggish than usual. The automatic doors slide open, spilling the smell of rain and asphalt into the sterile air. I turn once, catching one last glimpse of her through the small window in the door. I swallowed the lump in my throat. I should be with her.

"She's going to wake up," Joss says quietly, like she can hear the thought I don't have the strength to say.

"Yeah," I manage. "She has to."

The drive back feels endless, even though it's only a few miles. The world outside is washed in gray, rain streaking down the windshield in uneven lines. The wipers drag across the glass, squeaking every few seconds like a heartbeat that doesn't know how to keep time. The outside world reflects what I feel on the inside. How poetic. Joss hasn't said much since we left the hospital. She sits at an angle toward the window, watching the road blur by. The soft glow of the dashboard light paints her face in a tired amber. Her deep inhale and exhale are the only things audible.

"You don't have to keep driving circles around your thoughts, you know," she says finally, voice low.

I let out a half-laugh that sounds more like a choke. "Feels better than stopping."

"You can't will her to feel better." Joss pushes out

I grip the steering wheel tighter. "Yeah, well, tell that to my head. It doesn't seem to care."

The silence stretches between us, heavy but familiar. I pull into the parking lot behind Nonna's, the rain tapping against the roof like a thousand tiny reminders that the world's still turning, even if mine stopped six hours ago. I kill the engine, but I don't move. My hands stay on the wheel. My chest won't expand right. Joss has been quiet since we left the hospital. She's staring out the window, arms crossed, her reflection flickering in and out of the streetlights.

"I don't know how people do this," I say finally, my voice rough, quiet. "The waiting. Sitting in a room full of noise and not being able to do a thing." I run my fingers through my hair and drop them back to the steering wheel.

She doesn't answer right away. Just let the words hang there.

"I've never done this before," I continue, staring at the rain. "I've never… loved. I've definitely never loved somebody enough to be scared like this." The words catch on the way out. "And I hate it. I hate that all I can do is wait for someone to tell me she's okay."

Joss turns toward me, her voice low. "It's the worst part," she says. "The waiting feels heavier than the truth sometimes." Something in her face tells me this feels hauntingly familiar to her.

I let out a shaky laugh. "Yeah. It's like I finally found something that makes me feel alive, and now I'm terrified it's going to be taken away before I even understand what it is." My hand presses against my chest as I can physically hold the ache in. "It's not supposed to feel like this."

Joss looks at me, really looks at me. "It is," she says softly. "That's what love does. It makes you care so much it feels like it's breaking you in half."

I shake my head, blinking hard. "I just need her to wake up. I don't even care what she says when she does. She can tell me I'm too much, make fun of me for freaking out, I just …I need her to wake up."

The cab goes silent again, except for the hum of the heater and the rain against the roof. Joss reaches across the console, resting her hand on my arm. It's grounding, comforting.

"She will," she says. "Remi's too stubborn not to."

That's the truth.

Nonna's is mostly quiet, the kind of quiet that haunts you. The kind that gives space for the heaviness of something after it happens.

Rachel shouts orders at Joss and me, simple things like, "Dishes," "Roll silverware," "Bus tables," "Seat them at seven," "Take this to twelve," and my personal favorite, "Snap out of it and get moving."

I try. God, I try. Every sound in this place is wrong without her. The clatter of plates, the hiss of the espresso machine, it all sounds hollow, like the soul's been scraped out of it. Joss catches me zoning out more than once. She doesn't say anything, just hands me a towel or points me toward another table. We move around each other in a kind of half-silence, both pretending we're okay enough to function. It's muscle memory, that's all this is, even though I've never done this before. Wipe, stack, nod, breathe. Repeat.

My phone buzzes on the counter, but I ignore it at first. Rachel's already barking something about refilling the waters. The second buzz comes five seconds later. Then a third.

I glance down.

St. Mary's Hospital.

The whole room goes quiet in my head. Everything stops.

"Zane?" Joss's voice cuts through the static.

I answer, my voice shaking. "Hello?" Looking to Joss for an emotional grounding, I force down a lump in my throat.

"Is this Zane Carter?" A nurse's voice. Calm. Gentle. Professional.

"Yes." I say panicked.

"This is St. Mary's. I'm calling to let you know that Remilia Moretti is awake."

For a moment, the floor tilts. The sound in the restaurant fades. My breath catches halfway in and won't go anywhere. I hang up the phone, quickly throw it into my pocket, and strip myself of the apron tied around my hips.

"Zane?" Joss says again, this time softer.

"She's awake." The words quietly break out of me, shaking. "She's *awake.*"

Rachel gasps from behind the counter. Joss covers her mouth with her hands, her eyes glassing over.

"Go," she says, but I'm already running towards the back door. I'm leaving, I'm going to see my Polaris, my angel, my home.

I don't even grab my jacket. Thankfully, I put my keys in my pocket, slamming the door on my truck shut. I throw it in reverse and back out of Nonna's. The speed limit is just a suggestion at this point. Every red light feels like a personal attack, every turn too sharp, every second too long. The road's still slick from last night's rain, streetlights glinting off the puddles like broken glass. My hands won't stop shaking, so I grip the wheel harder until my knuckles turn white.

"She's awake." I keep saying it out loud like it's a prayer that might stop being true if I don't keep repeating it.

Panic sets in as I pull into the hospital lot, my chest's tight, and my throat burns, but I've never felt more alive. The automatic doors can't slide open quickly enough, and the smell of bleach hits me instantly. The same nurse from before looks up at the front desk, her eyes soft with recognition. She doesn't ask for my name. I don't need to. She just points down the hall. "Room 203."

"Thank you," I breathe, already halfway there.

The hallways blur together, white walls, shiny tiled floors, that faint hum of machines and muffled voices behind every closed door. My heart's hammering so loud I can barely hear anything else. When I reach her room, the door is cracked open just enough. I try to steady my heart and my breathing before I reach for the door and push it all the way open.

There she is.

Remi.

She's sitting up slightly, her hair braided to the side, the pale morning light spilling through the window and painting her in gold. Her Mammà's hand rests gently on her shoulder. Nico stands on the opposite side of the bed, his head bowed, eyes glassy but proud. Just then, she looks up, like she feels me before she sees me.

Our eyes meet. Everything in me stops, my lungs won't work, my feet won't move closer.

"Hey," I manage, voice strained, trembling.

She blinks, the faintest smile tugging at her lips. "Z," she pushes out.

My chest collapses in on itself. Relief, disbelief, joy. It all hits at once, a tidal wave I can't contain. My hands drop to my knees as I try to steady myself. I'm bent at the waist, and I'm fighting back the moisture pooling in my eyes.

"Yeah," I breathe out, a laugh, the tears spilling over. "Yeah, it's me." I stand, trying to appear stronger than I'm feeling.

Nico steps back, giving me a nod and a look that says, *Go ahead.* Elena squeezes her daughter's hand, then moves to her husband's side. I cross the room in two steps and take her hand, pressing it against my chest like I have to prove I'm real.

"You scared the hell out of me, Remi," I whisper, my voice barely holding steady.

Her smile grows just enough. "You worry too much."

"Yeah, well," I exhale, my forehead dropping gently to hers. "When you find everything you've ever wanted lying on the cold cement, worry is about the only emotion to have." Our eyes locked, neither of us wanting to be the one to break the connection.

"We are going to call the restaurant," Nico announces

"And get some horrible hospital coffee," Elena adds, her voice low.

They exit without a word. Remi and I are still suspended in time, eyes roaming each other, searching. I finally blink and exhale. Pushing out the air I think I've been holding since Joss yelled for help. My breath is shaky, unstable.

"Sit with me?" she quietly asks.

I open my eyes at the same time she scoots over in her hospital bed. She lets go of my hand and pats the spot next to her. Of course, I oblige. Kicking my shoes off one by one, I can feel her eyes on me. I climb onto the extremely small hospital bed and lay my head on her shoulder. Her warmth invades me in the best way.

"You really scared me, Rem." I push out.

"You've already said that." She says with a laugh.

"Yeah, and I'm probably going to keep saying it." I grab her hand, lacing my fingers with hers. I begin running my thumb up and down the length of hers.

Her head turns slightly on the pillow so she can look at me. "How long was I out?"

"Too long." I try to make it sound like a joke, but it cracks halfway through.   Her eyes soften. "You stayed?"

"Yeah, I'm always going to stay. I went to the restaurant for a bit to help, but I'll always stay."

That earns me a small smile. "Zane Carter, you care about me?"

I laugh quietly, but it catches in my throat. Turning to look her in the eyes, "Caring is too small a word for what this is, Remi."

Her head turns to face mine fully. "Then what is it?" She whispers.

I take a second before answering, my eyes searching hers. I want to tell her the three little words, but she's lying in a hospital bed. She studies me, the humor behind her eyes turning into something softer.

"It's not that I don't know what this is," I say quietly. "I do." I swallow down the nerves. "I just don't know how to say it out loud, not here."

Her smile fades into something gentler, uncertain. "Zane..."

I lean in a little closer, our hands still tangled. "You feel it too, Remilia. Don't pretend you don't." It's not a challenge, not really, just a dare wrapped in a whisper, an invitation to admit what's already living between us.

Her breath catches, and for a heartbeat, neither of us moves. The monitor beeps, the world narrows, and she whispers back, "Yeah." She leans in, resting her forehead on mine. "I do."

Something in me loosens. The fear, the waiting, the not knowing, all fade under the quiet truth of her voice.

"Good," I whisper, brushing my thumb over her knuckles. "Then I'm not crazy."

She pushes out a forced laugh, soft and tired, her eyes fluttering closed. "Not completely."

Within minutes, her breathing evens out, slow and steady. I shift just enough to let her rest against my shoulder. The monitors beep all around us, but there's nowhere else I'd rather be. My own heart rate slows, and the tightness that has been in my chest since she collapsed is loosening its grip.

I press a kiss to the top of her head. "Sleep, Angel," I murmur. "I'll be right here."

I stay that way, still as the dawn light creeping through the blinds, holding her hand like it's the only promise I know how to keep.

Twenty Five

☾

Remi

The living room smells like espresso and worry. Mammà's been on the phone with relatives all morning, switching between Italian and English so fast it makes my head spin. Papà is pretending to read the paper but hasn't turned a page in an hour. I'm stuck on the couch under enough blankets to smother a small army. A heating pad warms my lap. Joss and Maddie flank me like hired guards. Every time I move, someone flinches.

"I can walk to the kitchen, you know," I say.

"Nope." Joss doesn't look up from her phone. "Doctor's orders. Couch potato mode activated."

"Pretty sure the doctor didn't specify the potato." My eyes roll, and I'm quickly reminded why I'm here… that hurts.

"Close enough," Maddie says, flipping through TV channels until she finds an old rom-com. "You get romance, carbs, and supervision."

From the kitchen, Mammà calls, "Remilia, are you comfortable? Do you need another pillow?"

Sighing, "I'm good!" I yell back.

Zane's sitting on the floor near the coffee table, cross-legged, sketching absently on a napkin. He hasn't said much all day, just keeps glancing over like he's afraid I'll disappear if he blinks too long.

"Couch life suits you," he says finally, not looking up from his napkin.

"Yeah? Maybe I'll make it a lifestyle." My words are dripping with sarcasm.

From the side of his face, I can see that he smiles, but it doesn't reach his eyes. The TV plays softly, the signature smell of the Morettis drifting in from the kitchen, comfort scents, familiar ones, but the air feels stretched too tight. Everyone's trying too hard to act normal. Then the knock comes. Two short raps on the front door, quick and polite.

Papà answers. A nurse from the hospital stands there, clipboard in hand. Her smile is kind but careful. This is what happens when Nico Moretti calls in every favor he has, his daughter goes home to rest, and the results show up at his doorstep. The nurse is holding out a phone, the doctor said he needed to consult with a group of doctors to explain what the 'shadow' was on my MRI. That information alone sent Papà into a quiet spiral. The nurse approaches me and begins checking my vitals. Since when has the hospital been doing house calls?

"Mr. Moretti, I have Dr. Lane on the line with results from Remilia's MRI."

Everything in the room freezes.

Even the movie laughs fall silent.

Papà takes the phone and presses it to his ear. "Sì, Doctor."

Mammà races to his side and presses her ear to the other side of the phone. The conversation is brief, too brief, and when he hands the phone to Mamà, his knuckles are white. She listens, nodding slowly, murmuring a soft 'Thank you' before hanging up. The pause that follows is unbearable. Mammà and Papà stare at each other silently, neither of them speaking, neither of them moving. When the moment passes, she hands the phone back to the nurse standing in the doorway and gives her a quiet nod. The nurse gives her a forced smile and shows her out, making sure not to make eye contact with anyone else while she exits.

"Mammà?" I ask. My voice sounds small, far away.

She sits in front of me, takes my hand. "They found something, tesoro." Her accent thickens. "A growth. But the doctor said it can be removed." Her eyes fill with moisture.

The word *removed* should feel like relief. It doesn't. It hangs in the air like fog. Zane's sketch drops to the floor, and his head sinks. Maddie reaches for my other hand. Joss mutters a curse under her breath. The entire room stops breathing.

Papà clears his throat, too loudly. "We will listen to the doctors, sì?" He pauses, trying to compose himself. "They said it is operable."

I nod because everyone's looking at me, everyone except Zane. "Okay," I whisper.

All I can think is something in my head doesn't belong to me anymore. The world moves around me. Maddie changes the channel for what feels like the fortieth time, Joss brings down books and cozies up, asking questions and pretending to care. Zane hasn't moved from the floor.

After dinner, everyone drifts back into the living room. Papà insists on feeding us like it's Sunday dinner instead of crisis night: pizza, salad, enough bread to line the street. Now the plates are stacked in the sink, the lights are dimmed, and the movie marathon has become background noise. Joss is sprawled on the rug, Maddie curled up on the loveseat, both half asleep. Mammà knits on the other side of the loveseat, her needles clicking softly, and Papà has fallen asleep sitting upright in the recliner, glasses tilted on his nose.

Zane never took his spot back on the floor. He's on the ottoman beside me now, elbows on his knees, his eyes fixed on the glow from the TV but not really watching. Every once in a while, he glances my way, like he's counting my breaths. I wait for him to look over again, and I motion for him to come sit with me on the couch.

"Everyone's acting like I'm made of glass," I whisper.

"You're not," he says, quiet but firm. His eyes are full of something I can't quite put my finger on.

"Then why are you staring at me as if I might shatter?" I can feel the burn behind my eyes.

He exhales, running a hand through his hair. Closing his eyes, he confesses, "because it feels as if I look away, something could happen."

"Nothing's going to happen, Zane." I'm not sure who I'm trying to convince, him or me.

He looks down, hands clasped. "You don't know that."

The words land heavily between us. The movie keeps playing, but it's just noise now. I reach for his hand and lace our fingers together. His thumb traces the inside of my wrist, a nervous rhythm that feels like a heartbeat.

"The doctor said it's small," I remind him. "They can get it out. It's not forever."

He nods, but his jaw tightens. "They also said the surgery's near your temporal lobe. That's memory, Remi." His voice cracks slightly on my name, his eyes glistening, "What if..." He stops himself, shaking his head. "What if you wake up and you don't remember me?" He looks heartbroken, shattered.

The room fades, the ticking clock, the soft breathing of everyone else. It's just us. I'd be lying if I didn't think of that already. Losing him would be like losing a piece of myself. The world would have less color and seem less appetizing.

I squeeze his hand. "I couldn't forget you." My eyes started to gloss over, matching his.

He lets out a shaky laugh that sounds more like a breath breaking. "You say that now," he whispers. "But what if the part of you that remembers me isn't there anymore?" I lean into him, settling myself under his arm, my head lying on his chest.

I shake my head, the words catching in my throat. "Then I'll find you again."

He blinks, and for a second, all the air in the room disappears.

"How?" Defeat is the underlying tone of his words. He lays his head back until he reaches the back of the couch.

"By instinct," I whisper. "The same way I always do. You could put me in a room full of people, and I'd still find you, Zane." I lift my head to look at him, his head lifting to do the same. "I always find you, you say I'm the gravity." I pause, shaking my head gently. "But you've got it all wrong, babe, it's you." I look back up at him, seeing the terror in his golden honey eyes. "It's always been you, pulling me towards wherever you are."

His eyes close like he's trying to breathe that in. When he opens them again, the fear hasn't left, but there's something steadier underneath it now. At what point did it change for me? When did the line between trying not to care and falling for him blur so quietly that I didn't see it happen? Looking at him now, I see it so clearly.

"Say my name again," he says softly.

"Zane," I breathe out, my thumb brushing against his cheek.

He leans forward, just enough that his chin rests against my forehead. His voice trembles against my skin. "I don't ever want to be a stranger to you, Remilia."

"You won't," I promise, my voice breaking. "I'll remember the way you make me feel, even if I forget everything else."

For a long time, neither of us says anything. The only sounds are the hum of the heater and the steady rhythm of our breathing, syncing in the dark. He kisses my head, and when he finally pulls back, his eyes are red-rimmed but calm, like he's made peace with something I haven't yet. He moves my hand to his forehead, his eyes closing. I can't tell what he is thinking, but I'm hoping he can match my optimism. He pulls my hand back down to his mouth and whispers something inaudible into the back of my hand before pressing a kiss to my knuckles.

I think Mammà senses the thickness in the air because her movement catches in the corner of my eye. When I give her my full attention, I notice she has put down her knitting needles.

"You okay Mammà?" I hear myself ask.

"Okay, enough sad faces! This is not a funeral, it's a random Sunday."

She leaves the room and then reappears with a box in her hands, dusted off from the top of a cabinet.

"Board games," she declares, holding it up like she's solved world peace. "This is what we need, a bit of fun."

Zane lifts a brow. "Board games?"

"Si! When things feel heavy, we play. It's the Moretti rule." She sets the box on the table with a dramatic thud.

"Papà!" She claps her hands and announces. "Come, we are making teams!" Loud enough to wake the neighbors.

Papà groans from the recliner. "Elena, *per l'amore di Dio*, not Uno again."

"Yes, Uno again!" she fires back, already shuffling the cards with frightening speed.

Maddie stirs from the couch, rubbing her eyes. "What year is it?"

"Doesn't matter," Joss says, sitting up. "I heard games. I'm in."

Within minutes, the living room is alive again, blankets pushed aside, pillows on the floor, bowls of half-melted ice cream abandoned for stacks of cards. Papà ends up dealing even though he swore he wouldn't, Zane sits cross-legged next to me, pretending not to strategize, and Mammà keeps threatening to "reverse" anyone who looks too confident.

Joss is the first to get loud. "You definitely peeked!" She accuses Zane.

"I did not," he says, grinning. "You're just bad at math."

"You don't need math for Uno!" she yells, laughing so hard she snorts.

Maddie leans against the arm of the couch, shaking her head. "This is chaos."

I smile into my cards. "This is normal." I needed something normal, something to not make me feel like a sick girl.

The laughter grows until it fills every corner of the room, drowning out the sterile hospital words that still hang between us. For the first time all day, my chest doesn't feel so heavy. The pain in my head is still there, but quieter somehow, like it's lost in the noise of all this life around me.

Zane catches me looking at him and mouths, "*What?*"

"Nothing," I whisper back, a tiny grin forming. "Just glad you're bad at Uno."

He smirks. "I'm letting you win."

"Sure you are," I shoot back.

Papà pretends to clutch his chest. "She's flirting *and* playing cards? *Madonna mia.*"

"Papà!" I groan, hiding my face behind my cards.

Zane just laughs, that full, real laugh that reaches all the way to his eyes. I stare at him through my slightly embarrassed eyes, and I can't help but commit his laugh to memory. It's quite literally the most beautiful and comforting sound I've ever heard. It's not the first time I've heard it, though, it's Eli who makes him laugh.

For a little while, there's no fear, no hospitals, no surgery, just us, a messy living room, and the kind of love that sounds like laughter. The end of the game comes, and the coffee table looks like it survived a natural disaster, cards everywhere, half-eaten cookies, spoons sticking out of bowls like little flags of surrender. Mammà's laughing into her hand, Papà pretending to be mad about losing, and Joss is still accusing everyone of cheating.

"Okay," I mumble through a yawn, "new rule. The winner gets to pick the movie."

Zane raises an eyebrow. "You just made that up because you won."

"Exactly," I smirk, leaning back against the couch. "Now hush, or I'll revoke your popcorn privileges."

The TV flickers to life, bathing the room in a soft gold light. The others slowly fade, Maddie curls up on the floor with a blanket, Joss steals one of Papà's throw pillows, and Mammà dozes off mid-sentence against his shoulder. The volume of the world turns low and steady. Somewhere between the second act and my fifth yawn, I feel Zane shift beside me. I look up, eyes heavy, and meet his smile.

"Come here," he whispers.

I don't argue. He stretches his legs out on the couch, and I let my head fall into his lap. I'm immediately wrapped in his scent, and I'm tired of not knowing what the sweet smell is and why it pairs so well with his cedar and rain scent.

"What is that?" I sheepishly mumble. "The sweet scent. You always smell like cedar and something sweet. What is it?"

"Pear." He smiles down at me, stroking my hair away from his face.

His fingers were tracing slow, easy circles against my scalp. The rhythm's soft enough to make my eyes fall closed, but I fight it for a few seconds longer, just to memorize the sound of his breathing and the warmth in his chest when he laughs quietly at whatever's still playing on the TV.

"Hey, Remi," he murmurs after a while, voice barely there.

"Hmm?" I whisper, already halfway asleep.

"You better be dreaming about beating me at Uno."

Twenty six

☾

Remi

Morning comes too soon. The house smells like coffee and lemon cleaner, a cruel reminder that life keeps moving no matter how much you want it to pause. The laughter from last night feels impossibly distant, already slipping through my fingers, and the silence now is thick, pressing on my chest. The hospital bag sits by the door, packed, zipped, ready, a silent threat I can't ignore.

I hate it. It looks like it's waiting to rip a piece of my heart away, no matter how tightly I hold on.

"Eat something," Mammà says softly, sliding a plate of toast in front of me.

"Can't. Not supposed to eat before surgery, remember?" My eyebrows shot upwards in a fit of sarcasm.

Across the kitchen, Papà's pretending to scroll through his phone, but his eyes flick up every few seconds, checking to see if I'll fall apart. I don't give him that satisfaction. I've only seen this type of worry knitted between his brows once before, when my Nonna got sick.

"Nonna would be proud of you," Mammà says, reaching over to smooth my hair behind my ear. "She'd say you're strong."

"Yeah," I whisper, swallowing around the lump in my throat. "She'd probably also say I should've listened to her and eaten more vegetables."

That earns a laugh, but it dies quickly.

Papà sets his phone down, his voice breaking the air between us. "They said it's a small mass, Remi. They'll take it out, and you'll be fine."

"I know." I nod, lying through my teeth. "Totally fine."

When they both look away, my eyes sting. Someone cutting into your brain is totally fine, right? My fingers tap against the table, too fast, too nervous. I can't stop picturing the white walls, the smell of disinfectant, the bright light overhead. Being alone and scared, lying on an operating table.

The what-ifs that keep circling like vultures. What if I don't wake up? What if I do and I'm not... me? As soon as Papà finishes his juice, he packs us all up in the car. Joss, Maddie, and Zane are supposed to meet us there before I go back for surgery. Giving us a little time to get settled. I try to push the nerves down as we pass through town. I try not to think of all the great memories I've had here over the last six months, but I can't. Flashes of Zane and me come into my mind when we pass the square. The ferris wheel, running in the rain to find shelter at Nonna's, or when I caught him being a perfect human, helping an old widow load things into her car.

I shake my head and pull out my phone. Going over all the pictures we've taken together over the last few months. A smile sneaks onto my face as I swipe. I see Papà staring at me from the rear view mirror, and instantly my cheeks heat like I've been caught.

"There's lots of time left for love teroso." It's like he can hear my thoughts, nodding. "Lots of time," Papà shoots me a reassuring smile.

You would think hospitals should feel warm and welcoming. Not cold and dead. Everything in this room screams *someone died here,* but I push that to the back of my mind. The doctors are here, yes, I said doctors, talking to Mammà and Papà about the ins and outs of the procedure while I pick nervously at the frilly pink blanket I brought with me.

When the doctor finally leaves, and it's just us three, and I finally crack.

"Papà," I look up at him with glassy eyes. "What if I'm not me when I wake up? What if I forget everything? What if I don't know who I am? What if I can't talk, if I'm trapped in my own brain?" Frantically wiping fallen tears off my cheek.

"Oh, Teroso," he rubs my back. "That's not going to happen. The doctors seem very confident in their ability to get the mass out." His tone was low, comforting.

"What if they change their minds when they're in there? What if it's bigger than they thought?" I spit out, trying to control my breathing. "Im finally at a place where I can breathe again after Nonna. I'm finally okay. I don't want to do this. I changed my mind." I say, looking up at Mammà. "Take me home, Mammà, please." A sob breaks free from my chest.

"Oh, Remi." She grabs my head and nuzzles me into her chest while stroking my hair.

Zane

I'm early. I went home. Showered, packed a bag, and put it in my car just in case I was lucky enough to stay overnight with her after surgery. The hospital smells like what I would imagine anxiety smells like today. I stare at the shiny floor and count the lights hanging overhead while I make my way to the neurology wing. Hands stuffed deep into my jean pockets, my shoulders stiff with tension.

"What room is Remi Moretti in?" I ask the nurse at the desk.

"Six twenty-nine." She says to me without looking up from her screen.

I turn down the hall and see doctors coming out of the room Remi should be in. *Why are there so many doctors?* I think to myself as I quicken my steps, needing to be close to her. One, two, three lights until I'm outside her room. The door is cracked, and I hesitate. Hearing her cry to her parents about waking up from surgery and being trapped in her own brain, not knowing anyone. She begs them to take her home, to let her live with the mass in her brain.

"Take me home Mammà, please." Remi.

The sound of her sobbing breaks me. I slide down the wall, my elbows hitting my knees, and my hand finding my hands. I press the heels of my palms into my eyes, like maybe if I block everything out, the sound of her crying won't hit as hard. It doesn't work. Every cry she lets out feels like it belongs to me, too. I've never been good at praying, but right now, I don't know what else to do. Please.

I drag my hands down my face, the fluorescent lights buzzing overhead, cold against the sterile white walls. There's a nurse pushing a cart past me; she gives me that tight, practiced smile, the one they reserve for people sitting on the floor outside hospital rooms. The ones who've run out of ways to pretend they're fine. I stare at the space under the door where the light spills through, thinking that if I stare long enough, maybe I can see her shadow move. Maybe she'll laugh. Maybe she'll say my name. Anything.

"Zane?" Cami's voice pulls me back. I didn't even hear her coming down the hall.

She crouches down in front of me, resting a hand on my arm. "Hey. You can't sit here like this."

I shake my head. "I can't go in there either." My voice cracks on the last word, tears streaming down my face. "She's crying, I can't hear that, how am I supposed to comfort her when she's scared?"

Her eyes soften. "You love her."

It's not a question.

She doesn't try to fix it. She just sits there with me. Silent. Present. After a minute, the crying from the room fades into quieter voices. Her parents are talking softly, and the doctors are murmuring.

Cami stands, brushing off her knees. "They're moving her soon. Go get some air before they see you like this."

I push myself off the wall, my legs weak but working. "Yeah," I whisper, more to myself than her.

I walk until the hallway ends, until I find the nearest exit sign and push through the door. The cold air hits my face hard, but I welcome it. The parking lot glows in the orange wash of morning light. I lean against the brick wall, press my hands into my hair, and finally let it happen. The kind of cry that comes from somewhere you didn't know existed. The kind that doesn't sound like crying at all, more like something breaking open. I stay like that until I can breathe again. Until my chest stops aching enough to stand upright.

Joss and Maddie are standing near the door. They are both wearing oversized hoodies and holding coffees. Typical. When they see me, Joss gives me a nod and a tight smile, and Maddie looks back at her book.

"They should be taking her back soon," Joss whispers.

I keep walking, a nod is the only thing I can offer her for telling me. I round the corner of the room and see my angel. She looks calmer, her eyes are closed, and her head is resting on the pillow behind her. The lines in her forehead have smoothed out. Her brave face back as if she wasn't begging to go home twenty minutes ago.

"Teroso, your ragazzo just walked in," Nico announces, patting me on the shoulder as I pass him.

"I don't speak Italian, but I'm pretty sure he just said, ' *Honey, your devastatingly handsome boyfriend just showed up.*" I raise my hands and shrug my shoulders. Doing my best to conceal my true feelings.

"The only thing you got right was *your* figlio, and that was in English." Nico laughs.

"You came." Remi looks up at me, wearing a brave face. All fear and emotion I heard earlier is gone.

"Yeah," I manage. "I'll always come back." Reassuring her. I lean down and press a kiss to her cheek.

That earns me a tiny smile. I take it. The nurse wheels in a small tray of folded hospital gear, grippy socks, a hairnet, the works.

Remi picks up the socks between her fingers and laughs softly. "So this is it, huh? My big fashion debut."

Maddie groans, leaning against the wall. "You're lucky you can still make jokes. I'd be demanding Prada scrubs."

Nico chuckles, though his voice wavers. "We'll make sure to let the surgeon know, sì?"

Even Elena smiles through her worry, brushing Remi's hair out of her face, her hand trembling just enough for me to notice. The nurse starts checking boxes, explaining things we can't really hear. Time feels weird now, too fast, too slow, all at once. I just keep my hand resting on the edge of her blanket, grounding myself in the warmth coming through it.

When the nurse says, "It's time," everything in the room seems to still.

Maddie wipes her eyes. Joss mutters something about not crying, but she's crying anyway.

Elena leans in first, kissing Remi's forehead. "Ti amo, tesoro."

Papà follows, whispering something I can't hear.

Remi looks up at me, grinning nervously. "Guess this is it."

"Yeah," I whisper. "For what it's worth, I like the socks." A smirk tugs at my lips.

She rolls her eyes, that spark flickering back for just a second. I push the hairnet down over her hair and smooth it gently into place, pretending like it's something normal couples do before surgery. The nurse unhooks the bed's brakes, and it starts to roll her toward the door.

Remi squeezes my hand, hard. "Zane?"

"Yeah?"

Her eyes find mine, searching. "If I forget—"

"You won't," I cut her off, quick, almost desperate.

She nods once, biting her lip. "Okay."

"See you soon, Polaris," I say quietly.

She smiles, barely, but it's there. "See you soon."

Then she's gone. And all I can do is stand there, staring at the doors as they swing shut, the echo of them closing louder than anything I've ever heard.

Hospitals aren't built for waiting. They're too quiet, too clean. Every sound feels like a clock tick you can't unhear. I've been pacing for what feels like hours, shoes squeaking against the polished floor, tracing the same twenty feet back and forth until I can't anymore. Then I sink down, my back to the wall, head tilted up toward the buzzing fluorescent light.

Maddie's on one of the vinyl chairs, arms wrapped around herself like she's holding in her own nerves. Joss has her knees pulled up, her chin resting on them, eyes red but stubbornly dry.

"You know," Maddie says quietly, voice cracking around the edges, "when we graduate, I want to leave Copperridge. Maybe Boston. Or Greece. Somewhere with noise."

Joss nods, not looking up. "I'll come visit. Somebody's gotta make sure you don't get scammed by a European waiter. That's If Elizabeth and John let you go."

A weak laugh slips out of me before I can stop it. The sound feels foreign. They both glance my way, small smiles that don't reach their eyes.

"What about you, Zane?" Joss asks softly. "What happens after graduation?"

I shake my head, rubbing my hands over my face. "Ask me when she wakes up."

No one says anything after that. The silence stretches again, long and heavy.

The vending machine hums. A nurse walks past. Somewhere down the hall, a phone rings twice and stops. I close my eyes, trying to picture the last time I saw her, awake, smiling, rolling her eyes at me. The way her hand found mine without even looking. Now, the space between my fingers feels empty in a way I didn't know was possible.

"Zane." Joss's voice again, softer this time.

"She's strong. That's gotta count for something."

I nod, my head thudding back against the wall. "It's better."

Maddie stands and crosses the small space between us, crouching down to hand me a paper cup of water. Her eyes flicker to the hallway leading to the OR. "They said it's supposed to be two hours. It's been…" she glances at her phone, "almost three."

The air in my chest tightens. I stare at the clock on the far wall like it's mocking me.

"She's okay," Joss says again, maybe more for herself than me.

"She has to be," I whisper to myself.

We sit there, three kids who've run out of jokes, prayers, and patience. The floor is cold beneath us, the smell of antiseptic thick in the air, the world outside still turning while ours stands still. We sit in silence for another stretch of forever, the kind that makes you count every second in your head. The vending machine is louder than before, or maybe I'm just noticing it now. Maddie's foot bounces against the tile. Joss twists a napkin into knots. I trace a crack in the grout with my shoe. No one says it, but we're all thinking the same thing.

Finally, I break the quiet. "Someone should've brought the Uno cards."

Joss lets out a breath that sounds halfway like a laugh, halfway like a sob. "Yeah," she says. "She'd be mad she wasn't winning right now."

Maddie wipes her eyes. "She'd accuse us all of cheating before we even dealt the cards."

That gets a real laugh out of me, it's short, sharp, and gone too soon. The sound dies when a door creaks open down the hall. All three of us look up as the doctor steps out, mask pulled down, expression unreadable. His eyes sweep the room until they land on Elena and Nico.

"Family of Remilia Moretti?"

I'm already on my feet before the words finish leaving his mouth.

Twenty seven

☾

Zane

"Yeah, that's us," Nico calls out as we all stand. The air is thicker with anticipation. I don't think anyone is breathing, but we're all moving closer to hear what the Dr. has to say.

The doctor nods once. "She's out of surgery. Everything went well, the mass was fully removed." He pauses, studying our faces. "She's in recovery now. She's stable."

The entire room exhales at once. I don't realize how long I've been holding my breath until it comes out all at once. I gasp when the next breath comes in. Joss covers her face, crying quietly. Maddie sinks into her chair, shoulders shaking.

"She's asking for her family," the doctor adds softly. "Parents, you can go in first; the rest of you will have to wait until she's out of the ICU."

"How long will that take?" I hear myself say. Everyone's head bobbing from me to the dr.

"No more than an hour," the Dr nods in my direction and turns his body heading for the room. "Mr. and Mrs. Moretti, you two can follow me."

Elena and Nico take off toward the Dr. Elena stops at the double doors from which the Dr appeared. Her eyes filled with sympathy. "Zane, honey."

My head snaps up. "Yeah."

"Put your number in my phone." She pulls her phone from her pocket. "I'll send you a text to let you know how she is when I lay eyes on her, okay." Elena is rubbing my arm up and down, trying her best to soothe me.

"Yes, ma'am. Thank you." I hand her the phone and watch her disappear down the hallway.

Maddie's voice breaks it first. "Stable." She repeats the word like it's a prayer. "That's good, right? That's what we wanted to hear."

Joss nods, wiping her nose with the back of her hand. "Yeah. Stable is good."

I can't sit. My legs won't let me. I pace the floor, running a hand through my hair until it hurts. The clock ticks so loudly it feels like it's mocking me. Every second she's in there feels like one I'll never get back. I catch a glimpse of my reflection in the vending machine glass, wide eyes, shaking hands, a face I barely recognize. I can't tell if I'm relieved or terrified. Maybe both.

"Elena texted me," I say to the room. "She said Remi is waking up slowly. She's still out of it, but she appears to be fine."

I sink into a chair and bury my head in the palm of my hands. I sit there for what feels like forever until the sound of footsteps breaks through the noise in my head. I look up to see Nico and Elena coming back down the hall. Elena's eyes are red, her lipstick smudged from where she's wiped at her tears. Nico's hand rests on her shoulder, his own expression caught somewhere between joy and heartbreak.

"She's awake," he says.

Everyone stands at once. Chairs scrape, hearts stop again.

"She's asking for Nonna," Elena adds softly, her focus on the floor.

My stomach drops. "Nonna?"

Elena nods, her voice breaking. "She doesn't… remember things correctly. Not yet." Her gaze flickers to me. "I'm sorry, Zane."

The words hit harder than I expected. My throat burns as I try to find something to say, anything that doesn't sound broken. I can hear my heartbeat in my head, and my chest feels like I'm breathing inside a plastic bag. I hear Elena say that the Dr's say she just needs time, her memories should come back with time. I nod, because it's the only thing I can do. My voice wouldn't work even if I wanted it to.

When they walk away, I sink back into the chair, my head in my hands, elbows on my knees. I can still hear her voice in my head. The laugh that could undo me in a heartbeat. The way she said my name was like it was something holy. Now she doesn't even know it.

"Zane, are you coming?" Joss and Maddie stare at me from the doorway.

"Uh," I hesitate. "Is that such a good idea?" I look at Nico and Elena.

"We have told her that her friends are here. We think it should be okay." Nico's head is hung low, his voice apologetic.

My throat is dry, and I can't manage to form a sentence. A nod is all I can manage to give them. I stand, my feet unsure of themselves. Joss and Maddie must see it, because I'm immediately met with one of them on each side of me. Linking their arms with mine.

"It's going to be okay, Zane. She will remember, I know she will." Maddie lays her head on my shoulder as we begin our way down the hall.

My worst nightmare is unfolding right before me. I wasn't even this upset when I realized my parents weren't coming back for me. When I realized it wasn't that they forgot me, it was that they didn't love me enough to stay. I feel like I'm breathing through a pinhole right about now. I can't do this, there's no way I can go in that room and watch the love of my life not know who I am. How can I act like I'm just her friend? The moment I met her, I knew she was more than that.

"I can't do this." It comes out as a whisper. I don't even think Joss or Maddie heard me.

Looking down at my hoodie, I see spots begin forming. Little droplets hit my hoodie. A leak in the ceiling, I think, until I look up to see what it is. There's nothing there.

"Zane.." Joss looks at me with tears in her eyes. Her head snaps to Maddie. "You go in, I'm going to wait until he is ready."

"You sure?" Maddie asks.

The cool floor looks comforting from where I'm standing, my legs still too weak to move. I sit right outside of Remi's door. My knees tucked into my chest, my head finds solace leaning against the wall.

"Yeah, he needs someone too." Joss sits on the floor next to me.

Joss doesn't say anything at first. She just sits there beside me, knees pulled up, her shoulder pressing lightly into mine. For a minute, it's just the sound of the busy hallway, the beeping of the machines, the intercom, the shuffle of nurses' shoes against tile.

Then softly, "You really love her, huh?"

I let out a dry laugh, more air than sound. "Love. It doesn't even cover it."

She nods, like she already knew that. "You know," she says after a beat, "Remi once told me she didn't believe in fate."

That gets my attention. I look over at her. A look on my face that screams *what?*

"Yeah," Joss continues. "Said it was just the universe's excuse for chaos. That everything was random, and we just called it destiny when it worked out." Her lips curve into a sad smile. "But then she met you, and suddenly she started using phrases like 'meant to be."

"She never told me." I drop my head back to the wall.

"Why would she?" She deadpans. "The day she met you, she texted me and asked if we could go wedding dress shopping."

My head snaps to hers, still struggling to speak.

"She met you, and everything changed for her." She trails off, lost in a memory from a different lifetime.

My chest tightens. I press the heels of my palms into my eyes. "I don't know how to be somebody she doesn't know, Joss. I can't just walk in there and introduce myself like it's the first time."

"You don't have to."

I blink, looking at her. "What?"

Joss turns her body towards mine, excitement written all over her face.

"I know how to fix this, Zane. I know what to do." She reassures me.

Her sudden energy cuts through the fog that's been sitting heavy over both of us. I lift my head, confused. "Fix this? Joss, you can't just—"

She shakes her head hard, words tumbling out before I can stop her. "No, listen. You don't understand. There's something…something of hers that might help."

I narrow my eyes, watching her shift from heartbreak to purpose. "What are you talking about, Josselyn?"

"Okay, first of all, rude." She bites her lip, hesitating for the first time. "I can't explain it yet. Not until I talk to her parents."

"Joss." I can hear the desperation creeping into my voice. "I can't do false hope right now." I force out.

"I know. Listen," She cuts me off, eyes glistening, she places her hand on my forearm. "I can fix this. I promise. It's just a major privacy breach. I need permission."

I stare at her, trying to read whatever she's not saying. She looks almost afraid to move, afraid that if she breathes wrong, the idea might slip away.

Her voice softens. "You have to trust me, okay? Just… hold on a little longer. Don't give up on her."

A humorless laugh escapes me. "That's not an option."

Joss nods, her throat bobbing as she swallows whatever emotion she's fighting. Then she stands, brushing the dust from her jeans. "Good. Because I think…No, I *know*, she left herself a way back to you."

Before I can ask what she means, she's already walking down the hall towards the exit, her phone clutched in her hand, determination in every step. I lean my head back against the wall, closing my eyes. For the first time since she forgot me, something that almost feels like hope starts to stir in my chest.

The hallway lights dim sometime after visiting hours end, and the nurses start speaking in whispers. I've lost track of how long I've been sitting here, long enough for the vending machine to go dark, long enough for the coffee in my cup to turn cold. The door to her room is cracked again. I tell myself I'm just going to peek in, just make sure she doesn't need anything.

Elena and Nico are inside, sitting close together in the corner, their heads resting against each other. The glow from the monitors paints their faces in soft blue light. Nico glances up first when he hears me.

"Come in, Zane," he says quietly, voice roughened from too much worry and too little sleep.

"I didn't mean to—"

"You're not interrupting," Elena says gently. "She'd want you here."

I nod once, stepping closer. Every sound in the room seems amplified: the rhythmic beeping, the soft hum of the air vent, the rustle of hospital sheets when she shifts slightly in her sleep. Remi's hair spills across the pillow, a faint crease on her forehead that makes her look younger, smaller. I stop at the edge of the bed, afraid to get too close, afraid to break whatever fragile peace she's managed to find.

Nico stands, placing a hand on my shoulder. "She's strong, figlio. More than she knows. You stay close, sì?"

"Yeah," I whisper, my throat tight.

Elena offers a tired smile. "She'll find her way back."

I nod again, unable to speak. My eyes, already burning, are still locked on Remi. Her fingers twitch slightly, like she's reaching for something even in sleep. I want it to be me.

"I just wanted to make sure you guys," looking over at Elena and Nico, "didn't need anything. I think I should probably go home for a bit."

"We're good figilo, go home. Sleep." He puts a hand on my shoulder, giving me a sympathetic nod.

Then I step out into the hall, the door clicking softly behind me.

My phone buzzes in my pocket.

Joss: Meet me at Nonna's first thing tomorrow. I found it.

Twenty Eight

☾

Zane

This morning, I chose to park in the back of the parking lot. Like the fresh air I'll get can somehow prepare me for what's coming. This hospital is beginning to feel like a prison in some ways. As if breaking her out of here can somehow bring all her memories back. Bring me back to her.

It's sunny out today, and the air has officially turned cold in Copperridge. The birds have sought shelter somewhere warmer. The smell of pine and cinnamon fills the air. Why does this town always smell like cinnamon? I'm carrying two coffees with me this morning, and when I walk in, I know she'll ask where the third is. If she were her.

I round the corner and stop just outside of her room door. Six twenty-nine. I haven't seen her since she woke up. Maybe the universe will be nice to me, and she will have woken up this morning with all of her memories back. Maybe she will remember what love feels like, what I feel like.

"Figlio, come in. My wife is in desperate need of what you're holding in your hands." Nico shouts from inside the room.

That's almost enough for my lips to tug up into a smile, but it falls short. Everything seems to be falling short lately.

"Yes, Sir." I push the door open, careful not to spill the precious cargo I'm holding for Elena.

Elena is the first person I see, she is walking towards me. "Good morning, Zane," She pulls me in for a hug. "Thank you so much for bringing the coffee. The chairs they have in this hospital are terrible." She grabs the coffees from my hand.

Nico gives me a nod from his chair in the corner. Elena takes her seat again next to him and hands the other coffee over to him. Elena texted me this morning, and I thought it would be an update on Remi. No. It was a coffee order, nothing more. This family is extremely reliant on their morning fix.

Nervously, I push my hands to the bottom of my pockets. I can feel her staring at me from my side, but I'm terrified to bring myself to look that way. I swallow. Hard. Then I inhale and turn her way. Her eyes are wide, searching. As soon as our eyes meet, she looks down to her lap, tucking her hair behind her ears. When she looks back up, she is chewing nervously on the inside corner of her lip. She has blankets tucked around her waist and a line from her pillow on her face. She looks like Remi. Just not *my* Remi.

"Hi," my voice is timid. "How are you feeling this morning?" I rock from my toes to my heels.

"Um, I'm okay. Hi," Her eyes went from me to her lap.

"She is doing well this morning, Zane. She had a good night's rest, and the doctors are pleased with her progress so far." Elena chimes in from the corner.

My eyes snap back to Remi, shaking my head to let Elena know I heard the report. Remi's eyes won't focus on me.

She keeps flicking back and forth between me, her lap, and her mom. I feel so terrible for her. I wish I could go to her and hold her. I can't.

"My parents say we're friends." She says, but it sounds more like a question.

The word *friends* hits harder than I want it to, and my chest tightens. I swallow it down and nod, masking the ache. "Yeah. We are."."

She studies me for a moment, her brow furrowing. "Do we... go to school together?"

"Yeah." I step closer, careful not to crowd her. "Copperridge High. Same lunch table. Same friend group."

"Right." She fidgets with her blanket, looking down at her hands. "Sorry, I just" She pauses, looking down at her hands." My head feels like a fog I can't clear."

"It's okay," I say quickly. "You've been through a lot."

I reach into my hoodie pocket and pull out my phone. "I thought maybe pictures might help?"

She looks up, hesitant but curious. "Pictures?"

I point to the empty chair next to her bed. "Can I sit?"

She waves her hands towards the chair, giving me a nonverbal yes.

I swipe to a photo, one of us sitting at the Copperridge Fall Festival, her hand halfway to her mouth, laughing mid-bite of her favorite kettle popcorn. I hand her the phone.

Her fingers tremble slightly as she takes it. "This looks… fun," she says slowly. "But I don't…"

"Here," I swipe again. "Pumpkin carving. Trivia night. The ridge."

Every photo feels like a punch to the chest. Her smile in each one—once mine—now seems like someone else's memory. She shakes her head, frustration bleeding into her voice.

"I'm sorry, Zane. I don't remember… I don't *feel* any of this. It's like looking at someone else's life."

I force a small smile, trying not to let it show. "That's okay. You don't have to remember right now."

Her eyes flicker to mine, glassy and apologetic. "I can tell I meant something to you. I just.." Her words trailing off again.

My throat tightens, and I swallow down the pain. "You do."

The silence stretches, heavy and awkward, thickening the sadness. She sets the phone on her blanket and looks toward the window, blinking too fast. I can tell she's fighting tears, and the room's mood shifts from hope to helplessness.

Elena touches my arm gently. "Why don't we let her rest for a bit, hmm?"

I nod, slipping the phone back into my pocket and standing. "Yeah. Of course."

As I walk out of the room, her voice follows me, soft and confused. "I wish I remembered."

Me too.

I get back in the truck, and I lay my head on the steering wheel. My body is heavy with an emotion I can't quite put my finger on. My phone buzzes in my pocket.

Joss: Meet me at Nonna's. I've got an idea.

I don't even reply. Throwing the phone on the seat next to me, I put the truck in drive and head towards Nonna's. I need hope. I need something. I need her.

The bell jingles when I enter Nonna's. The scent of espresso, sugar, flour, and something citrusy from Rachel's baking fills the air. It's the scent I've always loved, the one Remi used to carry home on her skin. It feels wrong without her here—too still, too quiet. Joss is waiting at our usual window booth, hair in a messy knot, eyes red from crying or lack of sleep. She cradles a mug of coffee for warmth.

When she looks up and sees me, she doesn't smile. "About time, Carter. Sit down."

"Your text said you found something." I slide into the seat across from her, my voice rougher than I mean for it to be.

Joss nods, glancing at the counter to be sure we're alone. She reaches beside her and sets a small, dark blue box on the table. It's solid and carved with crescent moons and tiny, worn-smooth stars.

"She keeps this under her bed," she says.

The sight of it makes my throat go dry. "What is it?"

"Something she's had since she was little. The box belonged to her Nonna." Joss hesitates before she pushes it toward me. "It's full of letters."

"Letters?" I echo, like the word itself doesn't make sense.

She nods, her voice soft. "Remi used to write to someone called *L.* She said he was the boy from her dreams. He'd come to her when things felt heavy. When she woke, she'd still feel his warmth, like he'd just left."

I look down at the box. The carvings catch the light just right, and for a second I swear they shimmer. "Joss…"

"I know." She swallows hard. "It sounds insane. But listen, I started reading a few. And Zane, they're not just dreams. They're memories. Or something close to it." Her face pinches with confusion, like she's not yet sold the idea to herself either.

My fingers trace the moon etched into the lid. "What do you mean?"

"Little details," she says quickly, leaning forward. "She describes moments you've actually lived. Sitting on the swings. Sharing sandwiches. Talking about how home feels like a fairytale." Her eyes flick up to mine. "Zane, she wrote about you, *years* before she ever met you."

"Joss, that's private, and they're just dreams. This isn't real, and it's not going to bring her back to me." I stand to leave. This was a waste of my time. "Call me when you have a better idea." I slide the box across the table towards her.

Joss begins reading a piece of paper from the box. *"Dear L, The ridge was glowing tonight. The sky looked bruised."*

I stop moving, remembering how it looked that night we were on the ridge, not the first night. I couldn't tell you what it looked like that night. All I saw was her.

"All purple and gold, like the world, couldn't decide whether to end or begin again. You were ready for everything. You brought a blanket to sit on, jackets, and even a warm drink. You were sitting with your knees pulled up, and your head tilted toward the horizon, like you were listening to it breathe."

I close my eyes, the wetness making the world blur away, remembering how it felt to be up there with her. My hands stuffed in my pockets, standing right behind Joss as she reads the letter in the direction I was sitting before I got up to leave.

"You didn't say much at first. You never do. You just pulled out your guitar and let the music fill the space between us. It wasn't even a song I knew, but it sounded like something you'd written just for the sky."

The backs of my eyes are burning with unshed tears. I don't want to listen to this, but I can't force myself to walk away. She dreamed this? How long ago? I clear my mind and keep listening to Joss read the letter.

"We didn't talk about the future, or the kind of big things people are supposed to care about. You just said, "Do you ever notice how quiet the world gets right before the sun slips away? And I remember thinking that maybe the quiet isn't silence, maybe it's the earth holding its breath so it doesn't miss it.

The wind picked up right after that, carrying the smell of cinnamon and woodsmoke, and you turned to me and smiled. The kind of smile that feels like a secret. I swear for a second everything slowed down, the clouds, the air, even my pulse.

We sat there until the stars came out.

They looked different tonight, softer, closer.

Maybe because you'd been there to see them too.

If I ever forget what warmth feels like, I'll come back to this spot.

Because up here, with you, the world finally makes sense.

—R."

The air leaves my lungs. I blink down at the box again, feeling the weight of it like it's something alive. "She dreamed of me before she knew me?" I take a seat back at the booth, my eyes fixed on the blue box in front of me.

Joss's voice softens, breaking a little. "Or maybe she remembered you before she met you."

I open the lid slowly. Inside are dozens of folded pieces of paper, stacked neatly and tied with a frayed gold ribbon. The ink is faintly smudged in places, the edges curled like they've been touched a thousand times.

The first letter I pull out smells faintly of vanilla, her scent, always her scent.

My fingers shake as I unfold it.

Dear L,

Last night, we watched the sunset from the ridge again. You said the world looked smaller from up there, but maybe that's because you make it feel bigger. You played me a song on your guitar, something soft. When I woke up, I swore I could still hear it.

My vision blurs halfway through. Another moment from that day on the ridge. I blink hard, forcing the words to stay clear. "When did she write these?"

"She began having these dreams right after her Nonna died. So maybe thirteen or fourteen years old." Joss' voice is low, almost a whisper. "Every time she dreamed about him, she wrote it down. She said he felt …real."

I sit back, rubbing the back of my neck, trying to breathe around the lump in my throat. "All this time…" My words trail off.

Joss studies me carefully. "You said she told you once that you felt familiar, right?"

"Yeah," I whisper. "She said it the first night we met."

"She wasn't wrong," Joss says simply. "You were a familiar thing. The one she's always been chasing."

I laugh, but it comes out hollow. "So what now? I hand her a letter and hope the universe jogs her memory?"

Joss shrugs, tears welling in her eyes. "I don't know. But if she dreamed of you once, maybe her words can lead her back again."

I look down at the paper in my hands, at the handwriting that somehow feels like it's looking right through me. The words blur again, but I don't bother wiping the tears this time.

"She found me once," I whisper. "I guess it's my turn to find her."

Joss reaches across the table and squeezes my hand. "Then start with that one."

I nod, tucking the letter carefully back into the box, clutching it like it's fragile glass.

"Do you happen to bring anything to write on?" I look up to Joss.

Twenty nine

☾

Zane

The floor outside Remi's hospital room is practically mine. It creaks when I shift, hums as nurses roll carts by, and smells faintly of lemon disinfectant and burnt coffee. It's uncomfortable, but it's as close as I can get to her without breaking some unspoken rule.

The blue box sits between my sneakers, its paint chipped at the corners, tiny gold stars dulled with age. I run my thumb over the lid, tracing the little carved moon, trying to summon the courage to walk inside and hand it to her myself. Every time I stand, I see the memory of her face that first day after surgery, blank and polite. Like I was a stranger in her favorite story, and I sat back down again.

The elevator dings, and Joss steps out clutching two coffees, looking like she hasn't slept in days. Her hair is a mess, sweatshirt inside out, but she still seems steadier than I do.

"Please tell me one of those is for me." I plea

"Actually, no. When you texted me saying you couldn't do it, I knew the next text would be you asking *me* to do it. So I brought her favorite drink, to try to make her remember her favorite person."

I hang my head low. "I tried to go in, but my feet won't move. It's like she doesn't even know who I am, and if I go in there with that…" I point to the box. "She won't want to remember who I am; she will only want to know why I went through her things." I look up to Joss. "Me, a complete stranger to her."

Joss crouches down, pulling the box toward her knees. "I think she needs this, Zane."

Staring at the closed door just a few feet away, I swallow back the feeling bubbling inside me. "You're sure? I feel like maybe we should just give it time… It's not what I want, but I don't want to upset her."

"I've never been more sure about anything." She grabs the box and leaves the coffee. "Drink it, Zane, you look like crap."

I huff out a weak laugh, even though nothing about this is funny. "Yeah," I mutter. "You've mentioned that before."

Joss squeezes my shoulder. "You don't have to do anything right now, Zane. Time, it's just going to take some time."

She doesn't wait for me to answer. Just stands, box in hand, and starts toward the door. I don't follow her. I can't. I just watch her disappear into the room, my heart punching against my ribs like it's trying to get through the door before I do. My Polaris, always pulling me home.

Remi

"Hey, Rem." I know by the voice exactly who that is. My best friend, Joss.

"Come in," I call out.

Joss hasn't been in to see me yet. I know hospitals are hard for her; she has never talked about it, but some things you just pick up on. She panics at the thought of a doctor's appointment. She makes sure to cross the street whenever we walk past the clinics in town. She won't even go see the school nurse if she's sick. I know thereis an underlying reason for her being the way she is. I've never pried. So when she rounds the corner, and she looks worse off than I do, I don't judge her for it.

"Look what I found." Her voice is higher than normal.

I look up from my pile of blankets, which I'm fidgeting with. A small blue box sits in her hands, its paint chipped, tiny gold stars faded like old freckles. Something in my chest stirs before my brain can catch up.

"Nonna's box," I say when my mind catches up. "What are you doing with it?" My question comes off a little harsh.

Joss's grip tightens around the edges of the box like she's afraid I'll tell her to put it back.

"I, uh… I found it," Joss stammers. "It was under your bed. You told me once your Nonna said to hide your treasures there."

She sets it down on my tray table, her hands trembling when she lets go. Something twists in my stomach. *Treasure.* A distant pang in my stomach. It's like searching through your favorite book to read your favorite line again, only to never find it.

"You went through my room, Joss?" I arch a brow, but my tone softens halfway through.

Joss looks like she hasn't slept in days, her hoodie wrinkled, eyes red. She's probably been sleeping in my bed, too. She always does when her walls come crashing down on her.

"I didn't mean to," she blurts. "Zane was looking for a sweater for you, and I saw the box, and… I don't know, Rem, it felt important."

The way she says important makes my chest ache, but again, I can't figure out why. I hate this, I hate missing pieces of my own life. How long will it stay like this? Will I ever get the last year of my life back?

"Do you remember it?" she asks. Her voice is barely above a whisper.

"I remember Nonna's hands," I whisper. "The way she'd trace the carvings and tell me the stars were secrets worth keeping." The words slip out before I even realize. My fingers slide across the lid, tracing the little moon. "I know I put things in there, I just… can't exactly remember what. I haven't seen this since the sleepover debacle."

Joss sits beside me, fidgeting with her hoodie string. "Then maybe it's time to find out."

She sits across from me on the bed and opens it slowly, almost reverently. Letters spill out, folded, some worn soft at the edges, all in blue ink. The air shifts. The room feels smaller, fuller.

My heartbeat stutters. "I wrote these."

"Yeah," Joss says, her smile wavering. "You used to call them your dream letters. Said

they were from some boy who only existed when you slept."

Her words hit like static in my brain, flashes of color, laughter, a hand brushing mine under the glow of carnival lights. But the details slip away before I can grab them. I remember, just not completely. If I'm being honest, I tried to throw them in the trash. I was so humiliated when the rumors started swirling around the school. Why would Joss bring me these letters?

"Then let's start small," she suggests, pushing a letter towards me.

Her fingers brush mine as I take it. She hesitates, glancing at the door before meeting my eyes.

"He's right outside, you know," she murmurs. "Zane. He's been sleeping on the floor for days."

My heart trips over itself. "What do you mean by sleeping here?"

"He goes home to shower." Her face scrunches up. "I haven't seen him eat since the night before your surgery. The nurses keep putting snacks and drinks out for him, but he never touches them." She says, shaking her head. "Anyway."

I take a letter, unfolding it carefully. The paper smells like me and stale air, like something that's been waiting. Joss is silent now, leg bouncing as I start to read.

Dear L,

Last night, we rode the Ferris wheel.

You always let the silence do the talking for you. There's something about the way you looked at me, like I was magical.

I wanted to keep spinning forever, just to stay in that quiet with you.

The lights looked like fireflies trapped in glass.

You pointed out the ridge in the distance and said, "That's where home is."

I told you home wasn't a place, it was a person.

You didn't argue. You just looked at me the way people do when they already know the truth.

Love,

R

The words on the page tilt the world on its head. I can *feel* the sway of the Ferris wheel, the vibration of the metal beneath my feet, the wind tangling my hair. The smell of kettle corn, a hand brushing mine when the cart jolted. Flashes of my head on someone's shoulder, the charged air between us. It's all there. Blurry. Distant. But there.

Joss's voice is small. "Anything?"

"Yeah," I whisper. "Not all of it. Just… pieces. The lights. The air. Someone sitting next to me who made everything else disappear." I swallow against the tightness. "It's like remembering a dream right before it fades."

Joss nods, smiling through glassy eyes. "It's working." She squeezes my hand and nudges towards the box with her chin, "Keep reading, Rem, you're going to want to remember him."

"Who?" I ask, trying to make sense of it.

Joss doesn't answer, just pushes another letter towards me, old and worn. Like it's been read a thousand times. I rub my fingers over the indentation of the words on the inside. I'm nervous. I want to remember him. I know she's talking about Zane. I feel terrible. I don't want to hurt him. I just cannot control my memories. Sleeping on the hospital floor, not eating, I must mean something to him. These letters won't help me remember him. I wrote these before I met him. Pushing out a heavy breath, I open the letter and begin to read.

Dear L,
I think I fell for you between the noise.

Joss sits in the chair next to my bed, one leg crossed over the other, pretending to scroll through her phone. She's been here for an hour now, talking about everything except the box sitting in front of us. The door opens a few inches, and I hear that voice, the one that makes my stomach twist even when my head doesn't quite know why.

"Hey."

Zane's standing in the doorway, hoodie wrinkled, eyes tired, but soft. There's a folded piece of paper in his hand, the corners bent from being turned over and over again.

"Hey," I whisper, suddenly aware of how quiet the room feels.

He looks between Joss and me. "Can I...?"

Joss jumps to her feet before he can finish. "Yeah. I'll, uh...go get some coffee. Real coffee, not the motor oil they serve downstairs." She squeezes my hand, eyes flicking between us. "Don't screw this up, Carter."

"I'll try not to," he says with a half-smile that doesn't quite reach his eyes.

He smiles, just barely. "How are you feeling?"

I shrug, trying to sound casual. "They say I'm healing fast. I think the nurses like me."

"That sounds like you," he says, and there's something so sure in the way he says it that I can't help but look at him longer than I should.

A beat of silence passes before I ask, "You keep saying that."

"Saying what?"

"That I sound like me." I pick at the frayed edge of my blanket, pretending it's not shaking slightly in my hands. "But what if I don't anymore?"

I don't know why I'm confiding in him. I am not even sure I really know this guy. The me that I know won't give someone her all. She wouldn't be someone's all, either. That sets you up to live a long and lonely life. I saw it firsthand when Nonno died, and Nonna had to carry on without him.

His expression softens, and for a second, he looks like someone breaking in half. "You do," he says, voice low. "Maybe not the way you remember, but the way you are."

That does something to me, like hearing a song I forgot I loved. My throat tightens, and I have to look away.

"Everyone keeps telling me I'll remember," I whisper. "But no one tells me what happens if I don't."

He takes a small step forward. "Then we start over."

My eyes find his again. "We?" I pause. "You'd really do that?"

"I already did once." He takes a seat on the foot of my hospital bed.

I don't know what he means, but the way he says it sends a tremor through me. My stomach twists, not in fear, but in something dangerously close to recognition. Something inside of me wants him to scoot closer, but it feels unnatural, like distance is foreign between us.

"Joss said you read the letters," his voice comes out as a whisper.

I nod. "They're... familiar, but also not." I breathe out, "That was a long time ago. Not to mention dreams."

He studies me for a second, then sets the paper on my blanket. "Then maybe this one's for who you are right now."

I glance down at it, swallowing down the emotion making its way up my throat. "You wrote me a letter?" The back of my eyes is burning.

His throat works before he answers. "Yeah. You don't know me right now, and that's okay. I just need you to know that you once looked at me like I was home...and I've been trying to get back there ever since."

His words stir something inside me, and the air leaves my lungs in a shaky breath. I don't know what to say. I don't know how to feel about this, about him.

He shakes his head lightly. "Read it when I'm gone. You don't owe me anything, not recognition, not remembering. Just...give it a chance."

He stands, hands me the letter, and places a kiss on my cheek. Closing my eyes, I breathe him in. I inhale until my lungs won't expand anymore. He takes one step back, like he's afraid to break whatever fragile thing is hanging between us, his eyes searching for something in mine. He blinks, and it's gone. He turns on his heels and walks toward the door.

"I'll be right outside, okay?"

I nod, even though he can't see me. "Okay."

The door closes behind him, and I release the breath I was holding in. The air in here feels heavier, like he took the oxygen with him when he left. I don't remember him, but I want to so badly. There's something about the way the room changes when he is standing in it. Like everything leans towards him on instinct.

He doesn't feel like a stranger. He feels familiar. Like a scent I recognize but can't place where it's from, like a song I used to know the lyrics to. I close my eyes and try to remember what the room felt like before he walked in, but I can't. I can't remember him, but I can feel his presence, and it feels very familiar.

Looking down at my hands, my fingers have already begun tracing over the letter he handed me. The corners are sharp, the indentations from the words are soft. I take a deep breath and open the letter he wrote me.

Remi,

I don't know what you'll remember when you read this, or if you'll feel the same ache in your chest that I do when I think of you. Maybe not, and that's okay.

You once told me home wasn't a place, it was a feeling. You were right.

You were the laugh that made the noise fade, the warmth that found me when everything else was cold.

If the memories never come back, let this at least remind you that they were real. If you never remember what we had, I'll remind you of what we were. What we are.

I'll be here, however long it takes, for the day you look at me that way again.

Love,

Lennox.

The signature hits me harder than I expect. Lennox.

It's not the name that surprises me. I know this name somehow, I've heard it a hundred times, it feels like. Seeing it there, written in his own writing, curled in the corner of a page that sounds like forever…That's different.

Thirty

☾

Remi

Coming home feels strange. I can't remember the last time I
was here.

The scent of tomato sauce lingers in the air, music floats from
the kitchen, and the sunlight hits the wall where Nonna's cross
used to hang. Everything looks the same, but it feels *different.*
Maybe it's me that's different. Papà insists on carrying me up
the porch steps even though I tell him I'm fine. Zane's right
behind him, juggling my bag, the flowers from my nurses, and
what looks like three different kinds of soup my Mammà made
"just in case."

He's everywhere. Always there, always moving, always
helping, like he belongs, like he's been here all along. I've even
heard Papà call him figilo.

"Teroso, slow down," Mammà scolds me, fluffing the pillow
on the couch. "You just had brain surgery, not a haircut."

"I'm aware," I mutter, sinking into the couch cushions.

Zane lingers by the doorway, his shoulder pressed to the frame, head tilted slightly, that same unreadable look in his eyes.

When Papà hands me a glass of water, I lean toward him and whisper, "Is this… normal?"

He looks confused. "What?"

I nod toward Zane. "That. Him. Always here."

Papà glances over his shoulder, then smiles, soft, knowing. "Since the day you met, he's been here, figlia mia." He pulls a blanket onto my lap. "È normale," he adds with a small smile. "Some people don't ask to belong, they just do. And that boy, he fits. Like he was always meant to be at our table."

He squeezes my shoulder and walks off toward the kitchen, humming under his breath. The words replay in my mind long after he's gone. *Since the day you met, he's been here.* Zane laughs at something Mammà says. He moves through our home like he's memorized the floor plan. Like he knows how sacred this space is. I watch him hand Papà a towel, the two of them exchanging a few words I can't quite hear. My chest tightens at the sight of them.

Papà pats Zane's shoulder on his way out of the kitchen, muttering something in Italian that makes Zane grin.

Mammà catches me watching and winks, whispering, "He stirs the sauce better than your father ever did."

My eyes balloon. He must feel like family to them and to me because we have a rule. Guests don't cook in Papà's kitchen. Are they letting him stir the sauce? What else has he had his hands in cooking in that kitchen?

"Hey," I protest weakly, but the smile that comes after is real.

The warmth in the room thickens, softens. Everything feels slower: the laughter, the clink of dishes, the light spilling through the windows. My head starts to feel heavy, but I don't want to close my eyes. I want to memorize this moment, the comfort, the normalcy, the sound of Zane's voice mixing with my family's, like it's always been there. I want to know this version of my life.

Sharp pain hits the back of my eyes. It's so sudden that it has my hands racing towards my head. A pulse. A flicker of something behind my eyes. Ouch. I close my eyes hard, opening them back up, and the light dims, then brightens. *Oh no, this can't be happening again.*

Flashes of Zane's hand brushing mine on the ridge.

His hoodie slides over my shoulders in the cold.

Rain was soaking his hair while he laughed under Nonna's awning.

The Ferris wheel lights spinning above us, the smell of caramel and cedar, the warmth of his voice in my ear telling me I'm magical.

My heart stutters. My breath catches. I blink, and the room steadies again. Everyone's still talking. Laughing. Breathing.

The blanket slides from my lap as I sink back into the couch, dizzy.

"Remi, are you okay?" Slender hands touch my forehead. "Lay back, Bambina, rest." Mammà eases me back onto the pillow.

I remember. I try to tell her, but the words won't come out. I remember how he made me feel. The pull, the quiet gravity that only exists between us. I don't feel like a stranger in my own story anymore, I remember. Sleep takes me under before I'm able to say it outloud.

When I wake, the light in the room is different, late afternoon, golden and soft. Someone's turned off the TV. The house hums low with the sounds of forks clinking and faint laughter coming from the kitchen. There's a blanket draped over me again, no wait, a hoodie. His hoodie. It smells like soap, woodsy mixed with…pears. My fingers twist into the fabric on instinct. Footsteps creak against the floor. I know that rhythm before I even open my eyes.

Zane

"Hey," he whispers, voice rough, like he hasn't spoken in hours. "You need anything? Water? Food? Another pillow?" He pushes my hair out of my face, touching me with gentle care.

I blink up at him, slow and disoriented. He's standing a few feet away, hesitant, hands in his pockets, like he's afraid to step too close.

"No," I say, my voice thin. "Just… stay."

He nods once, stands, and then sinks into the chair on the opposite side of the room. The air stretches between us, full of words neither of us knows how to say yet. Neither of our eyes is moving from the other. I lean up onto my elbow, and he sits up straight, ready to jump if I need anything.

"Could you?" I hesitate, looking down at the ground in front of me. "Could you maybe come sit with me?" He doesn't move, just blankly stares at me.

I watch the sunlight catch in his hair, the small scar near his temple I've traced before, though I don't remember when. My mind flickers through flashes again: the ridge, the music, the hoodie, his laughter under the rain. Each one burns brighter than the last until it's almost too much.

He gets up and moves towards me, sitting on the opposite side of the couch. Something about his warmth and his closeness lulls me back to sleep. When I wake up, there's no more light pouring in from the windows, no more noise in the background. I can hear noise upstairs, probably Mammà watching her soap operas.

I blink the sleep from my eyes, disoriented for a second, and then I feel it, the steady rhythm of his breathing beside me. Zane's still here. Leaning forward, elbows on his knees, fingers intertwined. He's staring at the floor like the answer to everything might be hiding there. The lamp beside us throws a golden circle around him, soft and small.

"You're still here," I whisper, my voice rough.

He looks up, startled, then smiles a little, the kind of smile that looks like it costs him something. "I'm always here."

My chest tightens. "You really don't know how to give up, do you?"

He shrugs. "Not when it comes to you."

There's no reason that line should hit me as hard as it does. But it does. It hits like a memory I almost have, just out of reach. I wish I could remember it all; it's coming back in flashes, and I want to watch the extended version.

I shift, tugging the blanket up around me. "You don't have to keep babysitting me, you know. I'm fine."

He laughs under his breath, rubbing the back of his neck. "You're terrible at pretending to be fine, Remilia."

That name. The way he says it. Like it's sacred. Like it's *mine.* Something in me stirs, that same flicker behind my ribs. I never loved my full name, but the way he says it makes me want to use it full-time.

"Tell me something," I say softly. "Something only I would know."

His eyes lift to mine. There's a beat of silence, and then he speaks, low and deliberate.

"We went to a music festival one day." A smile sneaks its way across his face. "You were staring at me for some reason." He rubs his jaw as he pushes out a half-laugh. "You said you liked the color of my eyes, you were trying to say they look the color of honey, but instead," He pauses, rubs his hands over his chin in an attempt to conceal a laugh. "You called me honey. You were embarrassed for probably a week."

A small laugh slips out of me before I can stop it. "That's… oddly specific."

"You also tried to convince me that pickles didn't belong on burgers."

"Oh my gosh." I cover my face, shaking my head. "That sounds like me."

He grins now, fully. "Yeah. That's you."

"They get hot and soggy from the meat, it makes perfect sense." I shrug.

The room settles into a soft, glowing quiet. I can feel the weight of the memories pressing against the edges of my mind, not sharp enough to grasp, but enough to ache. My hand drifts toward his without thinking, brushing the back of his knuckles. Electricity. Warmth. Home.

He doesn't move. Just turns his hand over and laces our fingers together.

"I wish I remembered all of it," I whisper, staring down at our hands.

"You will," he says. "But even if you don't, I'll remember enough for both of us."

That breaks something open in me. My throat goes tight, and for a moment, I can't find air.

"I think…" I swallow hard. "I think I'm starting to remember."

"You remember?" he says. It's not a question, just awe. His eyes open, more tears threatening to fall.

"Not everything," I whisper back. "Just flashes, not full memories"

He exhales, a sound halfway between a laugh and a sob. "That's all I ever wanted."

Zane

The stars are out tonight, bright enough to make the porch look silver. Remi's sitting next to me on the swing, her legs tucked under her blanket, the same way she always does. It creaks a little when she rocks us forward, her rhythm slower than usual. She's eating pistachio ice cream, of course, from a tiny paper cup Elena brought out.

"I still don't get how you like that stuff," I murmur, nudging her shoulder with mine.

She looks up, the corner of her mouth curling. "If I remember right, you said that last time."

"I did," I push out matter-of-factly.

A soft sound escapes her as she dips her spoon back in for another bite. "Maybe it's not about liking it. Maybe it's about remembering that I do."

I look at her, loving the way the porch light hits her hair, the way her lashes flutter when she looks down at her ice cream. She doesn't realize it, but she's still *her*. Still, that same girl who'd dance barefoot in the kitchen, argues with her dad in Italian, and laughs at her own jokes before she finishes telling them. She's still in there, and she's still mine.

"How's your head?" I ask quietly.

She shrugs one shoulder, still looking out at the sky. "Heavy sometimes. Empty other times. But I think it's filling back up."

"With what?" I press.

She smiles, faint but sure. "You, apparently."

That one knocks the air out of me. I laugh softly to keep from breaking. "Guess I can live with that."

For a while, neither of us rushes for words. The night is alive around us, crickets chirping, the trees rustling, the soft thud of her spoon hitting the empty cup. It isn't until the thud stops that I look down at her. I find those stormy greys looking up, studying me.

"Zane?" she whispers.

"Yeah?" I push out breathy.

"If I forget everything again," she whispers, voice barely there, "will you remind me?"

My throat tightens. "Every time."

Her head drops to my shoulder. "Good. Because I think I'm starting to remember how good this feels, how good you make me feel."

I glance down at her, but her eyes are already closed. Her breathing evens out. The blanket slides a little, so I pull it up to her chin and let my arm fall around her shoulders. The swing keeps rocking, slow and steady. It doesn't take long before she falls asleep, her head on my shoulder. Her hand shifts, finding mine under the blanket.

I rest my chin against the top of her head, closing my eyes.

"Yeah," I whisper to the stars above us. "She's finding her way back."

Thirty one

☾

Remi

I wake to the sound of metal bashing together. Not the creak of the porch swing, that means Papà is up too early, clattering pans, not Mammà's soft humming from the kitchen. Just the small, ordinary sounds of home most people take for granted, not this freshly home from the hospital girl, though. Yawning and giving my body a big stretch, I notice what I'm wrapped in. Zane's hoodie still stretched around me from last night.

I'm on the couch, not the

swing. He must've carried me in. The throw blanket is pulled up to my chin, the hood over my hair. I blink into soft gold lamplight. The coffee table holds a glass of water, two pills, and a folded scrap of paper.

Meet me at our spot. Joss will pick you up when you're ready.

My chest pulls tight and then loosens all at once, like remembering how to breathe. Our spot. The ridge. I sit up too fast and the world tips, then right itself. The ache behind my eyes, the one that chased me for months, doesn't come. The room steadies. I glance toward the stairs, half expecting Papà to appear and say no, leaving the house, ragazza mia, not tonight.

There's a second note by the lamp I didn't notice. It's in Mammà's handwriting.

Rem. I had to run by the restaurant, be back soon.

I tuck the first note in my pocket and hover over the second for a heartbeat. Then I slip my shoes on, grab my keys, and step into the hall.

"Remilia?"

I turn. Papà is in the doorway with a dish towel thrown over his shoulder like a white flag. Behind him, the counters are clean; there's a single slice of leftover pizza on a plate. My eyes flick to his, begging him silently to let me go.

"You going somewhere, Teroso?" he asks, but it's the kind of question that doesn't want an answer.

I lift the note. "He asked me to meet him."

He studies me for a long moment, the hoodie, the way I'm holding myself, the way girls do when they're pretending not to shake. He nods once, slowly. "È casa," he says, in a low voice. "Se ti chiama, vai. Joss is outside."

Home. If it calls you, go.

"Be careful," he adds.

"I will." I slip outside, trying not to let the weight of what he just said slip out of my eyelids.

Joss doesn't say anything when I jump into the car. I give her a big hug, silently telling her thank you. Without her and those letters I wrote in the middle of the night, I wouldn't have remembered him.

"Take me to the ridge, would ya?" I say as I release her.

She doesn't say a thing, just nods and puts the car in reverse. We drive the entire way there in silence, me trying to replay all the memories I've gotten back of him over and over in my head. Committing them to memory so I never lose them again. I'm totally writing all of them down when I get back home. We stop at the ridge, and I reach for the handle, eager to get out of the car, eager to see him.

"Thank you for all of it, Joss. I mean it. Thank you for taking care of him and me." I shut the door behind me. Joss doesn't do emotions.

I climb the path we've climbed a dozen times, the one that smells like cedar and rain even when the sky's been dry. The wind tugs at my hair. The morning sun at my back, the gravel crunching beneath my feet. I finally get over the last hill, and I see him, his back to me, hands in his pockets, looking out over the ridge.

His face tilts up at the sound of my steps. When our eyes catch, the rest of the hill goes quiet. I don't think the world actually stops turning, but it feels like it lets us get ahead for once.

"You came," he says.

"I always do." I manage a smile. "Isn't that our saying?"

He pushes out a laugh and sits down on a rock. Knocking the back of his hand against the rock beside him. An invitation. I go, if my heart is telling my head the right thing, I'd follow him anywhere. We're close, but not touching. Not close enough.

"You moved me," I say, and then realize how that sounds. "I mean, you carried me in from the porch last night."

He nods. "Your Papà would have me served up on a platter next to the chicken parm." A beat. "I left you a note."

"I got it," I say softly. "Im surprised he let me leave the house."

He grins, half-wonder, half-relief. "They like me."

"They called you family." Saying it out loud makes my throat warm.

Something loosens in his posture, a worry unwinding. His hands settle on the guitar. There's a new scratch I've never seen. Or maybe I have and simply forgot it. I don't trust my mind or the memories; I'm not sure I even have them all.

"I brought you something," he says, voice gone careful.

He reaches into his pocket and opens his palm. The small black pick glows dull in the moonlight, silver crescent catching what little light there is.

"I think this is actually yours." He says, playing it cool.

My mouth parts. I don't move for a full breath, two, three. Then I reach out and let him drop it into my hand. The plastic is warm from his skin. My thumb rubs the shallow moon over and over. His guitar pick. I remember him giving it to me. It somehow makes me feel closer to him.

"You put it on a chain." It's more of a statement than a question.

"You deserve to have more than a string around your neck, Remi," he laughs out.

"Proof," I whisper before I can stop myself.

He looks at me like I just solved the last clue in a treasure hunt. "Yeah," he says, a little broken. "Proof."

"Are you going to play?" I ask. My chin tipped in the direction of his guitar.

His hand flexes, the way it does when he's nervous or bracing or both. Then he nods, shifts the guitar into place, and lets his fingers find where to begin. He doesn't look at me when he starts, and I'm almost grateful. If he did, I would fall apart too soon. The sound coming from the guitar feels like a story I've heard in my sleep, as my mind forgot, but my body remembered.

His voice comes in soft and mumbled. The way it did the first time he ever sang to me here.

"You were the light I didn't know I was chasing,

The warmth in the cold I was braving,

The map when I had no road,

The place that finally felt like home."

My eyes burn. The wind pushes my hair across my cheek, and I don't brush it away. I let everything touch me. Closing my eyes and soaking it all in. His voice is so sure now, confident. He keeps singing, and the memories begin to play like a trailer in my head.

I see the Ferris wheel, the way the town looked small and possible from the top. I see the music festival, mustard on Eli's face, and Joss trying to pretend she wasn't smiling. I smell rain and burnt bread and Mammà's perfume. I feel the porch swing, the weight of his arm, the taste of pistachio when he kissed me carefully. The hospital walls, the vinyl chairs, the terror of waking in a body that felt half-full.

When he finishes, I'm crying. Not hard, not messy. Just tears that belong to the moment. He sets the guitar down and watches me like any movement might doctor the spell.

"It's okay," I say, and I'm not sure whether I'm telling him or me. "I'm okay."

He lets out a laugh that's more like an exhale. "I didn't know," he admits, "if I should keep singing or…" He gestures at my tears helplessly, as if they're a fire alarm he doesn't know how to disarm.

Swiping at my tears, I push out a breathy laugh. We don't rush to fill the quiet; we just settle into it. I reach for his hand and put the pick between our palms. He closes his fingers around mine, the edges pressing into our skin.

"Tell me something real, Zane," I whisper.

"I love you," he says quickly, sure of himself.

The words arrive without warning. I've heard them before, though. Waking up after surgery, I didn't recognize the voice at first, but I do now.

"I thought I'd say them here," he continues, voice low, "the night I played for you before everything happened. I kept… waiting. I thought I should give a better speech forever." He smiles at himself without looking away from me. "But I don't think forever needs speeches, Remi. I think it needs to be shown up. Every day. Every minute. Every time you forget, I'll just… show up again."

He squeezes my hand, the pick digging deeper into our skin.

"I love you, Remi. I don't know when I started, but I know I'll never stop." He confesses.

My breath goes rough. The part of me that writes letters in the dark, the part of me that sprinkles stardust over paper and calls it a promise, wants to reach into the blue box and pull out every version of him I've ever imagined. I don't need paper. I have a hand and a ridge and a boy who sings to the sky like it's listening.

I swipe tears off my cheeks and laugh at myself. "I don't know why I thought I would need a thousand details to remember you. My heart remembered you. I just needed time for my mind to catch back up."

His shoulders drop like someone just unhooked a weight from them. He leans his forehead to mine. He breathes easier than I've seen him breathe in days, probably since I woke up in the hospital without my memories.

"Lennox," I say into the inch of air between us, letting the name sit on my tongue. He closes his eyes at the sound, the way people do at church when the hymn finally gets to the line their heart was waiting for.

"Remilia," he answers, and it doesn't make me flinch. It never will again.

I rub the pick with my thumb again. He notices.

"Let me help you put that back on." He grabs the guitar pick necklace and puts it around my neck. He touched my shoulders and placed a gentle kiss on my neck, where he just clasped the necklace.

"Here," he adds, reaching for my hands. He turns them over, tracing a crescent moon into each palm with the pad of his thumb. Left, then right. "So if you ever forget again," he pins me with a look, "which you won't. But if you do, there'll be a map."

"Does the map end here?" I ask, teasing to keep from crying again.

He shakes his head. "It starts here." I brush my windblown hair away from my face. "Polaris?"

"What did Nonna say about love?" he asks after a while, voice gone drowsy with peace. "You told me once, but I want to hear it again."

I swallow around the ache that comes when I think of her, the good ache, the one that means I learned how to carry.

"She always had a lot to say about love, but I think the answer you're looking for is that it's the ingredient you never forget," I tell him. "Even when you can't name it, you can taste when it's missing."

He hums. "Good," he says. "Then we're safe."

"We're safe," I echo.

We sit until the rumble in my stomach is audible. He stands and offers me a hand up, like it's something he's practiced a thousand times, because he has.

"I need to do one thing," I say, and he tips his head like he wants to ask me what it is, but he doesn't.

When we get back to my house, I take him up to my room, kneel on the floor, reach under the bed, and pull out the dark blue box. I reach my hand up, inviting him to come to me, to sit with me. When he sits down next to me, I lift the lid, running my fingertips over the grooves my pen left years ago. My letters to L. I don't need to read them all. I don't need time to make speeches. I pull out a blank page instead, click a pen, and write.

Dear L,

We found the place where the story starts and ends at once.

It smells like cedar and pears. It tastes like pistachio and sounds like the song you sang to me at our favorite space.

Oh yeah, I love you too.

Love, R.

I fold the paper, tuck it beneath the oldest letter, and close the lid. Then I stand, turn, and hand the box to him.

"Nonna told me to hide my treasures here," I say. "Turns out hiding them was never the point."

He looks like I've just handed him a galaxy he's afraid to drop. "Are you sure?" he asks, even though he knows the answer.

"Yes," I say. "It's time the box learned how to breathe in the open."

He nods, cradling it like something sacred. Because it is. We follow the music downstairs, which means the house is about to be filled with a heavenly fragrance. Papà is cooking, so we make our way to the couch in the living room. Zane sets the box on the coffee table in front of us, making sure it's perfectly centered.

"Tell me something real," I say.

He thinks for a heartbeat and then says it simply, the way he always does when the moment matters. "Forever's not a speech."

I smile into his shoulder. "It's showing up."

He kisses my hair. "Every time."

I turn my face toward him and find his mouth the way you find your way in the dark when you've mapped the room in daylight. The kiss is not fireworks or announcements. It's a door opening to the same room we've always been in, only warmer. It tastes like salt and relief and something we'll name later.

When we part, I tuck the pick back under my shirt and press my hand over it, feeling the shape through fabric, small and sure.

"I'm going to forget stupid things," I tell him. "Like where I put my keys."

"I'll hide them in the same place every time," he says.

"I might forget how I take my coffee," I add.

"Don't worry, your coffee order has become my favorite," he says.

Standing and offering his hand, "Ready, ragazza mia?" Zane smiles, super proud of himself for that bit of Italian. Making a mental note to work on the pronunciation later.

I take his hand, smiling to myself. "Always."

The End.

Epilogue

☾

Remi

Italy doesn't feel like I thought it would. I imagined that loud-chaos in the kitchen- feeling I grew up knowing and loving. I thought stepping onto the street where my Nonna lived would knock the wind out of me, the way grief used to. That's not what I feel here at all. Overwhelming peace, and a home away from home is how I would describe the feelings I'm experiencing.

The town is small, tucked into the hillside like it belongs there and nowhere else. Stone buildings line narrow streets that curve instead of ending. Laundry hangs from open windows. The air smells like bread and warm dust and something familiar I can't name.

My parents walk a few steps ahead of Zane and me. My dad points at something and my mom laughs, soft and real, the sound grounding me more than I realize until it's there. Zane stays beside me. Not holding my hand. Not pulling me forward. Just close enough that I know he's there.

"This is where she grew up, Remilia." His voice breaking, "Where she met your Nonno." my dad says, stopping near a narrow street that looks like any other.

There's no sign. No marker. Just a faded green door set into stone worn smooth by time. I take a step closer and press my palm to the wall. "I think she always knew I'd come here." I whisper.

"I think you're right Rem" Zane steps closer, placing his palm onto the stone next to mine. "Look, the door is even the color of that horrible ice cream you love so much."

Shaking my head at him, I huff out a laugh. That night, we sat on a stone wall near the edge of town while the sky turns a deep, lingering blue. Somewhere below us, music drifts upward in pieces, unfinished and perfect. The air is cool but gentle. Zane shifts next to me.

"There's something I've been holding onto," He almost whispers.

He pulls an envelope from his jacket pocket. The edges are worn, the paper creased softly, like it's been opened and closed more than once.

"You wrote this." He rubs his thumb across the crease. "A while ago."

Placing my hand over his, trying to calm the storm raging within. I know what's in that letter. A part of me wishes I would've read all those letters before I gave Zane the treasure box, but here we are. I wrote about my plans for Italy, about him. About being afraid I would forget him. About hoping he wouldn't stop living if I disappeared. About wanting him to love fully, even if it wasn't with me.

"Zane" I breathe out. "I wrote this before surgery, I was terrified. I'm so sorry I didn't take it out."

He pulls me closer to him, wrapping both arms around me and placing a kiss to my head. "I know Angel. I just hated reading how scared you were."

"I love you Zane." I move to look into those honey eyes i've been in love with since the day i saw them.

"And I love you, Remilia Guesepina." he says with a perfect Italian accent.

We stay there until the day settles and the stars appear one by one.

The next morning, I wake to voices outside the window. When I step onto the balcony, I see my dad and Zane walking ahead of the others, talking quietly. A warm smile settles on my face.

"So," I say later, falling into step beside him, "you gonna tell me what you and my Papà were talking about this morning?"

Zane glances at me, then away, like he's considering something carefully.

"Not yet."

I raise an eyebrow. "That's suspicious."

He smiles, just a little. "It's supposed to be."

I shake my head, laughing softly, and lift my camera. "Turn around."

He does without asking questions, standing where the morning light hits just right. Italy stretches behind him, worn and beautiful and real.

I bring the camera up, steady my hands, and frame the shot.

"Ready?" I ask.

He nods. "Whenever you are."

The shutter clicks. I lower the camera, my smile lingering on the photo of Zane, standing in front of the house my Nonna grew up in.

"You think we could just stay here forever?" I meet Zane's gaze over the top of my camera.

"I think one day we can make that happen." His smirk blooms into a full blown smile. "C'mon, let's go get some food."

It started with a boy I imagined, but it ended with him.

Thank you for choosing this story and carrying it with you to the end.

If this book made you feel something, I would love for you to share that by leaving a review. Reviews help authors more than you can imagine, and they help stories like this reach the readers who need them.

Thank you for being here.

♡ Kailey Brown.

www.ingramcontent.com/pod-product-compliance
Lightning Source LLC
Chambersburg PA
CBHW051259130726

47987CB00004B/1585